The Berliners

Emma Harding

The Berliners

JOHN MURRAY

First published in Great Britain in 2022 by John Murray (Publishers)
An Hachette UK company

This paperback edition published in 2023

3

Copyright © Emma Harding 2022

The right of Emma Harding to be identified as the Author
of the Work has been asserted by her in accordance with
the Copyright, Designs and Patents Act 1988.

A CIP catalogue record for this title is available from the British Library

B format ISBN 9781529376203
eBook ISBN 9781529376210

Typeset in Sabon MT by Hewer Text UK Ltd, Edinburgh
Printed and bound in Great Britain by Clays Ltd, Elcograf S.p.A.

John Murray policy is to use papers that are natural, renewable
and recyclable products and made from wood grown in sustainable
forests. The logging and manufacturing processes are expected to
conform to the environmental regulations of the country of origin.

John Murray (Publishers)
Carmelite House
50 Victoria Embankment
London EC4Y 0DZ

www.johnmurraypress.co.uk

for my parents, John and Anthea Harding

and in memory of Marc Beeby (1958–2020)

You're not yet cold; it's not too late
to dive into your increasing depths
where life quietly betrays its secrets.

Rainer Maria Rilke,
The Book of Hours

Irving Berlin: Bob, I wish you'd do that introduction
over again.
Bob Hope: Why? Is there something wrong, Irving?
Irving Berlin: Yes. You know you got the name wrong.
It's Irving Jones.
Bob Hope: Jones?
Irving Berlin: Yes. I changed it. Anything over here called
Berlin, they cut up into sectors.

Titania-Palast Theatre, Berlin, December 1948

44 days since she detonated her life and she's in the coffin acoustic of a phone box, pretending to search her pockets for change. Not that there's anyone to perform to. The road remains quiet. No cars pass. She checks her watch for the third time. 6.58 a.m. Only just daylight. A low grey mist melting the edges of things. Across the road, above the hedge, the rusted top bar of the swings and the slide's wooden scaffold. No sign of any activity there, which makes her heart thump with relief. Her nose itches, but it feels like a dangerous distraction to scratch it, so she flares her nostrils instead, takes in the call-box smell of metal and piss and the sweat of strangers' fingers. And then the phone rings.

In her panic, she nearly knocks the receiver from its cradle, but catches it just in time. Monika's voice. *They've left.* Then the dialling tone. She goes to replace the phone, but her whole arm is suddenly numb and the receiver misses, falling with a clatter. It begins to swing ominously on its cord, the dialling tone wailing out. Though it would take a matter of seconds to replace it, something tells her not to stop. As she pushes open the door and emerges into the cool wet-leaf air, she thinks the whole street will hear the phone's lament.

She has twenty-five seconds to clear the scene. In ten, she's crossed the road and is through the park gate. This is the signal for Kat. The purr of a car engine a few hundred yards away. She should keep walking briskly through the park, but something makes her turn, glance back towards the road. And then she sees it. Negotiating a pavement pothole on the phone box side of the road, a woman with a pushchair. Tonja stops. There isn't time. No time to shout a warning. And if she goes back, she'll be caught up in it. Even here, she's too close. Stands at the top of the path, paralysed. Kat in the distance calling *What the fuck are you doing? What the fuck, Tonja?* Tyres of a car on the wet tarmac. And then the street before her splinters.

She sleeps for hours. At least, that's how it seems. And then a long low note, as though from a stringed instrument – a cello, is it? The sound seems to oscillate. The light is very bright. She had thought her eyes were open, but now she opens them for real. On her back on the path. The sky, thick with clouds. The threadbare, late autumn trees. Still the impossible cello plays. But the birds around the park have fallen silent. And then a baby starts to cry.

She scrambles up, sways back towards the road. Kat has disappeared. The car is a mangle of twisted, blackened metal. Flames lick around its eviscerated engine. She doesn't need to look inside to know that no one could have survived that. And in the road, just beside the car, something she cannot understand. A woman's arm. Still sleeved in a pale-blue raincoat. On the middle finger, an outsized ring in daffodil-coloured resin.

Focus. Focus on the child's crying, turn towards the sound. A little way along the pavement, an upturned pushchair. A toddler, with its legs in the air, kicking furiously against the sudden wrongness of its world. And though Tonja's not aware of moving, somehow she is there, turning the pushchair right way up and propelling the child, still screaming, along the pavement and into the park. Her heart beats so loudly she thinks it must be audible. Passing the playground, she wonders absurdly for a moment whether she should stop to give the child a turn on the swings.

*

Behind her, the street is coming to its senses. Shouts and cries. Cars coming to a sudden halt. She waits for the footsteps that will inevitably follow her. But nothing. At the park's far gate, she dares to look back over her shoulder, but she's still alone. Jörg and Kat and the car have gone. This does not surprise her.

The only course is to keep moving forwards. She's no idea where she's going, but instinct tells her to choose roads that lead as far from the park as possible. After half a mile, the movement of the pushchair seems to calm the child and it falls quiet. A few streets later, she finally stops and peers over the hood to look at her loot. Oblivious to its own disaster, the child is asleep. It's a boy. About twelve, fourteen months old. His face still flushed from crying, snot crusted around his nostrils. An elderly woman stops to tilt her head down at him. *Aren't they beautiful when they're asleep?* Tonja smiles and nods before walking on.

She has to get him back to Friedrichstraße. Pushing the chair, she looks around for landmarks, but doesn't know this neighbourhood, has no way to navigate. She comes to a main road, and decides to follow it, although she's aware of all the cars passing. Of all the eyes inside the cars. She expects one to screech to a halt beside her, for someone to jump out and shout *That's not your child! What are you doing? What the fuck are you doing?* She cannot think about the thing she saw on the road. She spots the green and white of an S-Bahn sign ahead. Surges forwards.

Outside the soot-blackened sandstone of number 19, the child once more comes to consciousness. He looks up at Tonja as she navigates the front door, looks up at the grand archway with its oak-leaf decorations, its bas-relief head of a woman, whose mouth is slightly open, as though caught in mid-sentence. He takes in this unfamiliarity, knows he does not care for it, screws his face into a pre-emptive expression of complaint and then, after a dramatic pause, lets loose a piercing wail. Tonja feels suddenly exposed on the pavement, as bleary-eyed schoolchildren and workers hurrying south to Hallesches Tor station weave around her. Across the street, the owner of the small Turkish cafe is using a metal rod to pull out his pavement awning in readiness for the day. Muttering ineffectual words of comfort to the child, she struggles with the pushchair through the front door into the chequerboard-tiled hallway and up two flights of stairs.

On the other side of the flaking brown paint, she can hear raised voices. But when her knuckles hammer at the door, the voices stop and the door swings open. The apartment's narrow vestibule is suddenly full of people, staring at her, as she pushes the child forward into

RUDI, 1906

The Future, on four plates of silvered glass. But I was distracted at just that moment by the sharp teeth of Fräulein Gottschalk, clamped onto my lower forearm. Being a skinny boy, there was very little flesh to cushion my radius from her incisors, but despite my cry of pain, no one took any notice of me. They were too busy gazing at The Future.

Not unlike The Past, The Future was full of shadows, out of focus, indistinct. And yet, there was enough of an image on each of the four plates to suggest meaning. Enough to make the small group of people gathered in that parlour room, on the first floor of Friedrichstraße 19, take a collective breath. I'm not exaggerating this detail. Erholtz taught me many things about audiences, and this was one. That humans can act as a single entity, like a murmuration of starlings, relinquishing their individual consciousness to the will of the group. And as the twelve people assembled took this collective breath, the room's oxygen level for that moment was temporarily reduced by an approximate total of 216 mg. No wonder I felt a little faint.

Once Fräulein Gottschalk had released me, leaving the deep red impressions of twenty-eight small teeth on my flesh, I too felt compelled to see the images again. I moved forward, rubbing my arm, to hover at the shoulder of the diminutive Madame Czigany.

The first was unmistakeably the Brandenburger Tor as seen from the Tiergarten. But in front of it, nearly obscuring the view, were what looked like coils of barbed wire, chaotic and forbidding, like the brambles around Briar Rose's castle in *Kinder- und Hausmärchen*. The second appeared to be a curious, spindly tower, shaped like a hypodermic syringe, its topmost tier as thin as a needle. The third was practically a silhouette. A Totenkopf. A death's head. Like the insignia of the Black Brunswickers, although closer analysis revealed it to be a Totenkopf mounted onto a ring, like an obscene wedding band. But the image I found most compelling was of a human figure in silhouette, a diver falling through space, their body a perfect cubic parabola. But the light through which they fell was oddly patterned, so that their legs and torso were cast with curling shadows, like the marbled markings of a cat.

What was even more curious was that we would normally use these glass plates as negatives with which to print a positive image onto silver gelatine paper. But, astonishingly, Fräulein Gottschalk's visions were already in reverse. They were not a world we knew, but they were something like it.

Erholtz pulled away from the huddle and addressed Fräulein Gottschalk across the room.

'Do these photographs capture what you see? Are they a true likeness?'

*

He used the voice I had heard him employ in countless public demonstrations. Inhabiting the audience's scepticism before exploding it altogether. Several heads turned in the girl's direction.

She gave one of the solemn little nods I had already grown to despise. Without taking her eyes off Erholtz, and in a breathy voice barely above a whisper, she spoke with studied profundity.
  'They are the truth.'

She'd only been in the house two days and I was already aching for her to leave. Her appearance at the Academy made her the fourth newcomer since my own arrival, fourteen months and twelve days previously. I had learned to accommodate the previous three arrivals, even half-blind Meshkhenet, the Egyptian Mystic who, despite her milky cataracts, possessed an uncanny ability to see everything that a young boy didn't want to be seen. But as soon as I set eyes on Fräulein Gottschalk, I knew with certainty she did not belong.

The Academy of Magical Arts had first been established at Friedrichstraße 19 on 3 May 1903. Despite the name, and the red leather-bound register of thirty-one occasional students, its primary function was as a supplier of the latest tricks and contraptions to the magical fraternity. Workshops to the rear of the ground floor employed three craftsmen – Kurt, a skilled joiner; Otto, a metalworker, whose forearms were crosshatched with burn scars; and Hetty, a decorative artist whose plump fingers belied a painting technique of incredible delicacy and precision. Their work supplied the shop at the front of the building, as well as orders from all over Europe and Russia. Kurt and Otto lived elsewhere in Kreuzberg, while Hetty had a small room under the eaves on the fourth floor, next to Madame Czigany. The other Academicians formed a performance troupe of sorts, giving demonstrations at venues all over the city, usually compèred by Erholtz himself.

*

My own arrival at the Academy had occurred on 22 March 1905. Already a half-orphan, my mother having died of puerperal fever shortly after my birth, I was fully abandoned, at the age of twelve, by the death of my father. At the funeral, I met Herr Erholtz, my mother's brother, for the first time, and though we were strangers to each other, there was no question of his not taking in his sister's orphaned boy. And with the flick of his conjuror's cape, I was spirited away from sleepy Oranienburg to the clatter and smoke of Berlin.

Until that moment, my father and I had lived a quiet, contented existence in a small house in the district of Sachsenhausen. Vati had been a repairer of clocks, and I inherited something of his close focus, his love of detail and his short-sightedness, both physical and metaphoric. Though he surrounded me with books and encouraged me to read novels and histories well beyond my childish understanding, my father was a man of few words. But I knew his reticence did not represent a lack of love. Although I was young, I instinctively felt that my mother's death had robbed him of his essential spirit and I could never shake the sense of responsibility that my arrival in the world had resulted in her departure from it.

My apprenticeship began aged nine, when my father set me to practise disassembling a pocket watch and then putting it back together. Bent over his work desk, scarcely breathing, I used tweezers to replace first the regulator, then the fourth wheel for the second hand, overlaying these with the third wheel and the setter wheel, before slipping the mainspring barrel beneath. These were followed by the plates, which my childish imagination cast as a knight's breastplates, armouring the delicate mechanical innards. I'd attach the small plate first, then the large – gently tapping each one down before fixing into place with miniature screws. This was the most nerve-wracking manoeuvre, because if you didn't position the screws in the

7

holes just right before tightening them, you ran the risk of snapping off the pivot. These were followed by the tiny crossbow-shaped pallet fork and its bridge, the winding wheel and the balance, for which my young fingers had to learn precision and dexterity. After screwing in the balance cock, I would turn the watch over, oil it, push in the cannon pinion, and then fit the dial, followed by the case. Then the held-breath moment of truth as I wound the watch and waited – if all was well – for the pure joy of seeing the entire mechanism jump into life. I was alive to magic even then.

As I grew in confidence, I would time my reassembly, competing with myself to reduce it from 50 minutes to 48, 48 to 45. At my quickest, I could put together a pocket watch in 29 minutes and 34 seconds, but I was never as fast as my father, who was always a predictably sure-fingered 23 minutes and 8 seconds. The gentle smack of my father's lips as he squinted at my labours, his nod of approval – these were all I needed to understand of his love.

In Sachsenhausen, my father and Barbel, our live-in maid, had been my only company outside school. The Academy, in contrast, seemed at first a place of endless noise and commotion, with the constant to-ings and fro-ings, the production line of small boxes in and larger boxes out, the ferrying of props and drapes to party halls and theatres and Kabaretts.

Friedrichstraße itself was no less overwhelming. The carriages and automobiles that flared through its canyon of tall, elegant buildings brandishing, at every level, brightly painted hoardings and advertisements – all the way up to the roof gutters. From Oranienburger Tor in the north, crossing the Spree river and Unter den Linden, then a further mile south to the Peace Column in Mehringplatz, the street shimmered with people in motion – hawkers and newspaper boys dancing daringly around the hackney cabs and bicycles, shop girls trotting off to work in too-tight shoes, office clerks and paperhangers, men with stained caps and drooping moustaches pushing handcarts, last night's drunks sobering up in doorways, salesmen scurrying to buses and trams, their cases of wares bashing against their legs. It was a place of endless movement, a continuous present.

The Academy's home, number 19, was a handsome double-fronted Wilhelmine mansion at the southern end of Friedrichstraße, built for some nineteenth-century merchant who had over-estimated either his own fortune or the construction costs, and fallen bankrupt shortly after the building's completion. It was five storeys of golden Silesian sandstone, with bay windows on the first three storeys, ornamental stone balconies and elaborate relief work. Above the doorway's arch, crowned with the bas-relief of a woman's head, two words were carved into the stone: *Cras Tibi*. Erholtz had explained that they were an abbreviated form of a Latin motto *Hodie mihi, cras tibi* – *Today me, tomorrow you*, a phrase more commonly found on tombstones. No one at the Academy seemed to know why the mansion's owner would have commissioned such a funereal inscription.

I didn't know what to make of the Academicians on first meeting, with their odd costumes and odder manners. Knowing nothing of the city, I wondered whether all Berliners were similarly eccentric. There was Caspar the escapologist, whose 'laboratory' unnerved me with its chains and boxes and straitjackets. Madame Czigany, who read Tarot, lived at the top of the building in an attic room hung with red and gold tapestries. Maintaining her Romany looks required a great deal of black hair dye and stage make-up, which she often dispatched me to purchase from a small theatrical suppliers near the Admiralspalast. Beneath her, on the third floor, was the room of the Dutch numerologist Hannus de Groot. When we were first introduced, de Groot

9

dispensed with the usual formulations of greeting and immediately demanded my date of birth. And when I told him, he frowned. 'Very interesting. Very.' Though I pressed him for more detail, he evaded my request, saying he would have to give it further consideration. 'But it is all very interesting.'

Erholtz had decided that I should be apprenticed to the Academy's photographer, Wolf, whose quarters took up part of the building's second floor. It's possible he thought my clockmaker's attention to detail might translate well to the darkroom. And so it proved. From the first morning in Wolf's studio, I was enthralled – both to him and to the alchemy of the darkroom.

My mentor was a skilful teacher and professed himself delighted with my aptitude. 'They used to call photography "the dark art",' Wolf told me, 'on account of the silver nitrate stains on photographers' hands.' But to me it was only ever an art of light. The summoning to the surface of the hidden image, invisible but present.

Erholtz also published a monthly magical periodical, *Die Zauberkugel*, to which everyone in the Academy contributed material, although he, as editor, wrote most of the copy. Wolf's official role was as photographer for this publication, which chiefly served as a means of advertising the Academy's products and services. He also ran a sideline in portraiture, catering for those members of the middle classes brave or curious enough to enter a building with esoteric associations. Wolf, who had accompanied Erholtz on several tours of Europe, taught me the English phrase 'to keep the wolf from the door'. He liked to joke, 'That is what the portrait business is about, Rudi, "to keep the wolf from Wolf's door".' And he played up to his name, growing his salt-and-pepper hair to a wild length, teasing it up with a comb to create an impressive mane that seemed to alarm and titillate his female clients in equal measure.

*

Wolf became my de facto guardian, and my orphaned heart was primed to love him, although he could be quick to temper, fired with an emotional energy that sometimes frightened me. Erholtz himself was well-meaning and generous, and managed the disparate personalities of the Academicians with great skill, but he had no experience of children and their needs. It was Margo who saved me.

I was too young to have a term for her relationship to Erholtz, although I knew they were not husband and wife. She must have been at least ten or fifteen years his junior, but though they were curiously opposite in demeanour, they nevertheless seemed devoted to each other. Off-stage, he was serious, wired with purpose, never quite off-guard. When he joined the other Academicians after hours, I noticed that he sipped his Riesling slowly, eking out a single glass over the course of the evening. Margo, however, seemed to have an infinite capacity for delight – in life and in other people – and she alternated between maternal fussing and a mischievous brand of flirtation, a combination I found irresistible.

On winter mornings, she would creep into my room with a cup of steaming cocoa and once this was delivered into my hands, would crawl into bed with me and warm her icy feet on my thigh.

'I only bring you cocoa so that I can thaw out my toes.'

'Wouldn't it be simpler just to drink the cocoa yourself?'

'Oh no. It's too long a journey from my lips to my feet. I have to take a short cut.'

I wondered whether Erholtz allowed her to warm her feet on him. Though it was impossible to imagine him undressed, freed of his starched collars, waistcoats and jewel-coloured cravats.

Now I was fourteen, I was really too old for a woman to be bringing me cocoa and climbing into my bed, but we both chose to ignore this. It seemed Margo had decided to continue treating me as a small child, despite my broken voice and the curly fluff on my chin. She was amused by my hunger for books and my prodigious vocabulary, and went out of her way to procure a small library for me. She loved poetry and sometimes would ask me to read to her from Goethe, Hölderlin, Heine – a task I willingly performed.

> Tell me now the meaning of man!
> From where does he come? To where does he go?
> Who dwells up there in the golden starfields?

As she left the room each morning, my eyes would follow the white curve of her feet, their thin blue veins, the small cracks on the backs of her heels. And when I touched myself beneath the blanket, it was to an inner movie of Margo's white ankles and the curve of her breast beneath her cotton blouse.

It was Margo who gave me the account of Fräulein Gottschalk's arrival at the Academy. She'd been minding the shop in the early afternoon, when she noticed a motorcar draw up to the kerb. An exceptionally tall woman, wearing a hat of black damas dentelle (Margo included this millinery detail with shy pride in her own powers of discernment) had descended first, followed by a slight, angular-faced child with dirty blonde ringlets. As the pair entered the shop, the lady was required to duck slightly beneath the lintel, which momentarily gave Margo a better view of the hat.

'Their heights were so oddly matched, Rudi, I thought they might be about to offer some kind of comedic juggling act. But the fish-slapped expression on Madame's face said otherwise.'

I giggled at this, but Margo was clearly still resentful.

'The giantess then demands to see Herr Erholtz. I tell her, in my best la-di-da voice that he doesn't receive visitors in the afternoon and she says that, *on the contrary*, Herr Erholtz is expecting her and at this very hour too.'

And so it proved. Erholtz ushered the strangers into his office and instructed Margo to see that the first-floor back bedroom, usually reserved for significant guests, be aired and furnished with fresh linen for our new arrival, Fräulein Gottschalk. He indicated with a wave of his hand that he was speaking of the girl, and not Frau Gargantua. Margo did not much care for being talked to like a scullery maid, but unable to speak up in front of the visitors, she bit her lip and hurried off to prepare the room, calling on Casper to mind the shop.

'And all the while, Rudi, I was thinking, he'd better not be expecting me to nursemaid that child. Who's to look after her? Why are we providing a home for waifs and strays?'

'I was a waif and stray once, Margo.'

'Yes, but you're such a handsome Liebchen,' she said, pinching my chin, 'I knew you'd be worth it.'

Our new resident was officially presented at dinner. We were all seated and slavering over the smell of Margo's Sauerbraten when Erholtz appeared in the doorway. He waited till he had our attention, and then, with a showman's timing, stepped sideways into the room, revealing the girl behind him.

'This is Fräulein Gottschalk, the latest addition to our happy community. She will be staying with us for a few months, while her guardian takes a tour of southern Europe. She has remarkable talents, which I hope to reveal to their fullest expression. And when I say "remarkable", I mean astonishing, like nothing I have seen before. I hope to be able to show you the results of her demonstrations very soon. But for now, I trust you will all welcome her to the Academy.'

He turned to the girl with a smile that was intended to be avuncular, but which landed awkwardly, as though his top lip had become stuck to his teeth.

'Now, my dear, I think you should sit here.'

And he pulled out a chair to the right of his own at the head of the table, the chair on which Margo usually sat. I caught the expression of hurt that flitted across her face. No visitor had ever displaced Margo. But something in me was glad for Margo's pain, as I hoped to prove myself far more solicitous.

Through dinner, I felt the girl's eyes upon me. The first time, I looked up and acknowledged her across the table with a half-smile and slight nod. She did not return the smile, but stared stonily at me. *So much for her*, I thought. Although, as we ate, I stole furtive glances at the newcomer. I wonder now whether I was already wary of her, although I couldn't have known that she was about to fire a cannon through my life.

As Caspar, Ingrid and the others chattered on, I watched the little Fräulein work her way daintily through the food. I perceived her distaste at the meal before her, and immediately felt defensive of Margo. Now that I had determined not to like the girl, everything about her seemed ill-favoured and open to criticism. The ash-blonde ringlets were self-consciously childish around a face that was already moving to womanhood. Her cheeks had lost their girlish plumpness, her eyes were knowing and framed by long eyelashes. Her clothes suggested wealth but, like the ringlets, were some years out of kilter with the wearer, being in a style that a younger child of eight or nine might wear. In movement, she was tense and mechanical, like one of the wooden automatons in Erholtz's shop.

*

As the dinner ended and napkins were folded away, Erholtz called me to his side.

'Rudi, I thought – since you're of a similar age – that you might like to take Fräulein Gottschalk on a tour of our little establishment? I expect your company will be more to her taste.' The girl loured at me throughout this little speech, but the moment Erholtz turned to her, she simpered.

'Shall we begin downstairs?' I asked, as we walked onto the landing, attempting a manly swagger.

'You're the master,' she said, with unveiled sarcasm. Her voice was high, breathy. I started down the stairs and spoke to her over my shoulder.

'Where are you from?'

'Nowhere you'd know.'

'I'm not a Berliner either. I grew up in Oranienburg. Till my father died. It's a small town to the north of here, of approximately 8,000 cit—'

'I can't imagine why you think I'd be interested.'

We crossed the cream and black chequerboard tiles of the hallway towards the rear entrance to the shop. I could feel her eyes on my back as I fumbled for the key from my pocket and unlocked the door.

'This is the store,' I announced, needlessly. Fräulein Gottschalk walked the length of the varnished oak counter, her chin raised, as if she herself were the proprietor. I stayed in the doorway, aware that my right arm was twitching slightly. Outside on the street, a barrel organ started to play a waltz. I recognised the tune as one that Margo sometimes sang around the house. *Suse, liebe Suse, was raschelt im Stroh? Das sind die lieben Gänslein, die haben kein' Schuh.*

Rattled by the girl's obvious contempt, my words tumbled over each other.

'Several of us take turns to work here, but Margo – Frau Erholtz – does the lion's share. She's also the best at dealing with customers.'

Silence. I felt compelled to fill it.

'We have a number of regular customers, but people come from all over Europe. You wouldn't believe the distances they travel.' Who was I defending? Margo? Erholtz? 'We sell all kinds of things. Standard conjuring equipment, of course, but the real demand is for Herr Erholtz's world-famous magical devices, like these – err – dice boxes.' I pulled out a drawer to show her. 'And these most mysterious Kubuss Spiel. Or, one of the wonders of the Orient – some Chinese linking rings. Or these sense-defying mirror chests. Herr Erholtz has travelled all over Germany to seek out the most up-to-date contraptions. Like this . . .' I opened another drawer. 'This is my favourite. It's called "David and Goliath". It uses a very sophisticated clockwork—'

'Do you think about her naked?'

'What?'

I turned to her, the drawer open precariously far, balanced on my hand.

'You do, don't you?'

The drawer slid out of its moorings and nearly crashed to the floor. I caught it just in time.

'I don't know what you're talking about,' I said primly, but I could feel the colour rising from my chin to my ears.

I attempted to dissuade Fräulein Gottschalk from further questions by conducting a virtually unbroken monologue around the rest of the Academy.

'As you can see, the building is constructed in a square U-shape around a central courtyard – the smaller rooms to the rear were presumably built to house the servants, while the owner occupied the grander quarters at the front, facing west onto the street.'

*

I showed her the ground-floor workshops that opened onto the yard, the first-floor parlour with its bay window overlooking Friedrichstraße, and directly above, Wolf's second-floor suite, with its room for receiving guests and the large linen cupboard that had been transformed into a darkroom. I did not show her the two bedrooms, but hurried along the dog-leg hallway that led to the south wing and Wolf's studio, its large windows facing north onto the courtyard. When I explained that photographers favour northern light because it is the most constant and diffuse, the girl made no attempt to conceal her yawn.

As we emerged once more into the central stairwell, I caught my reflection in the gilded dragon mirror on the landing beside the studio door. Pale and skinny, my forehead an eruption of acne. The contrast between the fearless golden dragon, whose claws clung fiercely to the top of the deep-red lacquered frame, and the pitiable spectacle presented by the glass was laughable. And I could see the girl thinking it too. The mirror reflected her smirk, and a barely energised wave of the hand.

'That's enough. You can go now.'

I was grateful to be dismissed. Too rattled for sleep, I went into the studio and sank into the high-backed armchair, grateful for solitude, for the wide vista of the hand-painted backdrop that hung against the opposite wall. I could hear the Academicians moving around the house. The creak of floorboards, the opening of cupboards, the wooden swoosh of curtain rings. A score of bedtimes. My nostrils registered the chemical tang that always hung in the air, the scent of Wolf's favoured brand of furniture polish, the toasted-almond aroma of Erholtz's cigar finding its way through an open window. These were smells that had come to represent home to me.

We offered a choice of two painted backdrops for portraits. A *trompe l'oeil* Palladian villa, or a grove of Black Forest pines. My own preference was the forest, with its path winding upwards through the mountains towards some mystery. I'd never seen real mountains, but my future, I fantasised, might be at the end of that path. It seemed to me that whatever waited for me there was not paradise, but neither was it malevolent. The only thing I felt certain of was that it would be lonely, that the only traveller on that path would be me. Though I cannot say why I sensed this. But as it was, I sat in the chair and let my eyes follow this path towards its vanishing point

SIGI, 1948

& I stared at it for ages like I was trying to make it come into focus & the painting made me think of you but I couldn't think why at first & then I remembered of course it was the snowy mountains in your watercolours the ones I was so mean about that first time but you know how I always need to get in there first with a little barb a little test just to put myself at an advantage with new people not an admirable habit I know & I think you were a bit hurt really but you were too nice to show it & perhaps you already understood enough about me to see it was all front & anyway this painting today wasn't even a landscape really just an abstract arrangement of blocks of colour green & blue & brown & white with shapes in the distance that might have been mountains but there was something about them like a threshold I wanted to walk towards & cross over as if by crossing I might be able to find you

& by the way in case you're wondering we had to break up the frames for firewood the glass was all cracked anyway but I've packed the prints away carefully for you & one day soon I'm going to get them reframed

& yes granted it's mad I'm going to art exhibitions when we're half-starved & all anyone can think about is queuing for food or exchanging Western marks for Eastern marks for coupons because your brain is in your belly all the time & the streets are mostly grey or beige & the people are grey or beige & most of the trees have gone so just walking into the makeshift gallery it was inside a bombed-out bank & all the ornate plasterwork was fire-blackened just walking in & seeing these huge canvases with great swathes of colour felt like jumping into a rainbow like waking up something inside me that's been asleep for a long time

& God knows where some of those paintings have been hidden all this time but you'd laugh because Berlin's full of degenerate art again even if a lot of it is pretty shit really but I'm glad to see it rather than all that angular idealised Futurist übermensch rubbish even though the very idea of being degenerate now seems a bit beside the point since everything's degenerated into stink & rot & rubble so it's almost impossible to navigate the city & to think I once knew it like the back of my hand but at least several of the churches are still standing even if their domes are just shells so I use these to find my way the Heilig Kreuz Kirche the Gedächtniskirche the Neue Synagoge too all still there like broken miracles on the skyline

& every three minutes the drone of a plane heading to Tempelhof which is a noise to reawaken nightmares though Eric says he doesn't hear it any more but for me it's the stink of bodies in air-raid shelters crying babies bronchitis coughs all of us sweating in the damp heat listening to engines trying to calculate how far away death might be but this time the Yanks & the Tommies are dropping coal & food & medicines & sometimes little parachutes of candy

& anyway I was looking at these paintings & of course most of them were painted before everything happened so it feels like their meanings are lost to us because all the symbols & colours & stories have taken on new associations so it's like their original ideas are trapped in amber I mean it's like you can see them but they're unreachable or like they're memorials to normality though if you try to remember when normality died you keep going back & back a year & then another year & soon you're back with the Kaiser & then you have to keep going back still further & you realise you're now in a time you don't even remember because you were too little to be thinking about making memories you were too busy building snowmen or swimming in the lake or hating the stiff-collared dress your mother forced you to wear & it's been really bothering me because I can't remember the name of the village you grew up in & it might be important because then I might be able to trace you & also when they asked I couldn't remember your maiden name which is just slug-brained of me because you must have told me all these things that are part of you & I've lost them just like the meanings of the paintings & I don't know why I talk to you all the time & maybe this is just another sign of my craziness are you kidding you say you've always been spider-brained ha ha but you're still the most real thing that happened to me so I have to keep talking to you or else I really would lose it

& because of the exhibition I was late getting to the bread queue & it seemed to take longer than ever though it was probably exactly the same as most days but anyway I was late getting home with my rock of bread I swear they're making it out of acorns & the teeniest tiniest pat of margarine in greaseproof paper & mother was all agitated & that made me agitated you know how I can't stand being in the wrong & I couldn't help shouting with frustration which isn't fair because she's hungry & shivers all the time despite the warm weather & though she's only seventy-two she looks about a hundred & I worry she won't make it through another winter even though the boys are a big help & they're really kind to her even when she's rude she can say the most vile things even though she's pretending not to know that we're all queer as queer & of course we're all driving each other crazy being cooped up together & mother never gets out she doesn't know her way around this new city of ruins

& the planes the planes every three minutes for three months so we've begun to think the blockade might be permanent after all you can get used to living with anything still I can't believe the Americans will stay for ever & most of us assume one day they'll just give up & let us be swallowed up by the Soviets or worse that there'll be another war though what kind of skeleton soldiers would there be left to fight

& I keep thinking we should leave but where we would go & would Mother even survive the journey & air passage costs 28 dollars even though the possession of dollars is illegal & it's not like I have anything like that amount of money anyway & even if Berlin is a prison if I leave Friedrichstraße I leave all hope of finding you & I choose to stay here because

& it's funny how when you lived in this apartment it seemed palatial compared to my tiny attic flat but with four of us it's like living in a cupboard with Eric & Gerhard sleeping in the drawing room & mother & I sharing the bed your bed in the front as the windows at the back are all missing so we've had to board them up as best we can & of course half the plaster has fallen off the walls you'd weep to see it & there's a huge hole in the kitchen wall so we can see right through into Frau Kowalcyzk's

& we're squatting here really as the Schreibers never came back they're the family who moved in after you I mean when he

& the Yanks took the top two storeys off the place so my cosy nest under the eaves was evaporated into dust all my posters & music & costumes although the only thing I ever really mourned was the little photograph of you in the peacock frame looking so shy & lovely

&

& anyway

& yes can you believe it the building's still standing or at least the first three floors of it are just about habitable despite the best efforts of the Allies & our stairwell is open to the elements but can you believe that revolting Chinese mirror on the landing you know the malevolent dragon with the googly eyes somehow survived the bombs with only a couple of cracks bloody typical so when I look into it I see myself with a crack down the middle which is a good metaphor for something & I kicked in the door of your apartment or Gerhard did it's always been your apartment to me so the boys & I have lived here ever since we're looking after it for you & then mother moved in with me that freezing winter of '46 as she couldn't cope on her own any more & even a dissolute daughter is better than no daughter at all but even though we've sold off most of the furniture or burnt it in the stove but not the table as mother said she'd rather burn her own body than destroy that beautiful mahogany we still get on top of each other even though three of us are out during the daytimes there is still the cooking we have to plan that carefully because the electricity only comes on for two hours in the middle of the night so one of us gets up at 1 a.m. to boil some potatoes & then cover the pan with newspaper & a blanket to keep them warm & sometimes all of us get up in order to savour that brief moment of electricity & light & radio because this is when we feel most human I guess & it's important to remember we're still alive

& then of course there are all the small indignities of sharing a bathroom & we all eat together in the evenings not that I have much energy for conversation after a day of work & we light a single candle & eat our bread & margarine with chives & the boys & I share whatever cigarette stubs we've managed to find & smoke them down till the last few millimetres but I try to keep things lively for mother's sake you know make an effort & we are all attempting a kind of normality in this parody family of ours & at least mother doesn't have to work like the old women you see scraping bricks in order to get ration cards I just can't imagine her doing that don't think she'd last long but even buying simple things is bewildering because matches have to be paid for in Western marks but sugar & soap in Eastern marks while onions are half East & half West & you have to have the memory of a gambler in order to hold all of this in your head & of course the only people who do well out of the whole thing are the racketeers at Zoo Station or Potsdamer Platz

& loudspeaker vans from American Sector Radio drive through the streets as a substitute for the wireless shouting out the news & prohibitions or the exchange rate or General Clay's latest assurances which we try to believe even though the Four Power conferences never seem to achieve anything & the Russians have said they will dry out the Western sectors like a tied-off wart

& of course most of Friedrichstraße has been obliterated all its lights & hoardings all those vast canyons now all gap-toothed & if you squint the whole city looks like something geological like great limestone cliffs with deep caves & crevices like something that no longer bears any relation to human beings

& gangs of kids just see it as an enormous playground climbing all over the exposed joists & the metal scaffolding like masts of ghostly ships or they build dens in abandoned cellars or sometimes I see them playing football with the Yanks using their metal helmets as the ball & occasionally a daring little tyke will run off with the helmet & the soldier will chase him down the street for a bit before giving up the kids know all the best hiding places so you can never catch them

& there are still mounds at the side of the road covering God knows how many unexploded bombs & shells & of course we rubble women find bodies too though they've mostly rotted into nothing or been picked to the bone by rats but slowly slowly things are being cleared & when the evenings start early we carry on working by arc light even if the rubble seems endless to the point where I think I'll spend the remaining decades of my life hauling it

& somehow the city carries on & people find ways to put on concerts & plays though you don't want to go out after dark as there are hardly any streetlights & it's too easy to stumble over loose bricks but women still take an interest in fashion even if they have nowhere to go no means of buying it not me of course & anyway I'm permanently covered with a film of dust I've given up trying to get rid of it from my hair just as well I keep it short as even with a headscarf on the dust combines with my sweat & forms a kind of sticky cement which just adds to my own grey hairs & makes me look like some little old man

& though my biceps are thick & strong with all the lifting & carrying my thighs like cart-horses I feel vaguely unwell all the time you know I've never been too kind to myself all those fags all the booze but still it mostly bore me along without much bother but these days my body's more questionable no longer a solid house more a flimsy Japanese paper thing I've started to think there may be something properly wrong with me but I don't want to find out so I haven't been to see a doctor & don't intend to but I'm aware of how other people around me walk in a full-blooded kind of way even if they're half-starved they still they have a sprightliness they never stop to think about it because they live in the land of the well but most mornings when I wake up I have to do a survey of my body each new ache each new unexplained pain & once I've run through the inventory of all of these I force myself to get up & I can't seem to stop myself from groaning as I push my limbs out of bed I mean we're all getting on but I didn't expect to feel quite this clapped out at forty-seven

& a couple of days ago some men in a building around the corner found a dead horse in the street & they chopped it up & Gerhard got a leg & brought it home & though it had been dead a few days we cooked it up & it tasted all right pretty good really but since then my stomach's been rather unhappy though I still don't regret it as it was just good to taste something a bit different though we're lucky really because Gerhard has a new job as a fire officer at Tempelhof it's pretty hazardous at the moment because of the summer fogs & that keeps him busy & the Yanks sometimes sneak him wondrous gifts like oranges proper sweet juicy things that taste like a little piece of heaven & American chocolate though nothing like the hazelnut creams I'd buy for you from Rausch do you remember the ones you used to hold on your tongue to let them melt & then you'd smile at me as if

& your smile

　　　　　your

& I overheard Frau Genscher the other day saying the whole airlift was an Allied plot & I wanted to say oh would you rather we all starved then but I couldn't summon the energy yes I know that sounds very restrained of me ha ha though of course she's been cheerfully stuffing herself these last few years with extortionate black market white bread bought with her pension from the Führer you know there's a rumour she had an affair with Goebbels though it's quite possible she started that one herself as it's hard to imagine she was ever a looker though perhaps

Goebbels just didn't have any taste & okay I'm not so naive as to think this is entirely an act of pure altruism but it takes a certain level of craziness not to be grateful the Yanks & the British are keeping us going even if none of us could say where exactly we're going to

& the rumours are frightening sudden disappearances people being kidnapped & dragged into the Eastern zone there was a demonstration at the Brandenburger Tor a few days ago & protestors tore the Soviet flag from the gate & the Russian police fired at them & several people were arrested & I learned yesterday that the Soviet military court sentenced five demonstrators to twenty-five years in a labour camp we all know that means death but we're all trying to keep a lid on our fear there are women I know who say they'll kill themselves first before those rapists take over but we have to stay hopeful of course we feel so terribly isolated here

& it's like the tenses of my life have got confused who I am who I used to be

& this sounds like an excuse & perhaps it is but my memories aren't linear I get the impression other people's memories are arranged that way but mine exist in fragments with everything out of order & in a murk though occasionally one will be illuminated & come into focus & it will take me by surprise like the cognac polonaise I found myself whistling the tune last night in the bath & I hadn't thought of that in years

& perhaps we need other people to tell us who we are but my mother never really knew me & anyway her mind is wandering these days & despite our enforced intimacy the boys are still more colleagues than confidantes not that we've worked together anywhere in years & my voice is shot to pieces & Eric's piano was burned for firewood at the end of the war but what I mean is that I have no one to remind me who I am I don't recognise my own life any more it's like the ledger of my life is full of torn-out pages

& now I hear you saying something to the quick like you were the one who ripped them out because you couldn't own up to their reckoning

& you're probably right but I need someone else to be my book-keeper & I think that someone was probably you

& I've been on edge this last week because I saw you

& some days living feels like a betrayal so many deaths these last years & often so sudden with no time to prepare for the lightning strike the sudden unbeingness of someone you expected to be around for ever like Herta who I'd known since the Schwarzer Kater don't think you ever met her but anyway we were a thing for a bit you know not serious but the thing is we were caught up in Russian sniper fire in the last days of the war we were so stupid to have stayed in the city but anyway hindsight is a wonder-ful thing & I threw myself behind a low wall & Herta also hit the ground we stayed there for four hours not daring to get up & then once the shooting stopped I risked it but she did not get up she was my only friend back then she did not get up but still I left her body in the street I was too scared to retrieve it didn't know who to ask couldn't imagine anyone generous or stupid enough to risk their life for such a salvage act so I left her body in the street & I still wonder what happened did wild animals carry her off did someone throw her onto a cart for the dead there were corpses all over the city by then & of course this is the obliteration we signed up for but she did not get up

she

*

& I have so much to atone for darling but there are not enough hours left in this lifetime & I saw you I saw you

& it was late & I was just closing the curtains & I looked down on the street & there you were & I actually cried out & mother asked me what it was & I said nothing but she looked so like you & for a second she stopped & peered up at the window but it was like I was the ghost because she looked right through me

& I was about to wave but she'd already started to move on & I nearly I nearly ran down the stairs to chase after her but I

& of course I know the mind can want something so much it creates its own phantasms but I knew it was really

HEIKE, 2019

waking up in someone else's life. Heike felt it before even opening her eyes. The angle of the light was wrong. Still half-paralysed by sleep, she lay in bed and stared at the wall, her eyes taking time to adjust to the miserly February dawn. She could sense the furniture around her was not in its usual arrangement. And then the wardrobe came into focus, a Bauhaus rip-off with chrome handles, and she remembered. *I am divorced now.* Leonie had not woken her up demanding breakfast, because Leonie was with Martin. It was his weekend. Which meant a whole winter Sunday to fill on her own.

The light hemming the curtains was beige. The curtains she knew, although it was too dark to see, were the colour of kidney, inherited from the previous tenants. She hated them. They'd have to go. And then she remembered how much she hated Martin. And then she remembered to check this in herself, because what was the point, and she didn't want Leonie to pick up on any of that, even if Leonie wasn't here, and anyway it was all too exhausting, the endless picking over the past, her brain re-quoting some of the worst things he had said to her like 'you are an empty husk' and 'I can't remember why I ever found you sexually attractive', when they were both carefully pretending to the world it was entirely amicable, they were still friends, a lot of love remained, it had simply changed in texture etc. etc.

And she regretted her symbolic act of throwing her wedding ring into the Spree, when she could have made a couple of hundred euros selling it at the seedy little shop near Moritzplatz – *We Buy Gold! Gold Jewellery, Gold Bars, Ingots & Nuggets, Krugerrands, Turkish Gold, Italian Gold, Chinese Gold, Indian Gold, Gold Watches, Industrial Gold, Scrap Rolled Gold, Dental Gold. All carats! Best Prices! Guaranteed!*

She'd slept on her right cheek again. Shit. She put a hand up to the lines she couldn't feel, but knew to be there. Two lines, curiously perpendicular, like a map of the T-junction outside her window between Friedrichstraße and Hedemannstraße. She rubbed expensive cream into them every morning and evening, but the T-junction remained. Heike was still, psychologically, on the nursery slopes of ageing. Which meant she was at that point in middle life when she couldn't quite believe that such changes were permanent. Her English friend Alice had suggested a new compound noun for this. *Faltenverdrängung.* Wrinkly disbelief. Heike had tried to laugh.

Jesus. Alice. Alice had talked her into a speed-dating event on Sunday. Jesus. And now Sunday was here. 'Who goes speed-dating on a Sunday night in February?' she'd asked Alice. 'Bored men who live in cold apartments?' was Alice's not altogether encouraging suggestion.

Heike rolled over to squint at the alarm clock. It was just before 8 a.m., which meant she had eleven hours to prepare. Which meant she could lie back a little longer. Oh God. Should she bikini wax? Is that what men expected these days? Wouldn't that just leave her looking like a plucked chicken? And sore. She'd been astonished to read in a magazine that week that 69 per cent of German women shaved. Could that be true? 69 per cent? And why the hell had she bothered to remember that statistic, when it would be far better to commit brain space to something useful, like her mother's cellphone number, or perhaps a few verses from Rilke, *You must change your life*, or the number of seats held by the AfD in the Bundestag. Ninety-two, was it? Ninety-one? And after three decades of sleeping next to the same man, was she really going to take her clothes off in front of some stranger she'd talked to for just three minutes? But then, if she did, what did it matter?

But it did matter, somehow. Because even living alone she felt the presence of an unseen audience. This audience was sometimes sympathetic and sufficiently engaged in the drama to will her on, but more often than not she felt them to be quietly censorious. They occasionally coughed, but they never applauded.

Outside the window, the city was snorting into life. Her apartment building stood a few blocks south from the larger shops and cafes, and the tourist honeypot of Checkpoint Charlie and the Wall Museum, so that by this point on Friedrichstraße the flow of traffic and pedestrians dwindled considerably. But it was the right level of noise – the reassuring percussion of other humans going about their lives. Heike had always given primacy to sound above all other sensations. When she was a child, growing up in a quiet suburb of East Berlin, her sensitivity to sound, her awareness of high and low pitched noises that no one else was able to hear, her ability to differentiate and pull apart the layers of birdsong, insects, distant voices, had given rise to a family nickname, *Fledermäusi*, 'Little Bat'. Sounds conjured for her something visual – nothing concrete enough to put a name to, and not synaesthesia exactly, as Alice had once suggested, but something simultaneously emotional and palpable.

No one was surprised when Little Bat opted for a career in radio as a sound engineer. Now she worked shifts at a speech radio station and, on her own time, constructed projects that might be called sound art. Though this was not a term she'd use with her more literal-minded family. These projects were labours of love – collecting, editing, shaping and layering sounds into works that were essentially musical in nature, sound portraits of the city. The air held it all. Sound waves travelling across the city containing whispers and arguments, jokes and insults, lies and promises, all criss-crossing and bouncing off walls and windows and roofs. She thought of her microphone like one of those geological drills that go deep into the earth and twist back up to the surface with exquisitely shaded layers of the earth's history.

And Friedrichstraße's multi-track pleased her. After years in the too-quiet suburbs, this apartment – only the third she'd looked at – had been an impulse buy, facilitated by a small inheritance left to her by her father. Events had colluded to create the momentum she needed. Her father had died and with the hammer blow of grief came sudden clarity. Heike understood for the first time that life was finite and that she was more than half-way through. *You must change your life.* And then she told Martin she was leaving him.

For the first few months, she stayed with friends or in cheap Airbnbs. And then she saw a card for the apartment in an estate agent's window and knew it was meant to be hers. An ornate Wilhelmine sandstone mansion built in a U-shape, its three wings now divided into flats. Outside, linden trees shed their yellow leaves onto the pavement and the stonework was elaborately carved – a Latin motto, *Cras Tibi*, oak-leaf decorations and the head of a woman with eyes closed but lips slightly open, as if about to wake from sleep. There were two retail units on the ground floor, one currently empty, while the other housed an intimidatingly expensive private gallery, with a window display of abstract sculptures that had titles like *Chronology II* or *facets of the heart*.

Friedrichstraße was an East-to-West Berliner, just like her. She'd been raised as a child of the DDR and the maps of her Berlin had ended at the Wall – the streets in the West a cartographer's mystery. But the year she turned twenty, this street, once bisected by the US Army checkpoint, the border between two Germanys, had been stitched back together.

Thirty years after the Wall had fallen, being able to travel the breadth of Berlin still felt like freedom to her. The city a teeming miracle, the human body in macrocosm. The regular pulse of the trams and the U-Bahn, the intestinal complexity of cabling and sewers, pipes and fibre-optics, the flow of people, the apparent self-organisation of it, the unspoken conspiracy to get along, to make it work, to somehow find one's own space within it. She loved travelling through the city on the elevated sections of railway, gazing out on all the streets and apartment blocks, dazzled by the imaginative impossibility of all those millions housed, bedded, washed. Flushing toilets and gas stoves and ten million electric lights. But neither was it cosy. The brightly lit interiors, satellite dishes, pot plants on balconies, graffiti tags – these were just the visible sedimentary layer over scores of buried decades, buried lives. Berlin had her heart, not just because it was home, but because of the way it had built its own annihilation into its very walls.

She'd had grand plans for the apartment before she moved in. For the first time in her life, she'd have a space that was entirely hers. Perhaps at last she could live in a self-governed state, no longer under siege from the expectations and unwritten rules of others. As she climbed the curving staircase, lit from above by a skylight, her heart pumped with possibility.

The apartment was on the second floor, with bay windows that looked out onto the street. The main bedroom was at the front of the building, while Leonie would have the smaller room across the hallway. The window here offered a view of the paved terrace at the back, where unknown hands cultivated box and cypress.

As the estate agent showed her around, she'd mentally started to paint the walls a dove-grey blue, to hang delicate white curtains that let the light through, to buy sleek, minimalist furniture that would counter her natural inclination to clutter. But once she was installed and surrounded by boxes, all the detritus from her married life, she lost heart somehow. Seven months later, most of the boxes remained taped and piled precariously in a corner. The notion of going to the hardware store and purchasing paint and brushes and rollers exhausted her.

Soon she grew used to the musty damask curtains left by the previous tenant, the wardrobe too heavy to move. Once, in a burst of cleaning mania, which she told herself was preparation for painting, she'd scrubbed down walls and cornices, picture rails and skirting boards. As she balanced on a stepladder, with a bowl of sugar soap and water, she discovered a pile of framed prints on top of the wardrobe. They were sticky with cobwebs, but she pulled them down to examine in the light. Their mounts were yellowed and water-stained, but a couple of the landscapes – turn-of-the-century Alpine scenes – appealed to her, so she had them re-framed and hung to cover the fade marks on the bedroom wall she'd so far failed to paint.

Now, as she shivered out from beneath the bedclothes, the glass of the mountain prints ghosted her reflection, her insane Miss Havisham hair. Age. What a scam. What a goddamn swindle. It didn't matter what all those feminist bloggers said – sexual desire in a forty-nine-year-old woman was a shameful absurdity. A neediness that made one laughable, that translated into the predatory harridans of 1970s sitcoms. As Heike padded to the bathroom, she wondered whether menopause might not be a good thing. Perhaps menopause, like breastfeeding, would kill her libido. She had her work, which occupied her intellect; she had Leonie, who occupied her emotions – she wished she could focus her life on these two things, not long for some soupy romantic subplot. Martin had always blocked her inarticulate attempts to express this need. Whenever she tried to hug him in their last few years together, hungry for any indicators of residual affection, his body would stiffen and his arms remain by his sides. She'd long given up on kissing him, not being able to bear the coolness of his unresponsive lips.

The speed-dating event was in the basement bar of a large chain hotel just off the Ku'damm. As Alice and Heike queued up to register, she took a furtive look at the competition. She immediately regretted her dress choice. Alice, standing next to her, looked effortlessly pretty in a silk blouse and black trousers. Her own costume, the sixth she had pulled on in front of the mirror, discarding all the others in despair, was too figure-hugging, too low-cut. On the faces of other women, she recognised the constipated look of flesh squeezed into shapewear.

Heike took Alice's arm. 'I can't believe I let you talk me into this.' But before Alice could bat back an unassailable answer, they reached the front of the queue, and had to give their names to the pixie-cut blonde running the event.

Heike looked down at this girl who, despite her lanyard, looked barely out of her teens, her black dress and slender arms, her nectarine breasts and unused face. Standing above her, Heike felt overripe, her perfume sickly like rot. Pixie-Blonde handed her an adhesive label to stick to her chest and waved vaguely in the direction of the dating tables. As she and Alice moved away, Heike looked over at the parallel queue, where the men were signing in. Next to the compressed, coiffured women, the men looked loose and haphazard.

At the bar, Heike bought two glasses of red wine. She tried to picture one of these heavy balding men taking her to bed. Is that why she was here? Was it sex or company she sought? Affection or affirmation? Standing here, in her tight purple dress, her balcony bra, she'd been co-opted into the societal value system that made fuckability the measure of a life. God, she hated herself. Or she would if she had the energy to hate anything. She turned to Alice.

'I'm not sure this is such a good idea.'
'No getting out of it now.'
Alice placed her hand in the small of Heike's back and pushed her forward towards the circle of tables.

When they were first married, people had reacted to their conspicuous happiness by asking how she and Martin had met. Heike would smile and say, 'I jumped over the Wall into his arms.' And this was almost entirely true.

On that evening, 9 November 1989, she'd been in the library of Humboldt University, feverishly writing an essay due in the following day. There was a sudden commotion at the library door and she looked up to see her friends Litzi and Erwin. 'What are you doing?' Erwin didn't bother to whisper. 'Haven't you heard?' Heike hadn't heard. Intent on her essay, she'd not been listening to the radio broadcast of grey-suited Günter Schabowski, accidental man of destiny, sight-reading words only half-comprehensible, words that rolled together would form the wrecking ball of history.

*

She grabbed her jacket and the three of them made their way down onto Unter den Linden, already loud with other students, all in party mood, clutching an odd array of chisels, hammers, cameras and beer bottles. Some walked three or four abreast, all moving purposefully in one direction, towards the Wall. The Wall that was already a relic.

Under the glare of the searchlights in front of the Brandenburger Tor, drunk now on the mood of the crowd, she'd let Erwin help her onto the shoulder of a tall stranger, and from there, another stranger reached down from the Wall and hoisted her up. And for a moment, she stood between Past and Future. The cheers and laughter seemed the self-realisation she had been waiting for. She looked down on the dark expanse of the Tiergarten and the lights of West Berlin beyond. Below her in the crowd was a young man with dark curly hair and a laughing face. He was calling to her, though she couldn't hear what he said. And then she realised he was saying 'Jump! Jump! I'll catch you!' And it seemed like the most obvious thing to do, to jump from an eleven-foot wall into the arms of a complete stranger from West Berlin. And so she did.

This had been their mistake. In that moment of giddy rewriting, of sudden and brutal re-fusion, they had both confused each other with The Future.

Pixie-Blonde now stepped up onto a small stage and picked up a microphone.

'Good evening, guys and gals!' Heike looked across at Alice and rolled her eyes. There followed some well-rehearsed patter. The gals would stay where they were, and after three minutes, a bell would ring, and the guys would move, in a clockwise direction around the room. 'Hope you guys all know which way is clock-wise!' And she enthusiastically rang a small hand bell. *Kill me now*, Heike mouthed across the room to Alice, and mimed hanging herself. Alice's shoulders shook with laughter Heike couldn't hear.

Number 32 came and sat down at Heike's table. 'You must be sixty-five!' And he held out his hand. Feeling the need to make sure her adhesive 65 sticker was still attached firmly to her dress, Heike pressed down its corners, before shaking 32's hand.

'You're looking good on it!'

'Sorry?'

'Sixty-five. You're looking good for sixty-five!'

'Ah, yes.' Heike felt a chasm of tedium open beneath her. 'Thank you.'

The man ran a hand through his mane of greying blonde hair with the coy smugness of the model in a hair restoration commercial. And the parade began. Man. Bell. Man. They played out old lines of flirtation. Echoes of their younger selves, or banter they'd learned from bad television drama. But there was a half-heartedness to it. Without the clumsy innocence of youth, the lines were self-conscious, banal. *We know too much*, Heike thought. She was also working her way through a lot of red wine. The waitress had refilled her glass twice already and they were only half an hour, or eight dates *Christ Almighty* in.

And that had been another mistake: to imagine that a single romantic act might be indicative of a person's essential nature. To imagine that a man who once urged her to jump into his arms might have been fuelled by anything other than a moment's drunken impulse. It took years of marriage for Heike to realise that Martin was essentially a pragmatic, self-contained creature. *Dependable* (her mother). *A cold fish* (Alice). But was it that, exactly?

*

When two years of trying for a baby had yielded no results, they'd sought medical help. And in their mid-thirties, when they'd exhausted all the drugs and alternative therapies, they strapped in for the roller coaster of IVF. Martin weathered these years of appointments and disappointments – *the weepy years*, as Heike thought of them – with stoic pragmatism. And Heike – bludgeoned with hormones and needles and the recurring language of blame – her womb was *misshapen*, her body had *failed* to respond – was grateful for his solidity, his refusal to contemplate defeat. But when, after two miscarriages, they were finally, viably pregnant, she wanted his emotions to mirror the trapeze-lurch of her own.

He was very pleased, he said. He'd been sure it would all come right *in the end*. If he wrestled with any doubts or fears, he never shared them with her. Heike thought of all the times she'd buried her head into his shoulder and soaked his shirt with tears. She'd imagined him to be by her side throughout, but now she saw that in some profound, essential way, she was on her own.

And as Leonie grew from scrappy baby into plump toddler, from kindergarten to elementary school, Martin receded even further into himself. They continued to have occasional sex, those first few years of parenthood, but they were not intimate in the truest sense, their bodies merely ghosting former passion. And then the sex stopped altogether. Martin still appeared glad of Heike's company, but he didn't need her in the physical, visceral way she needed him. There was something in him that could not show vulnerability or weakness. She felt excluded. And when she found a folder of porn on his hard drive – endless videos of permed, oiled Eastern Europeans, somehow cheesily anachronistic – it confirmed her own sense of superfluity. Sexually, emotionally, he was entirely self-reliant.

*

Number 44 sat down with a groan of pain, the thread veins on his cheek a red river delta of embarrassment. 'You remind me a bit of ... of ... of ...' As his comparison fell away into the polished wood of the table, the conversation became an extended game of 'Animal, Vegetable, Mineral'. At the end of three minutes, Heike had only managed to establish that she didn't remind him of a horse, Lady Gaga, Julia Jentsch or Angela Merkel. When he tripped over the chair leg as he got up to go, she felt ferociously happy.

Thread Veins wasn't the first stranger to think her familiar. The frown, the shaking of the head as if to dislodge a deeply buried memory. *You remind me of someone.* And this apparent recognisability depressed her. It happened so frequently she'd begun to wonder whether she could lay claim to anything of her own, or whether all her features were borrowed, a pale photocopy of somebody else. Perhaps she had no personality. *You are an empty husk.* Or perhaps Berlin was filled with her doppelgängers – all just a beat away from true individuality. *I'm sure we've met before.*

The next date only wanted to talk about music and his face flooded with joy when she nodded yes, she did like Miles Davis. He breathlessly launched into a deconstruction of *Milestones*, before Heike could confess to only a passing acquaintance with the album. But by this point in the evening she was grateful to have the burden of conversation lifted from her, so she encouraged him with smiles and nods.

'A piece like that,' he ended, definitively, 'it just makes me want to shit myself.'

There was a half-time break. Heike found Alice at the bar. 'Shall we make a run for it now?' she asked, hoping that her friend would agree. But Alice simply laughed her hearty English laugh. They'd instinctively turned their bodies in towards each other, sealing themselves off from the potential advances of free-ranging males, but the symbolic, gender-dividing wall of the dating tables appeared to retain its power during the interval. The men had gathered in twos and threes around the bar, simulating matey-ness, but visibly prickling with the need to outperform each other. The women stood together in semicircles, resentful at being pressed back into female company, sipping their wine with increasing urgency. Heike wondered how many people at this event were divorcees.

Divorce made you a disappointment. Heike had been shocked to discover that even in 2018, a woman with children was not supposed to opt out of marriage. If Martin had been unfaithful or abusive, her friends might have found it easier to accommo-date, but for Heike to choose to leave on the grounds that the marriage wasn't good enough – well, that just made her some kind of emotional snob. Especially after they'd endured the trauma of IVF together. It seemed that a man who'd stuck around for that had accrued some limitless amount of credit. Even the porn was dismissed as typically absurd male weakness. Her friends would never say it to her face – they were feminists, after all – but there was a strong implication that she had neglected her true female role of endurance. It seemed that even a sexless, bick-ering marriage of small stinging criticisms, endlessly re-spooled arguments, was a more acceptable choice than separation.

A number of friends fell by the wayside. Some made their criti-cism clear, or sided with Martin, the abandoned party; others stopped replying to her texts, or evaded her suggestions of meet-ing up. At first she tried to be bullish. But faced with three evenings alone each week, when Leonie was with Martin, Heike found a friend-shaped absence she hadn't anticipated.

'We're conformist creatures,' Alice had pointed out. 'We all pretend to be free-thinkers, but when it comes down to it, we don't like people to break the rules.'

*

40

The intermission almost over, Alice drained the last of her wine.

'I think I've already found yours,' Alice said. 'I'll just have to see if I'm proved right. He's very cute.'

Heike wrinkled her forehead in a simulation of raising an eyebrow. 'Cute' was not a word that could be applied to many of the men on the floor.

Pixie-Blonde reappeared, her smile tauter and toothier than ever. She rang the bell. 'Round 2!' Heike shook her head at Alice. 'You are never doing this to me again.'

A tall, rangy man in an ill-fitting suit confessed that he hadn't been on a date since his wife had died five years ago. And because they'd been together since they were sixteen, he had no idea how to chat anyone up. 'Don't try to chat them up,' said Heike, leaning forward. 'Just talk to them.' After that, neither of them could think of anything to say.

And now a man, with prominent freckles and a head of thinning wiry hair, sat down before her. He gave Heike an assured smile. In her peripheral field of vision, she could see Alice sit up suddenly. He held out his hand.

'Hi. I'm Yusuf. The only Turkish Jewish undertaker in Berlin.' She couldn't help but laugh. It must be a well-oiled line by now, but he'd managed to make it sound spontaneous, formulated only for her. There was a pleasing rasp to his voice. His eyes, she noticed, were somewhere between brown and moss-green and slightly lopsided. The creases on his face suggested warmth, good humour. A tuft of white chest hair sprouted from the collar of his shirt, in a way that was strangely erotic. Something in her stomach lurched. *Oh no*, Heike thought. *Oh no*. But she couldn't stop herself leaning forward a little.

'I guess I'll know who to come to when I'm dead.'

'How about you?'

Heike explained that she was a sound engineer. It still sounded too pretentious to say 'sound artist', even if that was how she increasingly defined herself.

'Oh. Great. Music or TV or . . .?'

'Radio. And sound art. Installations.'

She was usually reticent about her projects. When she tried to put them into words, she could see people's eyes glaze over. That was the point. They were experiential. They weren't meant to be described. But something about Yusuf's expression invited an attempt at explanation.

'I'm working on a piece about the buildings of Berlin. The way we experience buildings, interior spaces, through our ears – not just our eyes.'

'Okay. Like echoes?'

'Yes. Or the background noises we're not even conscious of. It's like every building has its own acoustic personality. And that's what I'm trying to capture. Its audio fingerprint. That's partly to do with the sounds that already exist inside the building – or outside – but it's also about the way that the acoustics of the architecture affect any new noises. Like if someone speaks, or coughs, or drops something. The smallest sounds can suddenly acquire huge dimensions.'

Yusuf convincingly assumed the face of someone who was interested.

'I guess different materials within a space reflect the sounds in different ways?'

'Yes. Yes!' The evening's earlier tedium evaporated. 'So it's partly about recording what's already there with different kinds of microphone, but I also experiment with generating sounds and then seeing what happens to them within a particular space – dropping a pin, perhaps, or ringing a handbell, smashing a plate, an air-raid warning siren even. It sounds a bit pretentious, I know. Kunstkacke. Art shit. But it's really just drawing people's attention to something they already instinctively know. We're constantly reading the acoustics of a space – we just don't realise we're doing it.'

She should really stop now. This was the problem with too much time on her own, talking to the walls of her apartment. But Yusuf tilted his head to one side.

'You think sound affects our emotions in the same way that colour or light does?'

'Yes. I hadn't really thought of it that way. But yes. I suppose that's what I'm trying to demonstrate.'

'So where have you recorded?'

'So far, the Berliner Dom, the Reichstag, Friedrichstraße Bahnhof, Hohenschönhausen—'

'The Stasi prison?'

'Yes. Also more fun places. The Fernsehturm, the Staatsoper, Bar Jeder Vernunft – you know, the Spiegeltent . . .'

The bell made her jump.

'Shit. I'm so sorry. You must think me very rude. Banging on.'

'No, no. Not at all.'

But he seemed eager to get to his feet. And who could blame him? Under the table, she pushed her spiked heel into the top of her left foot in self-punishment for being boring.

At the end of the evening, she was astonished to learn that Yusuf had given her a tick on the speed-dating form. It turned out that each of them had only ticked the other and no one else. Heike was surprised at how much of a victory this felt. Later, in bed, wearing a jumper to counter the chill that had eaten into her bones on the journey home, she continued their exchange of text messages. At 1 a.m., their capacity for cautiously flirtatious banter exhausted, they wished each other goodnight. In his final message, he signed off with his initial and a single kiss.

*

But by the following evening, after a day shift at the radio station, she was already questioning whether she had the stomach to date an undertaker, however charismatic. She nevertheless found herself walking home from work in order to burn off last night's wine calories. Just in case. It was raining and the insubstantial leather of her shoes was soon stained and damp, but she remained committed to impressing her Fitbit with her step count. As she crossed the windswept expanse of Potsdamer Platz, she passed a billboard poster advertising an exhibition.

The image made Heike stop, despite the rain. It was a black-and-white photograph of a figure in silhouette, a diver, falling through space, their body a perfect parabola. Heike's first thought was of Leni Riefenstahl's divers in *Olympia*, filmed so that they looked like angels flying through the air. Muscular shadows soaring against a darkening sky. But the light through which this figure fell was oddly patterned. Shadows cast abstract shapes across the diver's body, as well as the space behind them. On closer examination, it didn't look like an exterior shot, it didn't – come to that – look anything like a swimming pool. It looked like a person falling through a deep stairwell. Something inside Heike shifted and caught. She didn't remember ever having seen the photo before, but something about it seemed familiar, like an image from a recurring dream.

She read the accompanying text. *Wolf Bassermann: Magic and Mystery*, the dates of the exhibition and the name of the curator, Ilse Singer. She took out her phone and snapped a picture of the poster as a reminder, but then she realised she was too late. The exhibition had already closed. Perhaps she'd order the catalogue from Dussmann's.

There was a parcel waiting for her in her pigeonhole when she returned home. A new digital recorder. She carried it up to the apartment and, with a cup of lemon tea steaming on the table

44

beside her, unpacked it carefully. The hit of freshly unwrapped plastic, scent of Leonie's Christmas-toy excitement. She discarded the instructions without reading them, inserted batteries, mic, headphones. Her index finger hit record and the acoustic world of the room dawned in her ears.

The hot-water pipes ticking, Frau Meyer's feet on the floor above. Cupboards being opened. Cooking pans. She adjusted the recording level. A vacuum cleaner from one of the apartments at the back of the building. A pigeon flapping somewhere. She couldn't quite place it. Perhaps it was sitting on the roof of the bay window. Or in the main stairwell?

She picked out other sounds. A passing bicycle. A cafe awning being wound up across the street. A group of teenage boys swearing and laughing. Tyres on the wet tarmac. Branches moving in the wind. A single leaf from the tree outside fell against the windowpane and lodged in a gap between wood and glass, fluttering. A car drove by with drum'n'bass turned up to full volume so that the whole building momentarily pulsed with it.

Under all this was a sound she couldn't identify. She turned up the gain, her eyes squinting as though this would improve her hearing. Yes. There it was. A hum, a single sustained note, low, as though on a cello or double bass. Heike wondered whether it was the purr of a distant machine, some kind of construction vehicle, but the pitch never wavered, as she'd expect it to. Just as she was about to turn the machine off, her experiment complete, a voice spoke directly into her ear.

Was können wir sonst noch tun? What else can we do?
Heike instinctively turned around to see the elderly man who had spoken. But the room was empty.

She called out, 'Hello?' and then immediately felt foolish. Someone must have been speaking loudly on the landing outside, or accidentally turned their TV on with the volume at full. Whoever had spoken had gone quiet, moved off. But then, distantly, a woman weeping. Frau Meyer? But the sound seemed to be outside the door, not above. Still recording, but slipping her headphones down to her neck, Heike went to the door of the apartment and opened it. She stood on the landing, listening. But the only human sound was that of the vacuum cleaner being passed back and forth.

She put her headphones back over her ears, but the crying had disappeared.

Heike breathed in deeply, in an effort to wake up, to uncloud her senses. Everything in front of her felt oddly remote.

She pressed the stop button a little too hard and walked back into the apartment. Sitting on the sofa, she listened back to the track she'd just recorded. There it all was: pipes, floorboards, cupboards, pans, vacuum cleaner, bike, awning, leaf, drum'n'bass. She heard herself stand up and open the apartment door, heard her feet slip-slap out onto the landing. But this time there was no cello note, no male voice, no weeping. She pulled the headphones from her ears, threw the machine down on the cushion beside her. She was clearly going mad. This is where late nights and red wine and flirting with undertakers got you.

She sent the recorder back to the manufacturer. Reason for return: faulty treble and a strange

TONJA, 1986

humming 'There's No Business Like Show Business' the day she detonates her life. Irving Berlin. A song from childhood, from her father's vinyl stash of American crooners and Broadway musicals. A guilty, uncool pleasure. In the bathroom mirror, she admires her new Ulrike Meinhof fringe, steps over the large blue holdall in the hallway and goes to check on Kurt. He sleeps flung out like a starfish, his flushed cheeks puffing gently, as though turning over some difficult question.

It is this easy to go. To leave the nursery door ajar, pick up the holdall, close the apartment door behind her and pad softly down the stairs. The latch clicks shut and she's on the street, her own woman; nothing to carry but her own life. Picking up pace now, she swings her bag in an approximation of nonchalance. She feels strangely numb. What she ought to be feeling: liberation, purpose, the blood-heat thrill of risk.

Any minute now her mother will get back from her lunch and find the answerphone message. She'll call a taxi and be at the flat within half an hour. After his midday feed, Kurt is likely to sleep through the whole thing.

The warm air of the U-Bahn station pulls her down to the platform. She is vanishing. Stefan won't try to find her. He'll rail about her selfishness, her weirdness, her *unfemininity* to all who will listen; he'll exploit his mother-in-law's anxiety to maintain appearances so that Kurt will be passed between the two households in an uneasy, but entirely reliable, arrangement. Tonja knows she's not depriving Kurt of very much – she never made a convincing mother. It had all happened too quickly, too early; her body swelling before her mind had a chance to catch up. Kurt won't remember anything. And Stefan will rewrite her as a cruel, fairy-tale mother – a mother from *Kinder- und Hausmärchen* – and within a year, take up with some plump, compliant blonde who works in the factory office. Someone who won't mind the tedium of arse-wiping, food preparation, laundry. The office blonde will become Kurt's golden fairy. And this is all for the best.

*

Monika is waiting for her on the Hallesches Tor Bridge. A stomach-flip of disappointment. If she weren't there, loitering by the statue of the fisherman and child, Tonja would have an excuse to change her mind. It would not be too late to go back to the apartment, tear up the note she left Stefan, make up some excuse for the coolly scripted message on her mum's answerphone, pick up Kurt and sit out the rest of her life. But something restless and animal in her keeps her feet moving forward.

Monika looks pissed off. But then, she looks pissed off most of the time. The corners of her eyes droop downwards, giving her the permanent expression of someone who's just received bad news. In their three years of acquaintance, Tonja's managed to make her laugh exactly two times, and both experiences have been ridiculously gratifying. Even if the sound that she makes for laughing is something between a choke and a snort. Even if Tonja's not entirely sure she likes her brittle earnestness. Still. She wishes Monika looked happier to see her.

Instead, she flicks her cigarette to the ground and stubs it out with the toe of a scuffed DM. *Good to go?* she asks, which seems inadequate to the life-altering act Tonja's just performed. There, again, the schoolgirl need for a pat on the head. This is not about her. This is about trying to change the future. And Monika is already two paces ahead into that future, striding purposefully towards the concrete circle of Mehringplatz. With her heavy blue holdall, it's hard for Tonja to keep up. She wonders whether she's supposed to be trailing her inconspicuously, whether this is part of the initiation.

Past the Peace Column with its winged angel, past the dropouts and junkies of Mehringplatz, past the anoraked patrons of a small street market, stalls piled with knock-off Gucci and beige polyester knickers. A drunk man sitting on the pavement, his back against a graffitied wall, roars at her incomprehensibly, makes an obscene gesture. She tries to assume the bearing of someone who knows where she's going, while all the time keeping Monika in her sights, frightened of losing her among the crowds. Monika's black jacket and bobbed brown hair don't help, since that's the uniform worn by at least half the population of Berlin.

She realises they've come to the southern end of Friedrichstraße, just a few blocks down from Checkpoint Charlie. The area has an abandoned atmosphere – walls covered in fly-posters, a couple of cheap cafes, a discount store – as if being amputated from the rest of the street has cut off Federal Friedrichstraße's blood supply. She's not been allowed to know the address in advance. Although she's met most of its members, she knows the collective is slow to trust newcomers. She hopes she'll be able to keep up intellectually. So many of the activists she's met are frighteningly articulate – college graduates steeped in Adorno and Marighella and theoretical terms she only pretends to understand, like plutocracy and consequentialism.

The resolve that carried her out of the front door has begun to feel fibrous, liable to pull apart. She wishes Monika would speak. Although she still can't think of her as a friend exactly – she's too taut and unknowable for that – Tonja has come to regard her as an ally. Monika was the one who'd talked the collective into accepting her. The collective had voted. And now here she is, standing outside a late nineteenth-century building on Friedrichstraße, its ornately carved sandstone dark with soot. A freakish survivor between the undifferentiated post-war blocks of weather-stained concrete.

Monika pushes upon the front door and leads the way up two flights of a wide curving staircase with a curlicued iron balustrade. The lift is apparently out of order. The stairwell smells vaguely of piss. And now, a battered door, its brown paint peeling and key-carved with expletives. Beyond the door, loud voices in session; a percussive male voice yammering above the others. *The system can no longer hide behind its lies.* Entering the room at Monika's shoulder, she recognises the speaker as a man called Rainer. He does not break flow at the appearance of this newcomer, although a few others in the group – all variously sitting on tables, chairs and grubby cushions on the floor – look up. No one smiles. Everything in the room is impregnated with the citrus tang of stale pot . . . *if we don't regard this moment as a call to arms, we are acquiescing in the capitalist stranglehold of our culture . . .*

She had first met Monika on an anti-missile protest. This was pre-pregnancy, but post-marriage. Tonja wore a CND badge and carried a placard she'd carefully painted with a death's head and the words 'Atomic Death Threatens Us All'. She'd gone along with a skinhead called Christiane, but became separated from her in the crowd. But it didn't matter. She was caught up in the ebullient anger of the protestors, shouting in chorus until they were hoarse – *Rockets out! Amis out! No to Pershings, No to Cruise!* Someone set fire to a poster of Ronald Reagan. A few people threw rocks at a passing US army jeep. But the mood was mostly high-spirited, the air full of shouts and songs and whistles.

But as the crowd turned the corner of Kolonnenstraße, the texture of the sound changed. Tonja became aware of a commotion behind her and then the crowd of protestors began to surge forward, pushing past her, breaking into a run. Tonja stopped for a moment, confused, looking around for Christiane, but she was nowhere to be seen. This delay was an error. Too late, she began to run. As she tried to catch up with the protestors ahead of her, she looked over her shoulder to see a dark wave pushing forward – uniforms and helmets and raised billy clubs. A mist started to fall over the crowd. She screwed up her eyes, tried not to breathe it in. Ahead of her, young people scattered chaotically. She was only five-feet four and had never been athletic. Her legs couldn't propel her forward quickly enough.

The policeman caught her by the arm. Tonja tried to shrug him off, but his grip was too tight. She leaned forward with all her weight in a bid to release herself and the fabric of her jacket ripped from his grasp. But she couldn't right herself in time and stumbled forward, palms and knees scraping the tarmac. Before she could stagger to her feet, a boot pushed her to the ground. And that's when he started to kick her.

At first she couldn't believe that a man would do such a thing. The first blow found her chest, the second her stomach, and then a third and a fourth. I'm eighteen, she wanted to say. I'm a schoolgirl. You're kicking a schoolgirl. Instinctively, she curled up, knees to her belly, hands in front of her face. Through her fingers she could just make out a moustache, beetroot cheeks. How old was he? Forty? Forty-five? Same age as her dad. His blood was up and she was easy prey. And then he whacked her across the back with his truncheon.

All the air in her lungs was discharged onto the tarmac. She thought her entire ribcage must have cracked. Couldn't conceive that another person could think to do this to her. That her life was about to end, here on the filthy wet tarmac. But someone pulled him off and he was away. Raising his stick to hit someone else.

Now the kicking had stopped, the pain flared. Every inch of her torso shouted with the coming bruises. Vivid colours danced before her closed eyes.

A stranger knelt in front of her. Put a hand on her arm and pulled her upright. Somehow they hobbled together away from the street and into the shelter of an alleyway. Tonja leaned her back against a wall and sank to the ground. The stranger knelt in front of her, looked earnestly into her face. She had a fringe, wire-frame glasses, a trace of body odour and seemed impossibly glamorous.

Fucking pigs, Monika said. *The fucking pigs.*

Monika took her to the nearest hospital's emergency room. Sat with her during the long hours of waiting. She didn't say much. Her right leg jiggled impatiently, bouncing on the ball of her foot. Tonja found herself staring at it, trying to displace attention from the burning sensation in her chest and belly. She was glad not to be alone. She'd never been in a hospital before and she felt suddenly small and frightened. There were several others from the protest with bleeding heads, or swollen, torn faces. They acknowledged each other with nods or wry grimaces.

The emergency doctor clearly had little patience with protestors. He took a cursory glance at Tonja's bruises, prodded her belly, ignored her yelps of pain.

No damage done. Get yourself home. Take a bath. You'll be sore for a few days but it's all superficial.

It doesn't feel superficial.

The doctor tilted his head.

Your parents are going to get a bit of shock when they see you.

I don't live with my parents. I live with my husband.

She saw Monika's eyes widen.

You're married?

Tonja nodded.

Fuck me. How old are you? Seventeen?

Eighteen.

The doctor turned to Monika, but he was talking about her.

Old enough to be married, old enough to stay out of trouble.

*

She'd married Stefan to shock her schoolmates. Also to piss off her mum, though that soon backfired, as her mother thought the sun shone out of Stefan's arse. Tonja had left school the year before, relieved to escape the tramlines of education. She wasn't a natural troublemaker, she just wasn't engaged. And there was no one in her year group she felt drawn to, no intimacies of a best friend.

Her teachers interpreted her silence as sullenness. She had 'an attitude'. And because they saw her as a rebel, she started to behave as one. Voiced opinions she knew would shock, enjoyed seeing the effect words could have.

She knew her teachers wondered why she wasn't more like her older brother, Günther. He'd been the clever one, sailing through school and into university. From early on, it had been clear that she was never going to live up to him. Their parents made a half-hearted attempt to encourage her academically – they wanted something more for their daughter than their own energy-sapping jobs on the washing machine production line at Bosch Siemens. But her annual report cards were always a disappointment. She heard them say to their friends, *Ah, well, Tonja's more of an artistic type*, although she didn't know what they based this on, other than the desultory sketching she resorted to when bored. To her parents, the Arts represented anything alternative or youth-oriented. It became a convenient catch-all to explain their daughter's lack of direction.

Stefan was already at Technical College when they met, training as a mechanical engineer. Tonja was drawn to his groundedness, his maturity, his glossy black hair. He too wanted to frame her as an artistic type, his bohemian freethinker. And she played up to this by buying increasingly outlandish clothes – a scarlet velvet cloak, a feathered hunting cap, lacy petticoats worn as a skirt.

She found a job in a record shop and became knowledgeable about New German Wave, synthpop, ska.

When she began to show an interest in political activism, Stefan encouraged it, thinking it would bring her out of herself. He indulged her passionate but incoherent rants on social inequality, the oppressive state machine. They had nothing in common, really, but they told themselves this was the key to their mutual attraction – fire and ice, yin and yang.

Stefan qualified and immediately found a job at the BMW plant with good prospects and a decent wage. On the day of his first pay cheque, he took her out for a celebratory dinner, and between main course and dessert, proposed. They were both living with their parents at the time, frustrated at the lack of private space, sneaking around so that they could have sex on the rare occasions they were left alone in the flat. In two years of dating, they'd not spent so much as a single complete night together. Marriage represented the chance to escape. And their fierce hunger for each other's bodies carried them through for a while – an opiate that dulled any awareness of incompatibility. Although he joined the union, Stefan declared himself happy with his working conditions and with his fat, good-natured line manager. When Tonja pressed him on profit capitalism's exploitation of the labouring classes, he shrugged and said *that's just the way it's always been*.

After the hospital, Monika had walked her to a bus stop and shouted at the driver to look after her. Tonja didn't expect to see her again. She'd registered the judgement in Monika's eyes at her confession to being married. She could tell that in Monika's world, marriage was patriarchal repression, and marriage at eighteen the choice of country bumpkins or imbeciles. So she was startled when Monika turned up at the record shop a few days later, especially as she had no recollection of telling Monika where she worked.

Just wanted to check you were okay.

Tonja was flooded with gratitude. Her flesh was still swollen and tender, but she wasn't about to betray this.

Yeah. I'm fine.

What she didn't say was that her stomach was a fiery pit of rage. That she kept seeing the police officer's red face, moustache, the spittle on his lip. That his right boot had confirmed that the state did not exist to protect her. It existed only to suppress. To destroy.

She had crossed a threshold from a generalised anger at her own powerlessness to a sharply focused hate. Though her body ached like that of an old woman, her mind felt clear. For the first time she felt fully alive. And Monika's appearance seemed to her a sign.

We're going to the protest on Saturday. Want to come along?

She pulled out a dark pink flyer with details of a demo at the Olympic Stadium. Tonja calculated. She'd have to bunk off work.

Yeah. Sure. Where shall I meet you?

At the stadium, as Jesse Owens's widow unveiled a plaque in memory of her husband's four gold medals, watched by various American athletes and members of the Olympics committee, the two women stood among several hundred protestors. Between them, they raised a banner that read 'Athletes Against Atomic Weapons'. Tonja had painted the words in red on a white sheet, before adding the Olympic rings beneath. The paint had smudged a bit, but it didn't matter. That day, the police behaved themselves, no doubt conscious of the presence of international onlookers. But some older Berliners booed the protestors, saying they brought shame on Germany. *Nazi pigs*, Monika said. Every cell in Tonja danced with purpose. She was on the side of the good people.

*

In the months that followed, there were more demos, meetings, public talks, earnest discussions in bars and cafes, night-time missions to spray slogans on walls. Every few days, Monika would turn up at the record shop with pamphlets or books she thought Tonja would find interesting.

There were no confidences, no sharing of personal information. All that Tonja knew about Monika was that she'd grown up in a suburb of Frankfurt and studied philosophy at university. She also learned that Monika lived in a squat as part of a revolution-ary collective, but she didn't know where, although it seemed they'd managed to avoid the recent crackdowns on squatters, which had cleared many of the squats in Kreuzberg with tear gas and batons.

Monika never asked for Tonja's home address, showed no inter-est in her past and was quite open about not wanting to meet Stefan. Tonja had the impression that she viewed Stefan as an aberration who, if ignored, could be wished out of existence. As the months went by, Tonja sensed she was being assessed, though for what she wasn't sure. But she knew she wanted to pass.

After a demo against solitary confinement for political prison-ers, a few of the organisers headed for a local bar. When Monika suggested she tag along, she felt absurdly flattered. Over bottles of Pils, the conversation became fierce and sotto voce.

1977 was a complete fuck-up, Monika said. *The RAF was all over the place. Divided, muddled in their thinking.*
Tonja's heart hammered. *Is your collective allied to the Red Army Faction?*

A few of us used to be. But we got tired of their shit. We knew we could do better. So we formed this group and we're more focused than the RAF, more strategic. We have concrete, achiev-able aims.

*

It didn't occur to Tonja to interrogate what those achieva aims might be; she was thrilled to be entrusted with such confi- dences. She glowed with the ecstasy of the initiate.

It was because they were women, wasn't it? That the state hated them so much?

Monika tilted her head. *Go on.*

Because they saw them as unnatural – women committing acts of violence, Meinhof and Ensslin abandoning their children.

Monika put her glass down definitively.

Motherhood and political struggle are irreconcilable.

Are they?

Family is the main oppressor of women. Children are used as blackmail – women made to think that children are the primary function of their lives. That they have no business aspiring to political agency. The patriarchy determines that women can't be seen through any lens distinct from their private lives. They can only be one or the other – private or political. Never both.

Tonja shifted on her bar stool.

I'm not really into all that feminist stuff. I mean – I don't think men are the enemy. I mean – I don't think we should prioritise women's rights over workers' rights. We have to work for true equality first. For everyone.

Monika laid a hand on her arm. Other than that first day on the street, when Monika had helped her bruised body from the ground, they had never touched. Now the sensation of Monika's flesh through her shirt was like an electric jolt.

I'm going to stop going to demos.

The electric charge immediately subsided, went to earth.

Oh. Why?

I need to go underground for a bit. I think I can achieve more that way.

Monika drained the last of her beer.

Get me another, will you?

*

Tonja knew that if she spent the last few marks in her purse, she wouldn't have enough to buy dinner and then there'd be a row with Stefan. *Sure.* She clambered inelegantly up from the bench, tugging down the miniskirt that had proved inappropriate attire for four hours at a freezing barricade. *Anyone else need a drink?* she asked the rest of the group, hoping that no more than two of them said yes. Two of them said yes. At the bar, she counted out her loose change, relieved to find she could cover the total bill. The barman sniffed at the handful of coins poured into his hand, but tough shit. She returned triumphantly to the table with the four beers.

I'd like to do something, she told Monika later that evening. *I'd like to be a part of what you're doing. I'm sick of seeing the poor and vulnerable shat upon.*
Monika leaned in. Her clothes smelt of crystallised sweat. *How much are you prepared to lose?*
  Lose?
  The struggle demands selflessness, sacrifice, fearlessness.
  I think I'm pretty fearless. And as she says it, she believes this to be true.
Monika clinked her bottle against Tonja's. *Revolución o muerte!*
  Yes, Tonja said, not fully understanding the Spanish. Was mauerte something to do with the Wall? But she looked gratefully across at Monika and raised her beer. *Yes. Here's to that.*

The next day, Tonja handed a bottle of urine to a nurse. When the result was announced, she didn't know how to feel. It hadn't been planned, but neither had she taken precautions. She didn't tell Stefan immediately. She needed time to absorb this new reality, wanted the option of a secret abortion.

But one Saturday, lying in bed after sleepy morning sex, her back curved against the soft curls of Stefan's chest, she found herself

confessing, saying the alien words out loud for the first time into the bedroom's rose wallpaper. There was a moment's silence, then a strange choking sound. She rolled over and was astonished to discover him in tears.

It's all I've ever wanted.

She realised that should have been her line.

In the curtained gloom of the Friedrichstraße squat, Rainer is still talking.

It's time to open a new chapter in revolutionary strategy at the centre of imperialism! Protest is not enough. Too many on the left are prepared to live vicariously – to let others do their fighting for them, to let others go to prison for them, endure hunger strikes and force-feeding and beatings, while they stay cosy and cocooned in their lives of privilege. But everyone here knows that the only way forward is targeted direct action.

Tonja's been sitting cross-legged on the floor for forty minutes and her thighs have started to ache. Something in her feels reckless.

And what does that mean?

What do you think it means?

Rainer fixes her with his protuberant eyeballs. She can see white all the way around his brown irises.

You know what we're about, Tonja. And if that's not for you, you can walk out that door right now. I haven't got time to babysit you, or to justify our methods. But if you want to go back to your kid and your husband and your bourgeois life, go now. But if you stay, you're involved. No backing out. So. What's it to be?

She holds his pop-eyed gaze.

I'm staying.

After the meeting, Monika gives her a tour of the apartment. The main living space is at the front of the building. The grand bay window would look out onto Friedrichstraße, but the curtains are drawn and — she discovers later — never opened. Several members of the collective also sleep in here, as evidenced by the sleeping bags and cushions piled against one wall. Next to this is a large, windowless cupboard, which might once have been a pantry, or a linen cupboard. This is where Rainer sleeps — the only person to have a private room.

In the kitchen, Jörg and Kat sit at a large dark-wood table, surrounded by wires and cutters and plastic bottles. The coils on the table remind her of intestines. Her arms feel weak and prickly, her head suddenly emptied of thought. A fierce thirst makes her reach for a glass on the drainer, which she fills from the tap. As she raises it to her lips, Kat springs from the chair and makes a lunge, dashing the glass from her hand to shatter on the tiled floor.

What the—?

That had sulphuric acid in it a minute ago. Jesus.

Tonja instinctively creates a space between herself and every surface in the kitchen, raising her hands defensively.

Sorry. Sorry.

Just be careful for Chrissake. And don't even think about smoking in here.

Monika puts a hand on Tonja's shoulder and guides her past the bomb-makers and back into the hallway. She nods to indicate the door to the main bedroom and Tonja feels duty-bound to take a look inside, like a prospective tenant assessing a prime piece of property. There is no furniture as such. A stained double mattress, an equally stained futon unrolled on the floor, piles of books and magazines, drinks cans and abandoned clothes. She tries not to let any hint of bourgeois revulsion show on her face.

There is a second bedroom across the hall. The door stands open at 45 degrees — the widest possible angle, as the room is crammed with two mattresses and a single bed with a broken spine. A pile of bedding, the colour of rotting leaves, is stacked by the head-board; the window is covered with a paisley shawl. Before Monika speaks, Tonja knows that this will be her bunk.

She sleeps badly that night, between a waifish young woman called Angelika and a snoring Kat. Unused to such close proximity with other women, she's too self-conscious to take off her clothes, so leaves them on to wake up at 2 a.m. in a sweat. She wonders whether Kurt has noticed her absence. She wonders if Stefan is also lying awake. Whether he'll get out of bed in the morning, wash, shave, dress and go to work, as normal. Whether he'll come to see their marriage as an odd blip in his life.

Since Kurt was born, their relationship has become one of daily fights over trivial, impersonal things – the true meaning of a pop lyric, the best brand of margarine, the most efficient way to fold baby clothes. These small tussles a distraction from the larger chasm into which their marriage was slipping. There was no longer that physical urgency that had once propelled them to fuck in shop doorways, in parks and car parks, in his parents' bathroom. Instead they lay at the furthest reaches of their double bed, a no-man's-land of polyester sheet between them.

Stefan hadn't forced her into parenthood, but still she resented that the consequences of parenthood were for her so fundamentally life-changing, while his day-to-day proceeded much as before. She'd thought her maternal instincts would kick in once the baby arrived, but there was none of the euphoria she'd expected. Kurt would lie in her arms after a feed, drunk with milk, feather-soft, but she felt only bone-tired, blank. She did her duty by him, but it was mechanical. Without her job, without the company of other activists, she felt stranded. She'd long lost contact with her schoolmates and Monika never visited, presumably too deeply underground. Her mother's visits felt oppressive and judgemental – *why hadn't she attended to this? why was she doing it like that?*

But life in the squat brings a new kind of isolation. She knows the other members of the collective don't think her clever enough. Never mind, she tells herself, she can learn. And she's stirred by the group's discussions of social justice and wealth redistribution, of the need to quash the country's latent fascism, of their commitment to removing US forces and their nuclear arsenal from Europe; she's moved by their eloquent visions of what the world might be, persuaded by their logic that the only way to counter a militaristic regime is with military action. But her attempts to contribute to the debate feel banal, borrowed. Occasionally Monika appears to sense this and is generous, encouraging her to speak up and then nodding in support. Tonja craves their approval, tries to demonstrate that she is the most hard-working, the most committed. She's also the only one who ever cleans the bathroom.

There are no leaders in the collective, but there is a tacit acceptance that Rainer is at the centre of any decisions. He's bright and articulate, and though his features are too oddly proportioned to be attractive, he carries himself with the confidence of a film star, sporting a Trotsky beard and a red and white keffiyeh around his neck. His fingers are yellow with nicotine. He also possesses an unerring ability to have the last word in any argument.

Like most of the other men in the collective, Rainer had drifted to Berlin in order to avoid national service. Tonja has to push hard against an instinct deeply ingrained in her – something rooted in her parents' sense of social duty – that can't help but see this as shirking, as a form of privileged laziness. She also questions how he can understand the working-class experience when he receives a monthly allowance from his parents. But she knows these are impulses that need re-educating.

*

Tonja spends exactly forty-four days in the squat. Thirteen people share the four rooms and single bathroom. It's a warm autumn. Because the windows are never opened and laundry is not a political priority, the apartment is stuffy and rank-smelling. There are protests and sit-ins. There are meetings. There is a lot of soup. Tonja begins to think if she has to drink any more Kartoffelsuppe she might self-immolate.

Although Rainer's windowless sleeping space is cramped and smells of unwashed clothes, most nights some girl seems prepared to share it with him. Over time, Tonja learns that he's slept with most of the women in the squat except Kat who, at thirty-eight, is the oldest member of the group and a lesbian. *Though that didn't stop him trying*, Kat tells her, with a look to the heavens. *He's an arsewipe, but he's a charismatic arsewipe.*

He's not slept with Monika either, because it's very clear to everyone, including Rainer, that Monika's in love with him. Tonja can see he's turned on by the power of denial. And because she's Monika's friend, or project – Tonja still hasn't determined which – it's not long before Rainer turns his attentions to her.

One morning, he's in the hallway as she emerges from the bathroom wrapped in just a towel, and he makes it clear that he's looking her up and down, grading her. He even lets his tongue play briefly on his bottom lip. She avoids his eyes and hurries into the cramped bedroom, stubbing her toe on the foot of the bed which makes her curse loudly.

That evening, as everyone sits on cushions, passing around a joint, discussing the latest bomb attacks in Paris, Rainer reclines on the floor beside her like a Roman emperor waiting to be fed grapes. He somehow contrives to position his body so that she's cut off from the others. She hopes he's not about to ask searching ideological questions. But no. He doesn't require her to speak,

63

he simply wants her to listen. *The trouble with Berlin,* he says, *The trouble with Berlin is that it's like a city in waiting. But the real Germany's happening over there.* He gestures west. *In boring bourgeois bureaucratic Bonn. We've become bystanders. The resistance is losing momentum. Apathy has crept in. We need to do something to reignite the will to political struggle.* Rainer's protruding eyes hold her in what she assumes is meant to be an intensely sexual gaze. She's reminded of nature documentaries. A praying mantis on a stalk of grass. *It's up to us. To bring Germany here. To make them pay attention.*

She knows it's a game. She also feels a loyalty to Monika. But it's hard to work out what the consequences of rejecting him might be. His breath is stale with cigarettes. His face appals her.

After a fortnight of sustained attempts to get her into the suffocating little cupboard, she decides on her own compromise. One evening, when the squat is quieter than usual, she drinks several shots of cheap vodka and gives him a blow job in the bathroom. On her knees, the full olfactory force of a shared toilet hits her, quite literally, in the face. But at least she doesn't have to look into Rainer's mantis eyes.

After this encounter, he leaves her alone and makes her insignificance clear. If Monika knows about her betrayal, she never says anything.

On Tonja's thirty-sixth day in the squat, there's a meeting about the intended target. A list has been drawn up and the name of a man she's never heard of is at the top. Photographs are passed around. In every shot, he seems to be rushing somewhere, his limbs blurred, his eyes blank with purpose. He has a small bald patch. He is the CEO of a construction company that has won more than half of the contracts for building yuppie housing on the ruins of bulldozed homes. He looks entirely ordinary. But according to Rainer, he is responsible for *actions hostile to the people*.

On the thirty-seventh day, she goes out with Monika to scout the intended location, a task for which she is told to wear her most middle-class clothes. She's never seen Monika in a skirt before and the effect is unnerving. She looks like the receptionist in an undertaker's. They travel together in silence to the suburbs. Monika, who's been here before and committed the route to heart, leads the way confidently from the U-Bahn station through tree-lined suburban streets towards a small park and children's playground dotted with small, bright bodies and their hovering mothers. They head for a bench, well out of earshot.

His house is just around the corner. Every morning he's driven to work by the same route. His silver Mercedes leaves the house at 6.45 a.m., and they drive up this road, past the park and take a left at the junction. Kat's planning to set off an explosion just across the road, controlling the timing from here. She can conceal herself in those bushes there.

What about the children?

What about the children?

Well, the playground—

At 6.45 in the morning? There won't be any children here then.

And the . . . Tonja gropes for a word she can say out loud. *The device. Is it accurate?*

It should be. Kat trained in Iraq. She knows what she's about.

They sit in silence. Tonja's cotton dress is too thin for this October day, but she does her best not to shiver. She listens to the squeals of the playground toddlers, the iron strain of the swings, a blackbird's warning call from the tree behind.

*

Beyond the park, over the tops of the aspens that are just starting to turn to gold, she can see the upper storeys of the detached houses. She thinks of all that vacant space; all those unoccupied guest bedrooms, playrooms piled with discarded toys, grand dining rooms employed once in a blue moon to impress colleagues with catered dinner parties, gardeners tending vast lawns for owners who rarely venture beyond the patio. The greed and emptiness and waste of it all.

She thinks of the house around the corner, the people inside it who don't know what's coming. She reasons that this is true of everyone, that no one knows their own destiny. She reasons that he deserves what is coming to him, reminds herself how many people's lives he has made miserable, in order that he might have that oversized house, a driver to take him to work each morning, a glamorous trophy wife. These people were oblivious to the realities of ordinary people's existence. Blind to petitions, deaf to the voices of protestors. There were no options left if you wanted to change the future.

Alone with Monika, she dares a question.
Who decided that Rainer should be the leader?
There's no leader. We're all equal. Everyone contributes to the struggle.
But that's not really true—
Each of us is responsible for our own actions.
Well, yes, but someone ultimately takes control. And that's usually – always – Rainer.
Not always. Kat's the eldest. Though she's more at the practical end.
Tonja feels foolish for not knowing the answer, but asks anyway.
Have you done this before?
Monika checks that there is no one nearby to hear.
We targeted a US checkpoint. But there was a problem with the detonator and the timing went wrong.

What happened?

Nothing much. Premature ejaculation. So to speak. Rainer blamed Jörg, but I think it was just shoddy materiel. Belgian.

There is something sacred about the way Monika says Rainer's name.

Does Rainer ever take part in . . . she stumbles for the right word – *actions?*

There is the briefest twitch in Monika's left eyelid.

He's the strategist. We're the army.

At a meeting of the collective that afternoon, they report their findings, present a sketch of the road and park. They have timed all movements as precisely as possible. Roles are agreed. Just before dawn, in the only car owned by the collective, Monika will drive Kat, Jörg and Tonja to the road behind the park. The four of them will then split up. Jörg will lay the explosives and Kat will install herself in the bushes with the remote detonator. Tonja will act as lookout while Monika drives the short distance to the target's house and parks up somewhere where she can discreetly monitor all movements on his driveway. They never refer to him by name. He is simply 'the target'.

The group has invested in a Philips car phone and at the moment the target's car leaves the house, Monika will phone through to the phone box opposite the park, where Tonja will be waiting. As soon as she picks up, she'll have exactly twenty-five seconds to head into the park, where her appearance will be the cue for Kat. She won't stop, but will walk to the gate at the far end of the park, where Monika will be waiting with the car to pick them up.

Tonja wasn't originally implicated in this operation, but she finds herself volunteering. When Rainer asks her to confirm that she understands the plan, as though her participation in the conversation has been that of someone speaking a second language, her mouth is so dry she can barely answer. *Yes. Yes, I understand*

SARA, 1929

but now he was on top of her, inside her. Murmuring something in her ear. She used to strain to catch each phrase, listening out for the key, the word that might unlock it all for her and help her achieve the pleasure all those yearning love songs suggested was possible. *Eine kleine Sehnsucht*. Maybe then it wouldn't be so painful. She tried to remove herself from her body, as though she were watching this event from above, but that just made it absurd, humiliating. She wondered why God hadn't designed something more elegantly ritualistic for the continuation of the species. Like one of those eighteenth-century dances in the movies, all bobbing and grace.

At least Matz was kind and had relented to her once-a-week suggestion to give her body time to recover, but this meant each Friday had taken on a special texture, an involuntary sense of growing dread, a ticking down to his return at six from the office. Then the ritual of wine and dinner before the event towards which the whole evening leaned.

She tried delays. Extending conversations beyond their natural span of interest, prattling on about the small encounters of her day, the people she had met on the stairs, on the street; something interesting she had heard on the Telefunken. She always meant to make an effort to remember the jokes in particular, she liked to make him laugh. But the comedic stories on the radio ran off her mind like heavy rain from leaves, or she would only partially remember them and deliver them badly, fumbling the punch line, and Matz would ruffle her hair and laugh at his hopeless Kabarettist and use this as the moment to initiate a caress.

*

And she'd try to respond in the ways she imagined he wanted. She let him put his tongue in her mouth, although the reptilian darting about and taste of onions made her want to gag. And she let him squeeze her breasts, even though they were often tender. And she knew by now to prepare ahead and smear Vaseline down there to make the pounding easier to bear.

But there was no getting away from it. Married love was disappointing. The novels she had read as a girl had filled her with all kinds of chemical lightness, had made her reach down at night, under the bedclothes. And this is what she'd thought marriage would release. All those forbidden, unmentionable sensations. But Matz's naked body was a difficult thing to desire. He was pale and thin, his skin surprisingly blotchy beneath his shirt. And she tried not to look too directly at his thing, which seemed like a creature apart from him; she could not connect it with the cheery, distracted man she shared a breakfast table with.

She wished she had a good friend to talk to about this. But the two school friends she still saw with any frequency were not, she realised, the confidantes she needed. Were Melita and Irmgard both as contented as they claimed to be, when the three of them met for their monthly coffee at the Café am Zoo? Was it all one big mutual lie? Did they both lie happily back in their marriage beds as their husbands ploughed away at them? Perhaps Irmgard, being four months pregnant, had earned a reprieve from sex until the baby was born. Sara wanted to ask so many questions. She wanted the guilty thrill of complaining about her husband or, at the very least, to giggle about the absurdity of sex. But they were shuttered on such intimate subjects.

Marriage is a conspiracy of silence, Sara thought. *We're all so desperate to believe in it, that we feed the fairy tale just to keep things pleasant, just to keep us all humming along to the fruit market and the laundry, just to keep us on our backs, enduring the—*

Matz finished, finally, with a guttural moan and rolled over beside her. Within a few minutes, he was snoring loudly. Sara tugged at the edge of her nightdress, which had become caught under him, and quietly pushed herself off the bed. She could feel his semen, already cold, trickling down her thighs.

She crossed the hallway into the small, cramped bathroom, sat on the lavatory and concentrated hard to make herself pee. The urine stung, making the soreness worse. She then used her flannel to wash herself carefully, outside, and as far inside as she dared. She stood for five minutes, leaning on the washstand, in the hope that it would all trickle out. It was a betrayal, she knew. She knew good wives wanted babies. But she did not want a baby. And maybe she didn't want to be a good wife either.

This rebellious thought summoned the image of her parents. They'd be horrified by the contents of her mind, by the waywardness of their only child. They loved her, but they had no idea who she was. She had no idea who she was.

Matz left early on weekday mornings, before sunrise. He was a salesman for Auergesellschaft, where his current product was radioactive toothpaste *for a naturally bright smile!* and in the course of his duties, he might travel all over Brandenburg. Sara liked to get up with him, to prepare his coffee and breakfast, even though he insisted there was no need, he could see to himself. But once he was gone, the time between breakfast and the start of the day proper felt sparse and restless.

Outside the drawing room's bay window, Friedrichstraße was already tuning up, preparing for the day's overture. The steady clip of a butcher's cart with its yellow and red wheels, the ascending scale of an approaching bus, the rattle of bicycles weaving their way through the humming baritones of motorcars, the squeal of a steel handle drawing out a shop awning, someone – a child perhaps – practising halting scales on a piano, a man hawking perfume at the corner of Hedemannstraße, the street sweeper with his two-wheel cart, dexterously employing brush and spade to scoop up the morning's detritus, while somewhere a man roared, 'Hey, Orge! Orge! Come back here, you sewage farmer!'

She retreated from the window to sit in the armchair and flick through a magazine, but her heart wasn't in it. She picked up a novel that Frau Kimmel had lent her, but the concierge's taste was for romantic adventures with titles like *The Blue-Eyed Captain* or *The Blonde Mountaineer* and the florid prose tobogganed off Sara's brain, so that after just a few pages she realised she'd no idea who any of the characters were.

A block away, but out of sight, a building was being demolished. Sara could hear the impact of the wrecking ball and the split-second hiatus before the collapse of bricks and plaster. The city constantly destroyed and remade, impatient to be in the future. There was something in her that understood its restlessness, its impulse to destruction.

She felt marooned, purposeless. The apartment was large and light-filled, but in the daytime, with hours on her own, Sara felt the claustrophobia of her own company. She wished she'd had the foresight to attend secretarial college, so that she could be one of those young women who clicked down Friedrichstraße clutching envelope bags, heading to the office. She imagined the demanding but fair-minded boss, lunch-hour sandwiches with the other girls, the ranks of filing cabinets, the ringing telephones and the relief of five o'clock, leaving the desk with aching shoulders. But somehow this was not a path that had ever been on offer to her.

At ten to nine, there was a loud crash on the landing outside. Sara pulled her housecoat cord a little tighter and hurried to the door.

Half on the stair, half on the landing, an angular young woman with a sharply cut bob of dark hair was muttering furious obscenities, apparently directed at the stairs. She wore black, with a flash of green silk scarf, her four limbs flung wide at strange angles. Insect-like. At first glance, Sara feared the woman's leg to be dislocated, but then she managed to pull herself up, still swearing.

'Did you fall?'

'No, I deliberately decided to sledge down here from the fourth floor.'

'Sorry. Stupid question. Are you all right?'

'No I think I've probably smashed both my kneecaps because I bet that old sow's been polishing the stairs again? I SAY' and she raised her voice to call downstairs in the direction of Frau Kimmel's apartment, 'HAS THAT OLD SOW BEEN POLISHING THE STAIRS AGAIN? and my stockings are in shreds and I only bought them yesterday and naturally I spent every last bloody pfennig on—'

'You're bleeding!'

'Shit. And I'm late already.'

'Come inside. Let me sort you out.'

For the first time, the woman looked directly at Sara, who immediately felt in the wrong. The stranger's eyes were bright, mocking. Sara's hand flittered uncertainly to her chest. The woman registered this tic, and bit her bottom lip with amusement.

'I could be anybody.'

'Yes.'

'Could be a murderer.'

Something in Sara rose.

'Well, if you are, I'll just push you down the next flight. You could try Frau Kimmel instead – she's a lot frailer than me. And she keeps her money in a tin by the kettle.'

The insect woman grinned.

'Do you have coffee?'

'I have coffee.'

Holding on to her torn stocking, she hobbled past Sara into the hallway and without needing direction, made her way into the living room. Sara followed.

'I don't want to mess up your couch.'

'Have that wooden chair, then. I'll go fetch some bandages.'

In the kitchen, Sara heated the kettle, found a clean towel and took out the tin of medical supplies, her ears alert to the presence of another human being in the flat. The woman's proximity filled her with a strange and sudden joy.

She found the insect still standing, despite her injury, squinting at one of the Alpine prints Matz had nailed to the wall. Sara had chosen the pictures, finding their expansive skies an escape from the horizonless city, but their pleasure was compromised for her by the tightly regular way Matz had chosen to nail them up, one above the other. The spacing was all wrong, but she had never had the courage to tell him. His lack of instinct for such things dismayed her and now the glittering peaks of the mountains reflected only irritation.

'Did your husband choose these?'

'No. Why?'

'I always think mountainscapes a bit macho. Phallic, you know.'

Sara wasn't altogether sure what 'phallic' was, but it didn't sound like a compliment.

'I like them. I find them uplifting.'

'I bet.' What did that thin-lipped smile mean? 'Not much like Berlin, are they?'

Sara knew she was being patronised and resented it.

'Well, I don't need a picture of the KaDeWe on my wall.'

'True. Or the Plötzensee Prison.'

Sara blushed and laughed.

'Do you want to sit down and let me look at that knee?'

'Sure.'

She limped over to the chair and sat down, unselfconscious and ungainly, her knees slightly open. Sara set the bowl and bandages on the table beside her, as she proceeded to unclip and roll down her bloodied stocking. The stranger's skin was pale, ghost-mapped with faint blue veins, the muscles clearly defined in her slender calves. For a moment Sara forgot to move. Then the woman looked up at her expectantly.

'Do you have a flannel? I can clean it up myself.'

'No, no, please let me.'

Sara knelt in front of her, wetted the flannel and carefully washed the wound. The woman sucked in her breath.

'Sorry. It's a nasty gash. You must have taken quite a tumble.'

'Practically the whole flight.'

'There's going to be a bad bruise. You don't think you should see a doctor?'

'Not when I have you.'

The tone of this last made Sara look up and then quickly down again, aware of the heat spreading in her cheeks.

'Were you on your way to work?'

'U-huh.'

Something told Sara not to probe further, but she couldn't resist an apparently innocent follow-up.

'Do you have to go far?'

'No. Not far.'

Sara unrolled a length of bandage and cut it carefully with a small pair of shell-inlaid scissors. She began to wind the cloth gently around the woman's knee, allowing enough slack to permit movement.

'I'm sure they'll understand when you explain what happened.'

'You reckon?'

'Well, I . . .' Sara, not for the first time, was aware of her own inexperience in the ways of the working world.

'I'll be keeping the pianist waiting. And he's on an hourly rate.'

'Pianist?'

'I'm a singer.'

Sara looked up from her bandaging at the woman's angular cheeks, cropped hair. She couldn't imagine this woman singing Schubert lieder. Her patient seemed to read her thoughts.

'Don't worry. We're not talking the State Opera.'

'What are we talking?'

'Zimze. It's a nightclub, up near Unter den Linden. I'm part of the Kabarett.'

The word found Sara's guts. It spoke of dark cellars and sex. Whores and transvestites and men with rouged faces.

'Are you any good?'

Where did this sudden boldness come from? Her cheeks burned with it. But the insect was unruffled.

'Yes. I am. Damn good.'

'I'd love to—'

'No you wouldn't. Your husband would have a fit.'

This conjuration of Matz made Sara feel suddenly at fault.

'What sort of thing do you sing?'

The woman grinned.

'If you want to find that out, you'll have to come by. All I can tell you is that it's thoroughly disreputable.'

The following afternoon, Sara stood in her kitchen, slicing up beef flank for a Rouladen. The kitchen was to the rear of the building and had been constructed from the division of a larger room when the house had been converted to flats. The wall between Sara's kitchen and the adjoining apartment was made of thin, insubstantial plasterboard and she could hear her

75

neighbour, Frau Kowalcyzk, singing along to the radio. *There's something idiotic in the air! There's something hypnotic in the air!*

The window looked down on the yard that served the draper's store on the ground floor of the building. From where she stood, Sara could watch the vans being unloaded, Herr Brockdorff barking orders at the delivery men. And backing onto their yard, another row of mansion blocks, and beyond that Lindenstraße and the synagogue. She'd never been inside – that would have seemed a betrayal of Matz, of her new life – but she often found herself altering her route so that she could walk past and gaze up at the imposing Romanesque arch of its entrance. It was not a particularly attractive building – it had none of the unabashed orientalism of the Neue Synagoge's gilded Moorish domes – but something seductive and disquieting still pulled at her.

Rouladen was an extravagant dish for a weekday, but a lingering guilt in her felt the need to demonstrate wifely devotion. Matz had mentioned children over dinner the previous evening. He'd started talking about his own longing for a motorbike, machines that seemed to be breeding on the streets of Berlin this last year, and his plan to put a little money aside every month in the hope of being able to afford one in a couple of years – perhaps an NSU 251. And then he painted a picture of a future in which he took his son for a ride down to the Wannsee, or for a picnic in the woods. But voicing the word 'son' made him suddenly coy with her. They both knew the conversation was heading into territory usually avoided and Sara responded in her habitual way, deflecting talk towards something she'd heard on the radio.

She couldn't tell him that children frightened her. That she didn't know how to talk to them, didn't feel the soft-heartedness expected of a woman in their company, couldn't access the memory of how she herself had felt and thought as a child. And children had an unnerving capacity to discern her unease and play up to it. Even babies held no fascination for her. She sensed other women contained a physical longing for a baby, an urge to reproduce that was fundamental to their sense of themselves. But she could not feel it. The idea of being cooped up in the flat with a screaming infant only oppressed her. She hoped he wouldn't raise the subject again that evening.

She didn't hear the door at first. The thunk of her knife on the chopping board masked the knocking, but then a vibration through the floorboards alerted her. Wiping her bloodied hands on her apron, she hurried to open the door. She just caught the back of the insect's head disappearing down the stairs.

'I'm sorry. Did you call? I was chopping meat and didn't hear.' The woman came back up the stairs with a grin, her eyes flickering over Sara's stained apron.

'What are you carving up in there? The body of the Reich Chancellor?'
She leant down suddenly and picked up a small bouquet of cornflowers, left on the floor. She thrust them towards Sara.

'I'm glad I could deliver these in person, otherwise I might have started a rumour, leaving anonymous flowers. Your husband might think you have an admirer.'

'Oh. No. I don't think so.'

'Well. He ought to think it. He ought to be insanely jealous of his beautiful wife, spending hours alone. She could be getting up to all sorts.'
Sara felt the colour rise to her face. The girl waved the flowers at her.

'These are to say thank you. For saving my leg.'

'I'm glad to see it's still attached.'

'Only by a thread, but I'm quite redoubtable. At least that's what the nuns at my convent school used to say. And they didn't mean it as a compliment.'

'Thank you. They're lovely.'

'They reminded me of you. The girl with eyes of cornflower blue.'
Sara didn't know what to make of this and tugged self-consciously at the hem of her apron. She was suddenly conscious of the smell of blood on her fingers, the slight stickiness on her skin. But she said it anyway.

'Would you like to come in?'

By the time they were both sitting with their coffees in Sara's drawing room, the ease of the doorstep conversation had evaporated. Neither seemed to know how to restart. The woman openly checked her watch. A man's watch, with a thick black strap. And then Sara remembered.

'I don't even know your name. So stupid of me not to ask.'

'Sigi.'

'Sigi?'

'Short for Sigrid, but no one calls me that.'

'I'm Sara.'

'Is that Jewish?'

Sara hesitated for a moment. What was the girl's tone? She couldn't decipher it.

'Yes. At least, my parents were Jewish. Are. But I converted when I married.'

'Christ. Sorry what I mean is – having to learn two religions – I mean that's a bit much for anyone.'

'Well, not really. We were really only Yom Kippur Jews. You know – high days and holidays. My parents were never regular synagogue goers.'

Although, Sara reflected, that seemed to have changed recently. She'd begun to suspect that her own conversion had fuelled a renewed zeal in her parents, a need to assert their ancestry. Although her father only mumbled that it was important to prove the newspapers wrong. By this she'd assumed he meant the increasing frequency of anti-Jewish headlines.

*

They had married in church. Her parents had been sanguine about her converting. It was the way of the world. And Matz Babel was a good man, with good prospects, his family having weathered the inflation of '23. But after the wedding, her mother had fingered the new silver cross that hung around Sara's neck and cried. Her favourite aunt, Lilli, who'd come all the way from Paris for the wedding, hugged her close and whispered, 'If you ever need a refuge, you can always stay with me.' It was only later that Sara registered the oddness of her choice of noun.

The newlyweds spent two nights at a hotel on Lake Constance for their honeymoon. Sara had sat at a table with a red gingham tablecloth by the side of the lake, eating her breakfast, and when she looked across the table at this handsome stranger she had committed to spending her life with, something in her started to spin. It was as if she saw herself from a long way away – a woman sitting by a lake – and there was an urgent message she needed to impart to this remote woman, but she didn't know what it was. Or if she did, the words would not form into a meaningful line.

'Is that why you don't have one of those candle things?' Sigi was looking around the room. Acknowledging its absence gave the flat, despite its dark-green cushions and floral wallpaper, a sudden starkness.

Sigi wiped a line of coffee from her upper lip.

'You wouldn't think I used to be a good little Catholic girl would you and of course I was so pleased to take my first Communion perhaps it was the theatre of it all but now I'm afraid I'm not a believer in anything much.'

'That's all right.'

'Yes. It is.'

Sigi put down her coffee cup and went to the window. She gazed down at the street below.

'My father lost his faith in the war. Along with most of his friends. He found it hard to believe in a benevolent God after that. It was my mother who kept us on the straight and narrow.'

'My father was in France too. Though he never talks about it. I don't think he can.'

'We Germans are very good at that. Not talking about things. Which is a bit strange, given all the philosophers and poets we've produced.'

Something seemed to catch Sigi's eye out of the window.

'I have to go now.'

Disappointment twisted inside Sara, but she could only say stiffly, 'Well, it was very good to see you again. Do feel free to call in any time.'

Sigi turned to her with a grin.

'I think you need to see my act first. So you know what you're getting into. Thursdays, Fridays and Saturdays. I'm generally on just after ten. Don't bring your husband.' Sara followed her to the door. Sigi replaced her hat, and tugged its rim, raffishly. 'Toodlepip, as the English say.'

'Toodlepip.' The word like a thrilling obscenity in Sara's mouth.

She watched Sigi travel down the first flight of stairs before closing the door. Something told her to go to the front window. She hovered at its edge, out of sight, watching the street. She saw Sigi cross over and walk towards a young man, who was clearly waiting for her. He stubbed out his cigarette. They exchanged a few words and then Sigi pulled back slightly, chin up, laughing at something the man had said. Even from this distance, Sara could sense the ease between the two of them. They started up the street together and Sara, hovering behind the curtain, watched them head northwards, weaving through the daily parade of Friedrichstraße – the baker's delivery man balancing trays of loaves, a woman with dyed blonde hair and moleskin fur climbing out of an automobile, a limping man bearing the yellow armband of the disabled with its three black dots.

Sara tried to take comfort in the fact that the man had not taken Sigi's arm, but something inside her felt worked loose, clattering around her ribcage as she watched them

RUDI, 1906

disappear from view. Wolf found me at the window, gazing down on the street in its early morning flux. A river of umbrellas. The swaying passengers on the open decks of omnibuses, hunched against the sudden rain shower. Some became aware of my presence and looked up, so that I instinctively retreated further behind the curtain. So many pairs of eyes. Wolf came to stand at my shoulder.

'Looking out for anyone?'

'No.'

But I'm sure he'd also seen Margo's blue hat crossing the threshold of the grocer's opposite.

Wolf instructed me to prepare eight plates in readiness for an appointment at nine o'clock, but not to concern myself with setting out the camera, or lights. This struck me as a little odd, but in the red light of the darkroom, I set about loading the plates into their mahogany holders, two plates in each, and carried the holders through to the studio. There was a sharp rap at the door, which I sprang to open, and there stood Erholtz, in his grey tweed morning coat and the purple cravat he usually reserved for his conjuring shows. He smiled down at me and ruffled my hair. His eyes glittered. Behind him stood Fräulein Gottschalk, her ill-at-ease ringlets. Wolf nodded his hellos as Erholtz made a chivalrous gesture to usher the girl into the room.

*

'Where would you like us, Wolf?'

'I thought at the table over here, Herr Erholtz. Would that suit you, Fräulein?'

'No.'

'No? What would you prefer?'

'Somewhere away from the clock. It disturbs things.'

A Biedermeier grandfather clock stood in the corner of the room near the table. It was an elegant old thing, of pear wood and walnut veneer, and we often used it in backgrounds of portraits for added visual interest, particularly if the sitters were not in themselves picturesque.

'What about over there, my dear?'

Wolf indicated the opposite corner of the room, where the camera usually stood.

'Yes.'

Wolf indicated to me to clear that corner of equipment, which I did, with some ill will, thinking the girl was being deliberately demanding. I also didn't understand how we were to take a portrait away from the carefully draped backdrop, with its forest and mountains.

Wolf now lifted the table across the room, and set a chair beside it, which he gallantly offered to the girl. Erholtz took a seat on the couch, out of her direct line of sight.

'Extinguish the lights, please. And close the curtains.'

Her voice was authoritative, for all its breathiness. I pulled the heavy curtains across the windows and Wolf switched off the electric light. My eyes adjusted slowly to the gloaming.

'Are you ready for the first plate, Fräulein?'

'Yes. And no talking.'

This one certainly gave herself airs.

'Of course. Rudi? The plate?'

Not understanding what I was to do with a plate when the camera remained shrouded, I picked up one of the mahogany plate holders.

'Where should I—?'

'On the table please, Rudi.'

I found my way carefully to the table and set the holder down in front of the girl.

'Now, if you could remove the dark slide?'

Still mystified, my fingers found the holder's edge and I pulled up the dark slide to expose the plate beneath, before retreating a few steps. Even in the dark, I could see the girl close her eyes and throw her head back. Though Wolf and Erholtz were consumed by shadows, I knew that they too were watching her. I could sense the three of us check our breathing. In the presence of the wispy, ethereal girl, our bodies felt clumsy and out of proportion, so that even our breaths seemed noisy, uncouth.

For a good three or four minutes, nothing appeared to happen. Then the girl made a sudden surprised gasp. Then quiet, except for the dull ticking of the clock and somewhere, deep in the house, someone beating a carpet. But now I was aware of another noise in the room. A low note, like a drone, like a distant cello being bowed very slowly. I couldn't tell where it came from. Not from any of us. Not from a neighbouring room, or from outside in the street. But there was no question that it was in the room with us.

Suddenly she spoke.

'Another!'

None of us moved. Then Wolf whispered urgently to me, 'Another plate, Rudi!'

I stepped forward to follow this curious instruction and exposed the second plate in the holder.

*

The same process. The same silence, the same gasp of breath, the same long cello note.

'Another!'

I secured the first holder before fetching a second, which I laid down on the table before her.

After the fourth plate, the girl cried out, with a voice full of pain.

'Enough!'

And as I secured the holder and carried all four plates through to the darkroom next door, I was aware of Wolf drawing back the curtains. Returning to the studio, I hovered uncertainly in the doorway. The girl was slumped upon the table, her head in her arms, apparently panting with exhaustion, as though she'd just been running for her life. Wolf gestured at me to leave, so I returned to the darkroom and busied myself with preparing the trays. Although I couldn't understand what we would be developing, since the camera had remained untouched and the plates hadn't been exposed to any light.

I took down the two bottles required to make up the developing solution, and measured out the first, with its water, hydroquinone, metol and sulphite of soda, before combining it with a solution of water, carbonate of potash and bromide of potassium. It was a procedure Wolf had taught me in my first week as apprentice, and I took great pride in the precision of the measuring, and the steadiness of my hand with the chemicals. I then turned my attention to the stop bath, which I filled with acetic acid, before preparing the third tray with the fixing solution of hypo, water, sulphuric acid, sulphite of soda crystals and chrome alum.

As I worked, I heard low voices and finally the closing of the door. Wolf appeared at my side. I took the first plate from its cover and submerged it in water, before placing it in the developer.

I was expecting a blank image. And at first my suspicions appeared to be confirmed. But then, slowly, out of the murk, a shape started to emerge. A body in motion. A diver in freefall.

'What is it?' I asked Wolf.

'It's what's inside her head. She claims it's a vision of the future.'

'She can see the future?'

'That what she says.'

'And she can imprint her thoughts onto photographic plates?'

'You can see for yourself.'

'But the image is positive. How is that possible?'

'I don't know, Rudi. But I want to see the future too. Don't you?'

He placed the plate in the sodium citrate, before lifting it out and placing it in the fixing tray. When he was satisfied that the picture was fixed, he handed the plate to me to wash under running water for a few minutes, before blotting off the surplus water with a chamois. We then dried the plate next door, over the gas stove. On the glass, the diver seemed to move, the dark silhouette of the body stippled with sunlight like lace-work. But something about the image filled me with unease. It was Wolf who pointed out the disconcerting detail. The diver was fully clothed.

We worked the rest of the morning and through lunch. By the end, we had four images.

One was a view of the Brandenburger Tor from the Tiergarten. But this was a hellish, compromised Brandenburger Tor. To the foreground, coils of barbed wire, and behind these a wall, blocking the passage to Unter den Linden. Squinting at the image, I could also make out a row of small figures standing on the wall, but they were too blurred and indistinct to determine any detail.

Another image showed a shape like a hypodermic syringe. Wolf turned the plate this way and that, as we tried to decide which way up the image was meant to be. Was it some kind of medical or industrial instrument? Or perhaps a church steeple or minaret from a foreign land? It also made me think of the rocket in Méliès's moving picture *Le Voyage dans la Lune*. Could it be some mode of transportation for future space travellers?

The final image was easier to interpret. The skull and crossbones of the Totenkopf. But this was no military insignia stitched to a uniform, this death's head was mounted on a ring, like some malformed gemstone. The little darkroom was suddenly suffocating. 'Let's get some air,' said Wolf, opening the door.

After we'd presented the plates to a marvelling Erholtz, he summoned the other Academicians to the first-floor drawing room. As the other magicians gazed at the images laid out before them, I felt the chill of Fräulein Gottschalk's gaze from the opposite corner of the room and glowered at her in return. And then, in a moment, she was at my side, bending down as though to retrieve something from the floor. It took me a couple of seconds to realise that she had sunk her teeth into my forearm.

Erholtz was in a reverie. Famed as a showman he might be, but his true talent was for business, and the perfect business opportunity now, quite literally, stared him in the face. Madame Czigany, in contrast, looked haunted, her large eyes welling with tears. Perhaps her powers of augury were more than an act after all. But among the other magicians, the conversation grew louder, as people ventured opinions on the pictures' meaning. Did they represent the Kaiser's appetite for war? Did the barbed wire represent the defence of Berlin from the Russians? Did the hypodermic relate to the recent experiments with typhoid vaccinations at the Friedrich-Wilhelms? Or was it a vision of an alien civilisation, as from the fiction of H. G. Wells? Was the death's head a prediction of the resurgence of Prussia? Was the diver an athlete or a suicide? Opinions became louder, more assured in their interpretations. Erholtz clapped his hands.

'Time to go, my dears, time to go! Now she has had the opportunity to recover from the morning's exertions, I must speak to Fräulein Gottschalk alone. I'm sure you will appreciate the importance of capturing her thoughts as soon as possible. Wolf, Rudi, you may stay, so long as you remain silent.'

The other magicians and assistants clattered off to their various rooms, or downstairs to attend to the shop. Margo was the last out, closing the door quietly behind her. She glanced back at Fräulein Gottschalk with a thoughtful look. I wondered if she too had her doubts. Erholtz seemed possessed with a manic energy, which he was vainly attempting to conceal. He pulled out a chair for Fräulein Gottschalk and guided her into it, as though she were an old lady in need of assistance, and not a girl of thirteen. Then he took a chair for himself at the table next to her.

Wolf and I hovered awkwardly in the corner, incidental but necessary to the drama being played out before us. In silent agreement, we took a seat on the couch by the wall. Erholtz angled the four plates towards the girl, though she did not bother to look down.

'These visions, Fräulein. Do they come to you at particular moments in the day? Or after particular stimuli?'
'They can arrive at any time. I have no control over them.'
'And this vision here.' He gestured at the Brandenburger Tor. 'Do you understand its meaning?'
'I thought its meaning was clear.'

'It is a literal occurrence? You think there will be barbed wire in the Tiergarten?'

'I know it.'

'Can you say when this event will occur?'

'That is not explained to me.'

'But in my lifetime, perhaps?'

'No. Not in your lifetime.'

The girl raised her head a little then and looked at him with such meaning in her grey saucer eyes that I could see Erholtz shudder. A question passed through him, but he did not ask it.

'In your lifetime, then?' He attempted a smile. 'You are, after all, much younger than me.'

'Not in my lifetime, either. I do not live long.'

Erholtz leaned forward. 'Oh, my dear child, I sincerely hope you are mistaken in that.'

She kept her eyes steady, fixed on his.

'I am murdered.'

And then she raised her hand from her lap.

'He will murder me.'

And she pointed her sharp little finger across the room at me.

Both Erholtz and Wolf turned in the direction of her accusatory digit. I laughed. Surely, they would laugh too, at the absurdity of it all. But I could see from the expression in their eyes that her words had found their mark. Wolf didn't move an inch on the couch, but I could feel him pulling away from me. Somehow I managed to find my voice.

'What are you talking about? How could I murder you? I'm not capable of murdering anyone. Why would I?'

The little witch resisted the rhythm of my panic.

'For love.'

Her calm assurance made my blood surge. I sprang to my feet.

'This is ridiculous! You don't know anything about me! You can't come here, making false accusations about things that haven't even . . . What are you trying to . . . You took against me the moment you walked in the door. I won't have you—'

Wolf placed an admonitory hand on my sleeve.
    'That's enough.'

My body deflated into itself. Later, I realised that in that brief moment of inarticulate rage, I had wanted to put my hands around her throat and squeeze her till the bones snapped

HANS, 1969

in the long neck that made him think of a swan. That's when he first noticed her, crossing the street at the corner of Hedemann-straße. An adolescent swan, still a little ungainly, the curved shoulders of a girl who has always tried to disguise her height. Her hair looked unwashed, matted, but even in that state he could see it was a beautiful deep chestnut. He wasn't quite sure why he started to follow her, but it was as if he sensed that she was direc-tionless, lost in the city. And as he drew closer, he realised from her clothes that she was from the East. Which made the impulse to follow her even more urgent.

She walked quickly, perhaps to keep out the cold, as the coat she wore looked thin and insubstantial. He guessed she was sleeping rough.

This made him bold. He continued to follow her west, then north up Stresemannstraße, always just three or four steps behind. He could see her checking the reflection in shop windows, attempting to catch a glance of her pursuer. It gave him a little hit of pleasure to know that she was aware of his presence and he also glanced at the glass to see himself – tall and loping, the grey trilby he liked to wear on winter days. When the girl reached the temple-like shell of the Anhalter Bahnhof she turned around suddenly and confronted him.

What are you doing?

I'm following you.

Her face, now fully revealed to him, made him hold his breath for a moment. It was not exactly beautiful – the proportions were odd and her skin carried a layer of grime, but the combination of wide almond eyes, high cheekbones and a protruding bottom lip excited him.

Why?

Why am I following you? I thought I could help you.

I don't need help.

No?

No.

I could buy you a coffee and a sandwich. No obligation.

He took his hands out of his pockets to indicate – what? Harmlessness? He could see the hunger on her face.

No obligation?

No.

She shrugged. *Okay then.*

They didn't talk as they walked side by side, Hans a half-step ahead, scanning the building fronts for the likely sign of a cafe. A striped awning down a side street looked promising, so he indicated with a nod that this was the direction they should take.

It turned out to be a little Turkish place, where they were the only customers. The owner looked surprised to see them, but glad of the business. Through an archway that led to the kitchen, Hans could see the proprietor's wife, a toddler on her hip. Hans played chivalrous, pulling out a chair for the girl, as though he were taking her for dinner at some high-end establishment. He thought he saw her blush a little. When the man reappeared to take their order, Hans threw his hands wide in a gesture that indicated munificence.

Have whatever you want.

Her eyes devoured the menu. It took her some time to decide. He could see her weighing options – wanting the most substantial meal, but trying to find something mid-priced so she wouldn't look as though she were taking him for a ride.

No, really. Have whatever you want. It's too cold a day to be hungry.

She stabbed at the menu with her finger.

What's this?

Kofte. Grilled lamb on a stick. It's good.

Clearly East Berlin's culinary repertoire hadn't yet extended to the Orient.

Okay. I'll have that. And a Coca-Cola.

Hans ordered the kofte and Coke, and a Turkish coffee for himself. The owner seemed disappointed by the modest selection and his previous attentiveness sagged a little. He padded back beneath the archway.

You sleeping rough?

Uh-huh.

Must be hard.

She raised her eyebrows at the obvious banality of this.

You're from the East.

He could see her stiffen and half lift from her seat, ready to run.

It's okay. It's not a problem. You run away from home?

Yeah. My dad didn't like me much anyway.

What about your mum?

She's dead. Cancer. Two years ago. Her eyes watered suddenly.

I'm sorry.

She shrugged. *Shit happens.*

Yup. Sure does. My mum hates me too. So I guess we're even.
He was surprised to hear himself mention his mother. He never talked about her. Anyone who knew him would probably have assumed his parents to be dead.

How did you do it?

What?

Get over the Wall?

She narrowed her eyes. Her shoulders folded towards her chest.

Look. Honestly. Defectors are heroes over here. No one's going to send you back. I'm just intrigued. Must have been dangerous.

He could see she wasn't going to tell him. Never mind. Give it time.

When the food came, she fell upon it. He found himself smiling as he watched her unselfconsciously cram the bread and meat into her mouth. After sating her hunger, she turned to the Coca-Cola and sipped at it as though it were Communion wine. She met his gaze, a little embarrassed.

I've never had it before.

And is it good?

It's good.

And then she glugged it back thirstily, wiping the liquid from her lips with her sleeve. She was somehow out of kilter with herself, her movements ungainly and defensive. It was hard to age her. A beautiful woman in a body she did not yet know how to control. She had the clumsy self-consciousness of a fourteen-year-old, but the face of someone in their twenties, a face that had known loss. Even in the cafe's harsh electric light, the shadows played across her features in a way that made him regret not having his Rolleiflex with him.

After draining the glass, she seemed to remember her table manners, and dabbed at her mouth with the serviette. She then screwed it up, put it down on the table and looked directly at him for the first time.

I'll sleep with you for twenty marks.

——❖——

Hans was an early riser by nature and by first light the coffee pot was on the stove and he had started work, laying the pictures out on the kitchen's large mahogany table. He studied each photo with care and then began to arrange them. There was an art to collation. Although the pictures were unrelated, they needed to be presented in such a way that created some sort of narrative. The viewer's involvement should build gradually, their interest piqued at the start, but slowly teased along. He often started his editorial in the middle, with the centrefold, since this had generally been determined during the shoot.

The table had come with the flat, and its size proved ideal for his editorial process. He couldn't imagine the wealth or the sentimental determination of an owner who had not needed to burn this nineteenth-century behemoth for firewood. But, somehow, it had survived the war – unlike the upper storeys of the building, which had been reconstructed in the late Fifties.

It had proved surprisingly easy to find girls. At the beginning, he had simply advertised – 'Beautiful girls sought for glamorous shots' – and they had turned up on the step of Friedrichstraße 19, irritating his landlady with their tiny skirts and unapologetically modern attitudes. He'd had to reject at least half of them – their interpretations of beautiful stretched by wishful thinking. And definitions of beauty had changed. The robust, fecund German woman had given way to something more angular, gamine, long-limbed. Blondes were still popular, of course, but he'd recently found a couple of black girls too, which had led to a noticeable improvement in sales.

*

And now word of mouth was enough. His regular models would bring along their friends, which meant that his talent pool remained at largely manageable levels. And he had a good reputation. He could spend an hour rubbing ice on a girl's nipples to keep them pert in front of his hot lights, he might apply hands to her naked body to get her butt in exactly the right position, or trim her pubic hair, but at the end of the session, she was free to go. He would make no demands.

His studio space took up one half of his living room, with its backdrops, tripod and some old UFA lights he'd bought for a song from a little antiques shop on Bergmannstraße. They probably dated from the Forties, but they still worked perfectly, even if his models sometimes complained of the heat burning their skin. He'd made a darkroom from a large walk-in cupboard in the flat. And, for a cut of the profits, an old friend from printing school provided him with out-of-hours access to a print shop and a Rotaprint offset-printing machine. This was not where he wanted his career to be, but it would do for now.

The girl had crept up on him. She had slept late. Now she was barefoot and wearing one of his shirts over her knickers. She stood at his shoulder, so close that he could feel the heat of her through his sweater.

Is this what you do?
This is what I do.
And you can make a living from this?
It keeps the wolf from the door.
Do the girls get paid?
Of course.
How much?

No. *Don't even think about it.* He was suddenly sure about this, having not been until this moment. *Let me get you some coffee.*

You don't think I'm attractive enough?
That's not it.
My boobs aren't big enough?
Your boobs are fine. But you don't want to get into this kind of work.

The girl still hadn't told him her name. She had come back with him to the flat, eaten everything he offered her and curled up on the couch, watching West German television, wide-eyed and silent. When she fell asleep, the television still blaring, he had covered her with a couple of blankets, before tiptoeing off to sleep in his own room.

He cleared a space at one end of the table and set down two mugs of coffee, a plate of rolls. The girl ate hungrily, still apparently making up for lost time.
Are you ever going to tell me your name?
Ilse.

Ilse. Ordinary enough, but on her tongue it sounded exotic. It seemed to contain her eastern-ness and the unusual proportions of her face. That was the odd thing about language. It could slip away from you and make itself alien. He preferred images. You could manipulate a picture too, of course, but to him the rules of the visual seemed clearer, more in his control.

How old are you?
Nineteen.
He could tell by the way she said this, her eyes lowered, her mouth full of bread, that this was a lie.
Okay. You know you can stay as long as you want.
She finished chewing and looked at him.
We could do it now. I'm not tired now.
Do what?
Fuck.

I don't want you to do that. You can have the couch in the front room. Stay as long as you need to get yourself sorted out.

You really don't fancy me, do you?

You're very pretty. But you're not nineteen and you're certainly too young to be offering yourself to strange men.

Are you strange?

Her directness made him laugh.

Oh yes. Very.

You a queer then?

No. Though you'd be surprised how many homosexuals are in this game. Like vegetarian butchers.

She grimaced, but he could tell she was suppressing a smile. He refilled her coffee cup.

There is something you could do for me. If you'd like to.

Photos?

Yes. But not like that. More – fashion shots. With nice clothes. You know – like Veruschka and Donyale Luna. The girl's face was a blank. *You wouldn't know who they are, I guess. Thing is, I'm trying to build up a portfolio. And you've got a good face – I reckon you'd photograph really well. We could find some interesting locations, I could show you what to do.*

I don't have any nice clothes.

Then we'll go shopping.

At last, a genuine smile in her almond eyes.

Today?

If you like.

Ilse found it bewildering to be on Friedrichstraße, which she'd always believed to be an East Berlin street. Hans reassured her. *Most of it is on your side.* She insisted they walk the short length of Federal Friedrichstraße, but when they drew closer to Checkpoint Charlie and the American military police checking the short line of cars crossing to the East, Ilse froze for a moment before hurrying back the way they'd come. Hans jogged to catch up with her.

You okay?

Have you any idea what Friedrichstraße looks like over there?

I can remember what it was like before. And I can see some of the new office blocks.

You've never visited?

Not since '61. I don't believe in treating a population like a zoo.

He thought of all the times he'd sat on the roof of his apartment building. There was a section of flat roof around the glass dome of the skylight, which made for a pleasantly sunny spot to smoke a fag. Other roofs blocked his view of the world beyond the Wall, but if the wind was blowing in a certain direction, he could smell the East – a combination of adulterated petrol, disinfectant and vegetables.

They walked side by side. Ilse stared fixedly at the pavement in front of her.

And that graffiti? KZ? I see that everywhere on this side of the Wall. What does it mean?

He hesitated before replying.

Concentration camp.

Ilse turned her head away so that he couldn't see her reaction, but she carried on talking.

Around our Friedrichstraße, there are still vast areas of ruins. Whole fields full of rubble. Garbage. Weeds. Old men pulling handcarts with potatoes or coal. In fact, loads of old people, everywhere. We're still living like it's the war over there. But here – here it's like nothing ever happened.

There are plenty of ruins on this side. Empty spaces where there used to be buildings. Crater marks, bullet holes. There are some at the back of our building.

Our. How readily his tongue had found the plural.

But all these new apartment blocks. High rises. Offices. Coca-Cola signs. Everything's so bright and shiny. So much colour.

97

Hans shook his head.

Same scars. Just covered up.

Playing tour guide was a reminder that his whole world was an island of 481 square kilometres, surrounded by barbed wire and minefields. There might be slogans all over the city to reassure its citizens – *Berlin: Germany's capital* – and the West German constitution might call Berlin the eleventh state of the Federal Republic, but really the city was an outlier, a hot-air balloon tethered in enemy territory.

He took Ilse clothes shopping on the Ku'damm. She couldn't conceal her astonishment at all that was on offer, or her glee as she gathered up armfuls of clothes to try on, springing from the dressing room to show him each new outfit, posing and twirling. He was glad to see the pretence at worldly sophistication cast aside for a while and the teenage girl emerge, but he had to be careful not to capitulate to her enthusiasm, or he would have spent his entire week's earnings. Her delight made him laugh, but he tried to keep his professional eye for what would look good on camera. But then most things looked good on her. She was tall and skinny, with long, slender legs and, despite the shoulder-length hair, there was something androgynous about her – something cool and Londonish.

He was surprised when she agreed to have her hair lopped off and shaped into a sharp bob that framed her cheekbones. As they walked back to the U-Bahn from the hairdresser, Hans caught her admiring her reflection in shop windows. In her new magenta minidress and coat, she looked like something new-hatched.

For their first shoot, Hans took Ilse to pose in the ruins of a nineteenth-century hostel in Wedding. The way the light played against the red bricks and vacant window spaces worked well, but Ilse was stiff and self-conscious, her facial expressions curiously inanimate. Later, in his darkroom, he printed up the ten best shots to show her and though he did his best to take responsibility for their failure, Ilse could tell he was disappointed. She spent the day in a sulk, slamming doors and barely speaking to him.

So how's the new model coming on?
Pieter placed the second round of beers on the table between them.
What new model?
Oh come on. Katya told me all about her. I'm all for live-in servicing, as long as you can get rid of her when you need to.
It's not like that. She's from the East. Hopped over the Wall somehow and needed a place to stay.
Pieter whistled softly.
They were shooting again last night. Haven't seen the papers this morning, so I don't know whether they got anyone.

Pieter lived in an apartment that looked onto the Wall. It was not uncommon to hear machine-gun fire in the middle of the night from the East German posts. Hans sipped his beer.
And before you ask – no. She's not going to be in the mag. She's just a kid.
How old?
She says nineteen. I reckon more like sixteen. Maybe younger.
Well, if she says she's nineteen, go with that.
It's not like that.
So you said.

Pieter was his distributor. He worked the sex shops of Berlin, but also had contacts further afield, in Hamburg and Frankfurt. He would give Hans critical feedback on the content and design of the magazine, producing, with bureaucratic professionalism, detailed sales reports.

Guest-workers. They're the growing market. Take my word for it. All these Syrians and Jordanians and Turks. All they want are your German blondes. Can't get enough of them. Fascinated. All those golden pubes.

To Hans's irritation, such editorial advice often resulted in improved sales, although he sometimes wondered whether Pieter manipulated the data in order to prove his own worth.

Pieter dressed in the latest fashions, although they looked ill at ease on him – a balding man in his mid-forties, turning to fat. He was Dutch, but had been enticed to Berlin by the cheap rents, and the sparkling, resurrected buildings. *This is a little Manhattan!* he told Hans. *There's nowhere else in Europe that looks this modern. Skyscrapers. Plate glass. Concrete. Fat people. Consumption everywhere. Shops. Cars. Sex. Drugs. But even when the Germans let it all hang loose, they still do it in an orderly fashion. I love it. The compulsion to give orders. Even on the tourist signs. 'Achtung! Beautiful view to the right!'*

Usually Pieter's cultural generalisations amused him, but this evening Hans felt unsettled and defensive. He tried to turn the conversation towards football. Though he'd no interest in the sport, it oiled the wheels of male conversation, and since he had no desire to talk about girls, he made sure to stay sufficiently informed on the Bundesliga so as to have something to say. He'd never found the company of other men easy. Perhaps that was the result of being brought up a single child by a single mother. But it felt more deeply embedded than that – related to his lack of interest in sex, the absence of a libido that set him apart from his contemporaries. He worried that this was a deep psychological failing, perhaps even a sociopathic one. But he suspected it made life simpler. He could pursue his work with clarity and focus, free from distraction.

*

From school friends and workmates he'd learned enough to understand the mechanics of desire. Comically earnest text-books and well-thumbed porn mags gave him a sense of what he was expected to feel. But apart from the embarrassing surges of puberty, and a handful of half-hearted experiments to prove himself normal, the fuse of his sexuality had never ignited. Gradually, those who grew close to Hans would sense this differ-ence in him. Not just his failure to build on a dirty joke or to wolf-whistle at a girl, but something essential in his physicality, something controlled and quaint that ran counter to the world of free love and the pill and LSD. And once they formed this notion of him, they would usually back away, vaguely disgusted by something they couldn't quite classify. He tried to convince himself he didn't mind.

Whether his mother had any sense of this blankness in him, he didn't know. She'd never been overly demonstrative with him, and once he reached puberty she retreated to an even greater distance, as though it might be inappropriate to show physical affection to a child on the cusp of manhood. Conversations about girlfriends or sex were studiously avoided. He occasionally wondered whether she thought him a homosexual.

Pieter claimed to have contacts at the fashion magazine *Burda Moden* and had promised Hans an introduction. This had not yet materialised. As Pieter laid out his strategy for Hertha's defence, Hans's mind riffled through the best shots of Ilse. He knew none of them was good enough to include in a portfolio. They'd need to find a better location, somewhere Ilse might fully relax and cast off self-consciousness. Her arrival had intro-duced a new urgency to his sense of a career mislaid. He'd made some wrong turns, such as learning printing, rather than going to art school, which meant he now had a trade, but not an art. Sometimes the gap between him and all the bright young things emerging from art school felt unbridgeable. But why should money and privilege determine everything? The world was changing.

Pieter drained his glass with the speed of a man who senses that his company is no longer appreciated. He didn't suggest another round, and as he stood up to leave, asked Hans whether the next edition of the magazine would be ready on time.

Have I ever let you down before?

He had three girls scheduled for Thursday. Although Ilse had insisted on looking through back copies of the magazine, he felt uncomfortable about her being present for a shoot, but she insisted. *I might learn something.* He didn't want to know what she hoped this might be.

Trude was the first model of the day. She was old school. Buxom, full-lipped, at ease with her body, she had the amused pragmatism and large pink nipples of an Otto Dix prostitute. Hans suspected her of being on the game, although she claimed to work in a ladies' clothes shop. The clothes shop was apparently very accommodating about releasing members of staff for an occasional morning of moonlighting. She was getting on a bit for a nude model, and Hans had to be artful about disguising her stretch marks and thread veins with carefully placed shadows, but she was a reliable, straightforward presence in the studio and therefore a regular booking. And though they'd never discussed it, a morning in his studio was presumably a day when she didn't have to cater to her male clients.

At first he wasn't sure that Trude would take to Ilse. When they were first introduced, Trude put on a more refined voice, possessively making the longevity of her relationship with Hans clear to the younger girl. But once the session was underway and she felt assured of Ilse's deference, Trude relaxed and her Mitte garrulousness soon had the teenager in giggles. Hans had never heard Ilse laugh like that before. The sound, like a series of uncontrollable hiccups, made him smile, but it also made him feel curiously paternal. Was that what this was?

After the sessions, Ilse followed him into the darkroom. He talked her through the process – the exposure times, the various baths of chemicals, the making of the contact print. When it was developed, they emerged from the red-lit cupboard and laid the still-wet sheet on the kitchen table. They stood side by side, arms touching, and he could feel the softness of her skin through his shirt as she studied each image and gave her verdict. She didn't always call it right, but she clearly had a good eye.

Pieter collected the magazines on Wednesday morning and handed over an envelope fat with notes. Ilse was still sleeping on the sofa when he called, and Hans had hoped to avoid their meeting, but the activity in the hallway woke her, and she appeared in the doorway wearing, as usual, one of Hans's old shirts over her knickers. Pieter cast Hans a knowing look, before greeting the girl with three kisses, *in Dutch fashion*, he said with a wink. Hans saw his hand wander down to fleetingly cup Ilse's buttock. Something tightened in his chest, but he said nothing. He was glad when Pieter left.

By that point, Ilse was in the bath. Hans surveyed the clutter of the living room, the bundle of sheets on the sofa, piles of bright clothes draped carefully over a chair. He should really buy her a small wardrobe.

Although he found her presence in the apartment oddly comforting, the habit of solitude was hard to break, and he found himself going out more often just to be on his own. After Pieter's visit, he went to the bank to deposit the cash, keeping back enough to keep him going for the week. It was his ritual to celebrate payday with a lunch at Good Friends Chinese restaurant, followed by a movie.

He went to the Delphi Filmpalast to see *On Her Majesty's Secret Service*. The prefatory newsreel announced President Nixon's intention to bring home 50,000 American troops from Vietnam. The sinking of an oil tanker off the coast of Senegal. A speech to the American Geophysical Union by one Colonel Fletcher who warned that carbon dioxide pollution would have significant impact on global temperature, resulting in the melting of the ice caps. And then the narrator's tone became sombre. The week also marked the thirtieth anniversary of Eichmann's appointment to Referat IV B4, the department tasked with overseeing Jewish affairs and 'evacuation'. The chatter among the matinee audience died down at the mention of Eichmann's name.

The film cut to a rally. Goose-stepping soldiers, Hitler making a speech, gesticulating wildly. The machine-gun staccato of his voice filled the cinema. A few people in the audience tittered. Were they laughing off their old selves, the way people laugh over an old photo album, mocking the strange clothes and hairstyles they once wore? And now the film moved to Himmler's car arriving outside a public building in Berlin. Another man greeted him and took him up the front steps.

The script told him that he was looking at Eichmann but of course, since the trial, everyone knew that face, those amused, pursed lips. Everyone had seen the portrait of him in uniform from the early Forties, printed in the papers next to the photo of him sitting in a glass box in a Jerusalem courtroom, bespectacled now, but with the same twisted mouth. And here on the screen was Eichmann showing Himmler around the Reich Security Head Office. A row of smiling, neatly coiffured secretaries. Hans could sense their excitement, their hope that the Reichsführer would turn around and notice them. Eichmann's left shoulder was tilted towards the camera, and Hans's eye was drawn to the young blonde secretary just over Eichmann's shoulder, just behind the four silver pips on his lapel, the cap that bore the Totenkopf. And for a moment, it was as if the whole universe was sucked towards him and into his lungs.

But then the image vanished. It was only there for a moment. Other images followed, but he barely registered them. He sat through the film, but when it ended with James Bond weeping over the body of his murdered wife, Hans realised he hadn't taken in a word. The auditorium emptied around him, but he stayed in his seat, in shocked paralysis. An usherette came in to clean up, but she didn't ask him to leave, or check his ticket, so as the curtains parted for the next screening, he was still in place. He waited for the newsreel to appear, his heart speeding up as the moment of the image came closer. This time he was sure. He even nodded, as though the film merely confirmed a prophecy he had heard long ago. The air within the cinema suddenly seemed thin and he sprang up, stepping over people's feet without apology, pushing at the fire escape door to stumble out into the cold December air, which he inhaled with urgent gasps. This is what it was to live in Berlin. To be surrounded by a truth you don't acknowledge, that you refuse to see. But there was always going to be a point when it collides with you in the street and coughs in your face.

His mother had tried to love him. Her little Hans. She had given him the most unexceptional German name in an attempt to bury his origins and had moved into an ugly new-build apartment block in the suburbs, rarely venturing into the centre of the city.

He did not see her now. As though by mutual, unspoken agreement, they had removed themselves from each other's lives. There had been no rows, no emotional scenes – they had simply taken the decision to go their separate ways. And he had accepted the inevitability of this, supposing his presence, his face, was a constant reminder of the horror on which her whole life had turned.

She had been a virgin of twenty when she was raped by three Russian soldiers, one after the other, in the basement of a house in which she had been hiding. Hilde's mother had begged the soldiers to take her instead, but they were far more interested in her pretty blonde daughter. Since that time, Hilde had never had a relationship. No boyfriends, no marriage. Motherhood and the privations of war made her an adult before her time, but part of her emotional growth remained stunted, immature. Any romantic fantasies she had entertained as a schoolgirl had been irreparably corrupted.

Hans had learned all of this from his aunt, Gisela, the year he turned seventeen. His mother had never so much as hinted at any of it. She had spun him a story about an officer killed on the Eastern Front and when he grew old enough to realise that there were no pictures of this mythical father, she reminded him that they had lost almost all their possessions during the final bombardment of Berlin. When he pressed her about her experiences during the terrible months of 1945, all she would say was that it was a nightmarish time and one better left to rest in history.

As a child, he had believed himself responsible for his mother's remoteness. Even at kindergarten, he had sensed that he was simply not lovable enough. Perhaps it was because he'd thrown a tantrum when asked to share his toy train with his cousin. Perhaps it was because he'd once put a frog in a paper bag and accidentally killed it. Early proofs that he was undeserving of his mother's affection. And when his aunt, in the inebriate post-midnight hours of a family wake, had revealed the truth of his parentage, his sense of his own culpability was reaffirmed. His foetal self had had the temerity to survive. And because his features bore little resemblance to his mother's family, he had to assume his face was like his father's. What else might he have inherited? At least the sexual impulse wasn't present. Perhaps his developing body had unconsciously sought to correct the crimes of the past.

For years he had carried the shame of his paternity. For years he had carried his mother's suffering, silently, guiltily. She could not know that he knew. But now? Her victim past, though not quite rewritten, was suddenly more complex. It was hard not to feel, as he strode forwards, his breath forming pools of mist in the evening air, that the violence visited upon her was some kind of cosmic balancing. A reckoning with the psychopathic culture in which she had colluded.

Hans hurried along Friedrichstraße with an urgent need to disappear. He unlocked the front door of the building, took the stairs two at a time and flew into the apartment. As soon as he opened the door he could hear a male grunting in the last throes of sex, a woman pretending to enjoy it. On the couch in the living room, Pieter's bare arse, pummelling away, his trousers still gathered around his ankles. Fury carried him across the room and pulled Pieter off, throwing him into the lighting stands on the opposite side of the room. For a moment Hans glimpsed the dark curls of Ilse's pubic hair, the paper-white of her thighs. She hastily pulled down her dress.

What the fuck? Hans slammed his hand onto the table.
Pieter scrambled to pull his trousers up. *Take it easy, man.*
This is my fucking apartment. What the fuck?
Chill, man. Okay? It's cool.
No. It's not cool. She's too young. You have no right to lay a fucking finger on her.

She was up for it, weren't you, sugar?

Hans grabbed him by the shirt. He was gratified that Pieter looked worried.

Don't you ever touch her again. Or I will cut your balls off.

Okay, okay. It's a deal. Hans released him. Pieter backed his way to the door.

I didn't think it would be a problem. She was up for it, okay? Said she'd blow me for five, but I wanted the full works.

Hans ran at him then, pushing him against the door. The two men struggled. One fat, one weedy, pointlessly grappling with each other. Hans felt the humiliating farce of the situation and extricated himself. Pieter didn't stay to argue.

As the apartment door slammed, and Pieter's feet disappeared down the echoing stairwell, Hans turned back to Ilse. She sat on the couch, tugging down the hem of her minidress.

Don't let arseholes like that touch you.

It's my body. I can do what I want.

But you don't have to do that. I can give you more money, if you need more money.

You give me enough.

Then why?

I want to make my own way.

Then get a job. Go to college.

What if I like being a whore?

Hans flopped into the armchair. Was this his fault? Had he created this?

Don't do that. You're better than that.

Are the girls you photograph better than that?

They're not whores.

Aren't they?

They're models. Actresses.

You're happy to fuck them.

I don't . . . sleep with them.

No. You just pay them to oil their tits and spread their legs for the camera.

Yes. I pay them for that. I don't pay them for sex.

Yeah. You're such a fucking stud. They can't resist you.

No. That's not it. I'm not interested.

You're queer?

No. I'm just not interested. In sex. At all. With anybody.

Is there something wrong with you?

Probably.

He ran his fingers through his hair. He regretted starting this conversation.

Anyway. I'm not talking about me. I'm talking about you. You're too young to throw yourself away like that.

You want me to keep myself pure? Jesus. You're a fucking pornographer. You don't make sense.

They looked at each other. She was right, of course. He did not make sense, even to himself. But then, who did? At this moment, he could feel Ilse's anger, her humiliation, her fierce pride. But beyond that, he could not read her. He felt he knew less about her now than that first day, in the Turkish cafe. He had been hoping for something she could not provide – a person he might truly know. Those hours in the darkroom together had given him a sense of connection with her, a solidarity. But he looked at her now, with her flushed cheeks, her hair tangled from the couch, her eyes sparkling with defiance, and remembered that she was just a child, with all the beguiling, infuriating unknowability of a child. She was not a book to be read, or a puzzle to be solved.

He rose to his feet.

I'll get us something to eat.

He nearly said, *Why don't you get yourself cleaned up?* but checked himself in time. It was not his place.

I'm not hungry.

All right. I'll get myself something to eat.

He didn't even pay me. You threw him out before he had a chance.

Hans felt the urge to strike her. It frightened him. The anger he had. The urge in him to release it. He had to get out, climb up to the little terrace on the roof, smoke a fag.

How much?

Twenty. Same as I offered you.

He felt in the pocket of his jacket, retrieved a few crumpled notes, threw them on the table, and left, the slam of the door

HEIKE, 2019

ricocheting around the stairwell. But it was too late to turn back and change her too-loud shoes. She was cutting it fine as it was. Anyway. It was just lunch. She'd be sitting for the entire encounter. As she headed down the stairs, she pulled up her spine to adjust to this new centre of gravity. She rarely wore heels these days and the sensation was regrettably unbalancing.

She'd chosen the restaurant on the internet. When she saw its garishly baroque interior – the energy of the decor not reflected in the waiting staff – she realised she'd made an error and that she should have gone for the simpler, contemporary Italian next door. She hoped Yusuf wouldn't think her some sort of weird Prussian nostalgist. Having secured the table with the most flattering lighting, she went to fix her hair in the Ladies.

Back at the table, still five minutes before the agreed time, she agreed to a carafe of water, crossed her legs and tried to look insouciant. Uncrossed her legs. Leaned with one elbow on the table. Two elbows and her chin resting on her hands. No. That might emphasise her double chin. Sat back in her chair. Crossed her legs the other way. She gazed out of the window and tried to fix her face in an expression that said cool and wryly amused. Then she was flustered, because she saw Yusuf coming up the street and didn't want him to know she'd been looking out for him, so she turned her attention back into the room.

As he approached, she pretended to catch sight of him for the first time, and stood up. But the chair was heavy, and as he leaned in to kiss her on both cheeks, she was still wedged awkwardly between it and the table. Was she imagining it, or did he smell faintly of formaldehyde?

He handed his coat to the waiter and sat down. 'Nice place.'
She couldn't tell whether this was irony.
  'Regular haunt of yours?'
  'Only when I'm lunching with undertakers.'
Shit. She hadn't meant to betray her own unease. *Cool. Wryly amused*. She found herself staring at his hands. He laughed.
  'There are a lot of us about.'
She wondered whether those hands had, just an hour ago, been touching dead flesh.
  'I don't think I've ever met an undertaker before. Outside of a funeral.'
Clearly, her mouth had become disconnected from her brain. But he smiled.
  'We generally only come out after dark. Like vampires.'

Well. At least he was trying.

They ordered food. When Heike said she'd have a glass of red, Yusuf suggested they order a whole bottle. She liked him for that.

After the flirtatious intensity of their text exchanges, the reality of physical proximity made them both shy. They began cautiously, Heike leading the questioning, still embarrassed at her monopolisation of their speed date. Within a few minutes she'd established that he lived in Tempelhof, that his 'business' (she deliberately used a generic term) was in Neukölln, he had no children and a fifteen-year relationship had ended two years previously, when his partner left him for another man.

'I was numb with shock at first. And then I had a sudden moment of clarity. That I'd been released. From something stultifying. Now I feel actively grateful to her for cheating on me.'

Heike realised she'd strayed too quickly into the forbidden territory of previous relationships.

'Have you always lived in Berlin?'

'Is that code for "exactly how foreign are you?"?'

Heike flushed. Though it hadn't been that. Or not quite.

'No. I meant which part of Germany are you from?'

'Pretty much right here. I grew up about two streets away.'

'You're kidding?'

'How about you?'

'Köpenick.'

'An Ossi.'

'Yes. And a proud one.'

'Is that politics, or nostalgia?'

'A bit of both. Also an "up yours" at some of the Wessi entitlement I've encountered.'

Yusuf laughed at this. A loud, unselfconscious laugh that resonated from the very centre of him. It alarmed her a little, its volume out of proportion to the acoustics of the restaurant. But it was a sound that suggested life should be laughed at. And she liked the creases that deepened to the side of his eyes. She liked that his body suggested competence, warmth.

'I'll do my best not to conform to the stereotype,' he said.

'Oh, I'm afraid it's too late. You're the colonisers. We thought we were working towards reunification, but it's mostly been erasure.'

'Coke and Gummi Bears.'

'Coke and Gummi Bears.'

*

The food arrived, and Yusuf unfolded his napkin with a flourish.

'And you live in Kreuzberg?'

'On Friedrichstraße. A couple of blocks down from Checkpoint Charlie. The cheap end. Not Unter den Linden.'

'So you're a defector after all?'

'I guess so.'

'Kreuzberg 61. Bohemians and radicals.'

'That's me. I found out, the day after I signed the lease on the apartment, that it used to be a Red Army Faction hangout. Well, not exactly RAF, but affiliates – 2 June Movement or some such. Turns out they were involved in the murder of – what was his name – Schneider? – big property tycoon. Remember that? Back in the '80s?'

'Shit. Car bomb, wasn't it? Didn't they get locked up?'

'Yes. All out now, I think. Though one guy committed suicide in prison. At least, that was the official story.'

'And there's no plaque to them?' His smile was mischievous.

'There's no plaque. Though someone recently sprayed *RAF Forever* on the side wall.'

'Optimistic.'

'Yes.'

She wished she hadn't ordered a dish with so much spinach in it. Now every time she opened her mouth, she imagined Yusuf was being treated to a full set of green teeth. She tried surreptitiously to run her tongue over her upper incisors, but Yusuf caught her in the act and she immediately felt ridiculous, like she'd been attempting some bizarre sexual manoeuvre. She tried to keep her lips tight as she talked.

'You were never tempted to move away?'

'Oh sure. Especially when my parents took me back to Turkey for the first time. Berlin felt so grey when we got back. I've never really been able to shake that – the sense that this city is drained of colour.'

Heike, mouth full of spinach, nodded in vigorous agreement.

'But, I was an only child. There was the business. I wasn't about to run out on all of that.'

'Where in Turkey were your parents from?'

Exactly how foreign are you?

'No! That's not what I'm asking! I'm a hybrid too. My grandmother – my mum's mum – was Japanese.'

'That explains your beautiful hair.'

She affected indifference to this compliment.

'My grandfather worked as an aircraft engineer out there during the war. He came back with malaria and a bride who spoke barely ten words of German.'

'Postwar Germany must have been a bit of a shock.'

'Yeah.'

'But, in answer to your question – Istanbul. The northern quarter of Istanbul. There was a small enclave of Jews there, some who'd been there for centuries, some who'd fled Russian pogroms, or Hitler. But, economically, things were pretty rough, so my parents moved to Berlin in the '60s – when I was just a few months old – and within a couple of years were running their own cafe.'

'And from there it was one short step to undertaking.'

Another loud laugh. 'The cafe wasn't really paying its way, so they sold up, and Baba started a job with an undertakers. He was good at it and the owner practically adopted him, so when he died, he left Baba the business in his will. Then when I was old enough, I learned the trade and took over the company when he retired.'

'Did you have any choice?'

'I knew it was expected of me, so it was okay. I never resented it. We all have duties, don't we?'

Heike blinked a little too rapidly. The word *duty* made her uncomfortable. The unseen audience judging her again. It was a word associated with her failed marriage, the as yet unknown damage to her daughter, her residual sense of responsibility to Martin.

*

She took another swig of wine. 'How do you cope – with all that exposure to death?'

Yusuf dabbed at his lips with a napkin.

'I don't really think my business is with the dead. It's the living I'm responsible to. The ones left to grieve. People can go slightly mad after a bereavement. Behave unpredictably, thoughtlessly, angrily. It's a case of predicting what they need and guiding them through. They're the ones who need the rituals, the eulogies. They're the ones who carry us forward, who make sure we don't disappear entirely. Ultimately, they're the ones who make the meaning of our lives.'

'But that's a lot to carry – their grief.'

'Their grief is theirs alone. You can recognise it, you can empathise, but it's essentially a lonely business.'

Heike had a flash of memory. Sitting at her mother's kitchen table, a couple of weeks after her father died. Neither of them able to talk, wrapped up in their separate griefs, as though they were each mourning different people. And perhaps, in a sense, they were.

'Kids though . . .' Yusuf put his fork down. 'You never get used to that. Churns me up every time. It goes against everything those parents anticipated. Those speeches about how alive they were, how they brought such happiness . . .' He shook his head. 'Perhaps that's why I've never had kids. I'd be too fearful. Seeing dangers everywhere. Imagining every rash was meningitis, every water park a death trap. I'd be hopeless.'

'I'd say that was true of most parents.' *You always catastrophise, Heike.* 'I've lived Leonie's death a hundred times.'

'But I think good parents absorb that and let their kids take risks anyway.'

'I try. But I feel like I'm always rehearsing loss, just in case. Like if I rehearse it enough, if I fully imagine each possible disaster, it'll never happen.'

*

Yusuf glanced at his watch. Heike worried he was getting bored, but he merely poured out the last of the wine, giving her the lion's share. Neither of them said anything for a few moments. They both looked out of the window. A group of middle-aged Chinese tourists filed past in padded jackets, two by two, like kindergarteners. Their guide walked backwards at the head of the line, holding up a red flag, apparently able to navigate the street's obstacles by some mysterious sixth sense.

Yusuf broke the silence.

'I had a weird thing this week. A Facebook friend request from the Ravensbrück Memorial Museum. Don't you think that's a surreal idea? For a Jew to be Facebook friends with a concentration camp? My great aunt was a prisoner there. Which certainly makes "liking" their posts a bit problematic.' He sipped his wine. 'I can't decide whether it's tasteless, or whether it represents something rather wonderful and strange and forward-looking. I guess it's just another way of ensuring we don't forget.'

'What happened to her?'

'She survived. She was lucky. She only arrived there in late '44, which wasn't quite enough time to starve her to death. I only met her once, on a visit to Istanbul. I think she thought my parents were insane. Or traitors. Nothing would ever have induced her to come back to Germany.'

Heike was struck, not for the first time, by the miracle of migration. The sheer blind reckless optimism of it. The trust of Yusuf's parents that their adopted country wouldn't murder them, despite all the evidence to the contrary; her own grandmother, plucked from everything she knew and replanted, language-less, among the yellow and orange stucco-fronts of Zittau.

'Isn't it hard to live among all the . . .' Heike waved a hand in the general direction of the city outside.

'What else can we do?'

His choice of expression made her choke slightly on her wine. She heard again the disembodied voice on her recorder. *Was können wir sonst noch tun?* But Yusuf, oblivious, carried on.

'I imagine it's just as hard for the grandchildren of Nazis as the grandchildren of Jews. So much began here – or ended here – that's quite a burden for a place to bear. It's a city of hauntings, isn't it? I spend my working hours with the new dead and then, afterwards, as I walk the streets, I'm surrounded by the old dead. Perhaps that's rather fanciful, but there it is. Berlin doesn't offer tranquillity or simplicity or amnesia. And that's okay.'

'Do you believe in ghosts? Actual ones?'

'I don't think I do. But then I just used a metaphor about hauntings, so I guess at some level, I must accept the possibility of their existence.'

She nearly told him then about her unnerving recording experience in the apartment. The voice. The unaccounted for sounds. But she felt that saying it out loud would make her madness concrete. Instead she said, 'Perhaps ghosts leave undertakers alone.'

'Perhaps they do.'

She realised he was shifting in his chair, preparing to get the bill. He read the question on her face and smiled apologetically.

'I hate to leave an interesting conversation in the middle, but I have a client in twenty minutes. Shall we do this again sometime?'

They both stood and faced each other at the side of the table.

'Yes. I'd like that. Very much.'

'Me too.'

His lopsided eyes suddenly seemed to water slightly. Behind them, it seemed to her, a door opened onto a garden. Cool wet leaves, a fountain. The possibility that this stranger might already understand everything about her.

*

She could feel the tight ball in the core of her chest loosening. He was going to kiss her. She lifted up her face in expectation. But then he patted the top of her arm, like a colleague, said goodbye and turned on his heel, without looking back. She was left standing in the middle of the restaurant, her foolish, adolescent anticipation reflected in a wall of gilded baroque mirrors.

She picked Leonie up from school and took her for cake and a milkshake at Wilhelm & Medné, her favourite cafe on Friedrichstraße. It was a profligate treat for an ordinary school day. A mother's response to guilt, even if nothing substantial had yet happened. Despite the cold, they sat outside in the cafe's little makeshift garden on the pavement, Leonie scraping every last crumb of chocolate cake from the dish, Heike gazing up at the 1960s apartment block opposite, with its balconies and net curtains and satellite dishes. One balcony was filled with flowerpots, but all the plants were dead and withered. They must have been planted with good intentions, but then the resident had either lost heart, or health, and allowed them to die. Heike thought of all the cardboard boxes still piled to one side of her bedroom. There must be a way to override that sense of exhaustion – the thing that stopped you from opening a box, or watering a plant. Vitamin pills? Perhaps vitamin pills were the answer.

Her phone buzzed in her jacket pocket. She hoped it was Yusuf, but resisted the urge to check.

This was handover day. Martin dropped Leonie at school in the morning and Heike collected her. Handover days were often awkward. The first hour a stumble through oddly formal conversation, before they could relax with each other again.

Now Leonie looked up at her with a perfect ring of chocolate froth around her mouth. Heike felt the unread text pull heavy in her pocket.

'I'm getting very good at Minecraft. Daddy lets me play on his computer.'

'That's nice. How long does he let you play for?'

'Not too long. Sometimes I do it when he's sleeping.'

'You're on the computer at night?'

'No. Just the afternoon. When he's having a nap.'

'A nap?'

Heike realised her pitch had gone up several tones. She adjusted it back down.

'Daddy naps during the day?'

'Oh, yes. He's very tired. Do you think he's working too hard, Mummy?'

Heike, who believed Martin's job (Health & Safety consultant for a large accountancy firm) a constant jolly (what the fuck could possibly happen to six floors of accountants?), thought Martin didn't know what real work was.

'Perhaps. That might be it. Was that just this weekend, Leonie?'

'Oh no. He does it most days after lunch. Yesterday I built a tower that was taller than the Fernsehturm. And it had walls made of glass at the top. Just like the revolving restaurant.'

As Leonie went into great detail about her architectural projects, Heike swallowed back her anger at Martin for neglecting his responsibilities. Her phone buzzed again, like a bee sting in the skin of her thigh, and she had to muster all her self-control not to reach into her pocket. And then she realised she wasn't giving Leonie her full attention, so assumed her listening face. But then she felt guilty, because this was only a simulation of attentive parenting. In fact, she worried that much of her mothering was simulation. The love was real. The take-a-bullet conviction that you would die for your child. But in the day-to-day business of parenthood, she felt her displays of devotion were often strategic.

*

As they walked back to the apartment, Heike furtively retrieved her phone. A warm trickle of disappointment drained through her chest when she saw both messages were from Alice. The first simply read: *So????????* The second: *I want ALL the filthy details*.

That night, she lay in bed and stared at the ceiling. Perhaps it was just too late to be starting something new. On the phone, Alice had remarked, 'It's not like we're looking for someone to save us. Not at our age.' Out loud, Heike had agreed with her, but once she'd hung up, she was no longer certain this was true.

And now her heart flapped in her chest like a fish on the bank. She needed to ration her hopes. She didn't know this man. She was projecting too much on to him, on the basis of what? A ninety-minute lunch date and a thread of text messages? But it was possible to imagine understanding him. It was possible to imagine that he might understand her, with all her fractures and skitters and longings. Something to do with the directness of his gaze, the trace of shyness she detected behind the outward confidence. For years, she'd contained a well of feeling that had no place to go. And now. Here? Was this the vessel into which to pour all of that? An undertaker with a paunch and lopsided eyes?

She thought about Martin and wondered whether he was depressed. When she'd last seen him, he'd looked tired and grey, dark circles under his eyes, a rash of acne on his chin. And if he were depressed, what was her responsibility to him, to this man who'd never really let her in? On her bedside table, her phone vibrated. The fish in her chest did a full flip over.

Thank you for a lovely lunch.

That was it. No follow up. No kiss. Still. *Lovely*.

She looked up at a crack in the ceiling that ran from the point directly above her head towards the overhead light, before making a dog-leg towards the window. She imagined Yusuf balanced on a ladder, painting the ceiling. She imagined herself smiling up at him, while she rollered the wall, her hair tucked inside a red bandana, a single curl . . . Fuckssake. What kind of middle-aged DIY-store TV-ad fantasy was this? Her phone vibrated again. The screen shone.

'I wanted to kiss you earlier. But I bottled it. Sorry.'
Something detonated in her chest. There was no going back from this. She texted back.

'You can kiss me next time.'
There was a long delay before his reply lit up her screen.

'Yes. Next time. Sleep well, beautiful woman xx'

She mustn't fall too quickly. Something teenage and obsessive was threatening to emerge and it would be all too easy to humiliate herself. She was aware of her tendency to commit wholeheartedly to new projects, new people, as though her entire circulatory system wanted to surrender to some external river. *Hold back, hold back.* It would be so easy to frighten him off, if he sensed the urgency of her need for him. *Stay present.*

She slept badly. The buzzer went at 8.30 a.m., depressed for a little longer than necessary, enough to trigger a synaptic spark of anxiety. The accent on the intercom was not Berliner – Bavarian perhaps – and Heike didn't catch most of what she said, apart from something about an email. Not quite awake enough to interrogate the reasonableness of the woman's request, she buzzed her into the building.

She opened the apartment door to a tall, striking-looking woman in her sixties. The stranger's clothes were stylishly eccentric, her white hair cut short into a 1920s crop, high cheekbones, almond eyes. Heike's irritation gave way to intrigue.

'How can I help you?'
'I used to live here.'

For one panicked moment, Heike thought she might be about to produce title deeds and announce a legal claim to the apartment.

'I'm sorry, I . . .'

The woman had an amused glint in her eye.

'Back in the '6os. I lived with a guy who produced dirty magazines.'

This was unexpected. 'I'm afraid he's not here now.'

The stranger laughed.

'I'm not looking for him. Though I should probably track him down and apologise for being a class one bitch. No, I'm looking for you.'

In person, the woman's accent was not quite Bavarian – there was a trace of something else there, something more familiar, even East Berliner. But Heike was still unsure where this conversation was going.

'Sorry, I don't—'

'You emailed me. About the exhibition.'

Heike had almost forgotten. She'd picked the book up from Dussmann's just over a week ago. *Wolf Bassermann: Magic and Mystery* – the catalogue of the photography exhibition. The back cover showed a man whose face was crowned with a wild mane of salt-and-pepper hair that belied the youth of his face. She'd curled up on the sofa to flick through the pictures. Studio portraits of Berliners in the early 1900s that seemed fairly conventional; street scenes with trolley buses and hawkers, women in striped skirts and tall hats, shopkeepers and grinning street urchins. Evocative but unremarkable. There followed a series of images that were more murky, but which contained enough detail to suggest more familiar images. The Brandenburger Tor with what might be barbed wire in front of it; an SS Totenkopf ring; a shadowy shape that was somewhere between a hypodermic syringe and the TV tower; the eviscerated, fire-blackened skeleton of a car; a black athlete in white vest and shorts caught mid-leap – Jesse Owens, perhaps? And then the picture she'd seen before. The silhouetted diver, executing a perfect fall, down through the sun-dappled stairwell.

When Heike finally read the introductory essay, she'd learned that Bassermann had lived and worked for a time in Friedrichstraße 19. This coincidence did not seem all that extraordinary; she accepted it readily, like a truth she'd known all along. But still she felt compelled to turn back to the picture of the diver, experiencing once more the sense of recognition and unease.

That evening she'd emailed the exhibition's curator, explaining the coincidence of location and, attempting a lightness she didn't feel, asking whether there was any more information about the diver image. And now, presumably, this was the curator standing at the door before her, but Heike was struggling to recall her name. Ilse something, was it? If she wasn't going to introduce herself, she'd have to sneak a look at the catalogue's cover.

Heike realised the woman was slightly breathless after climbing the stairs.

'Please, come in.'

As they stepped inside the apartment, Leonie appeared at her bedroom door, bleary-eyed, still in her pyjamas.

'Morning, sweetheart. Do you want to make yourself some toast? I won't be long.'

Leonie padded off to the kitchen. Heike beckoned the stranger into the sitting room, where she took a seat on the couch and looked around the room with an expression between regret and amusement.

'I wish I'd known about Bassermann, when I was staying here. Not that his name would have meant anything to me then – no one was really talking about his work in those days – he was horribly out of fashion this place has changed completely.' She altered subject mid-sentence. 'I like the knock-through. It makes the whole place much lighter. Did you do that?'

'Oh no. I've only recently moved in.'

'This building was laid out rather differently in Bassermann's time and we're not quite sure where his studio would have been, but my hunch is that it would have been at the back of the building somewhere – perhaps even on the top floor. He would have wanted somewhere with northern light. More reliable.'

'Yes. I see.'

'He went blind, you know. In the war. The first one. He ended up destitute, on the streets. No one even knows how or when he died. Just disappeared.'

A pauper's funeral. Anonymous. Heike imagined herself in the cheap coffin, Yusuf in his funeral director suit, looking bored during the perfunctory crematorium service, flicking a cigarette to the ground and grinding it with the heel of his polished shoe. Yusuf not knowing the identity of the person in the coffin. Forgetting her. *You remind me of someone.* She realised that the woman was waiting for a response.

'How terrible,' she mumbled, obligingly.

'Anyway. Your email made me realise something. Something I hadn't thought of before.'

The woman opened her bag and took out an iPad. She scrolled to find something and then passed the tablet to Heike. It was the photo of the diver.

'This. You asked about this.'

'Yes. Who is it?'

'It's one of a sequence of images Bassermann published in 1906. There's something of a mystery surrounding them, as they were said to be visions printed onto the photographic plates by a telepathic young girl.'

'Yes. I read that.'

'Nonsense, of course, but no one's really figured out how he made the images. There's some kind of trickery at work, but I haven't yet read a theory that's convinced me. But I'm determined to crack it.'

The woman gave Heike a look that felt suddenly too intimate.

'Do you recognise it?'

'Only from the poster. I don't remember having seen it before.' The woman held her gaze. 'The location.'

Heike peered at the image. Unease pulled at her belly.

'It's the stairwell of this building.' She said this with a certainty that surprised her.

'Yes. That's what I think too.'

The diver was just a silhouette, impossible to age, impossible to sex. The shadows stippled across the image made it hard to determine detail, although she could just make out that the figure was wearing trousers and shoes. But it was the pattern of shadows that Heike suddenly recognised. The tablet trembled slightly in her right hand. She placed her other hand on the wrist to disguise this sudden palsy.

'Do you know who this is?' she asked.

The woman shook her head.

They went out onto the landing. The woman held the screen up and kept moving position until she was satisfied she had the angle right. She called Heike to her side, and together they looked from photo to stairwell, heads tilted up to the skylight. And just then the sun came out, like a winter miracle, and the curlicued patterns of light appeared on the wall behind the stairwell's banisters. And for a moment, Heike saw the falling figure.

She turned to the woman at her side and realised she looked strangely flushed. Heike touched her arm. 'Are you all right?'

'You know,' the woman said, taking a step back, consulting the picture and then tilting her head to one side to study Heike's whole frame, 'it really could be you.'

On their third date, she went with Yusuf to the cinema museum. This after a jokey WhatsApp exchange about doppelgängers, in which Heike had tried to mask how unsettled she'd been by Ilse Singer's visit. This text conversation had developed into a two-hour phone call, which encompassed a discussion of doppelgängers in early German films and a confession that neither of them had ever been to the Filmhaus on Potsdamer Platz.

The way in was through a corridor constructed entirely of mirrors. On every side, infinite repetitions of Heike and Yusuf, disappearing into some kind of never-time. Doppelgängers that made them unreal to themselves, like endlessly replicating tiers of dancers in an old Hollywood musical.

Heike looked up at the mirrored ceiling and the unfamiliar vision of them as a couple – the copper sheen of her black hair pulled back into a ponytail, the heart shape of his small bald patch. Yusuf too looked up at the ceiling and smiled at her. All the liquid inside her seemed to tilt towards him. Happiness, she knew, was not a permanent state, not a country to be reached and settled in. There were only small happinesses, stations along the way. It was important to recognise them when they came along.

Although it was a Saturday morning, the cold weather appeared to have deterred visitors, so other than a few French tourists, they had the museum to themselves. They wandered through the rooms, self-consciously standing close together in front of each exhibit. She longed to take his hand or squeeze his arm, but some deep reserve took hold of her.

*

They exclaimed with pleasure over a scale model of the set of *The Cabinet of Dr. Caligari*, at a 1920s camera, at the set designs for *Metropolis*; they watched Marlene Dietrich's screen test for *The Blue Angel*.

'You can see why she got the job.'

He nodded. 'Her face works so beautifully in the light. All angles and shadows. And yet she's a real woman. Not too skinny.'

Yusuf talking of bodies made her think of the morgue. Despite all the flirtatious texts, neither of them had so much as suggested that sex might one day be on the cards. The result was that Heike thought about sex obsessively. Visions of Yusuf doing unknowable things to the naked bodies of dead women kept forming in her mind.

'Is there a sexual element to your work?'

'What?'

She hadn't meant to ask so directly. She hadn't meant to ask on the third floor of the cinema museum, in front of a billboard of antique posters for the films of Oskar Messter – *The Robber Bride*, *The Wandering Light*, *Life is a Dream*, *The Man in the Mirror*.

'I mean. All those naked bodies.'

There was an appallingly long pause. Yusuf leaned forward slightly to squint at the wording on one of the posters.

'Trouble is, they don't love you back.'

He said this deadpan. Heike caught his eye and seeing the laughter dancing there, giggled in embarrassment. They moved into the next room.

'But yes. Sex can come into it.'

Again, Heike noted Yusuf's lack of volume control. Two well-heeled French women, who had been looking at a display of Dietrich's personal items, turned around at this pronouncement, and moved away. Yusuf seemed to take the hint and came to stand at her side in front of a glass case displaying exhibits about the director F. W. Murnau (1888–1931). He lowered his voice.

'Of course, I mostly deal with the elderly. But a younger female body . . . Apart from thinking about the sheer waste of a life cut short, I'd be lying if I said I don't imagine what has been done to her. What it might have been like to kiss those breasts when she was alive.'

They both stared purposefully forwards at the display. Heike read that Murnau's 4 *Devils* told the story of four orphans who form a high-wire circus act but that the film itself is now, regrettably, lost.

'That makes sense,' Heike said politely. 'Thank you for being honest.'

'Of course, I prefer a nice pair of warm breasts.' He did not look at her.

It was the most suggestive he'd ever been. She felt simultaneously turned on and panicked. Suddenly all those dead breasts felt like competition.

They emerged into the vast spaces of Potsdamer Platz. When the Wall existed, this had been on her side of the city, but now it was entirely alien to her. All the old buildings of the East had been torn down. The plate glass of the Daimler building reflected the blue December sky, while just across the street, the red-brick cladding of the Kollhoff Tower resembled the Futurist structures on the film posters for *Metropolis*. Yusuf caught the tenor of her gaze.

'You think it's ugly?'

'Yes. But I also think architects face an impossible task in this city. Do you turn your back on the past, or honour it? Do you deliberately throw out every principle that Speer might have espoused and design buildings you're sure he'd have hated, even if they're eyesores? It seems each time an architect submits plans for a new building, another architect will claim it's fascist. Stone is fascist, pillars are fascist, height is fascist.'

'Though not plate glass, apparently.'

'But who decides?'

He took her arm. They were walking into the wind and instinctively pressed together for warmth. The delicious solidity of him, the unfamiliar proportion of muscle to flesh.

'At least they keep asking the question.'

She thought of Yusuf's great-aunt in Ravensbrück. Although she'd visited the museum as a schoolgirl, she couldn't remember being told about the presence of Jewish prisoners there. Her East German guide had been far more keen to talk about the memorial site as a camp for anti-fascist freedom fighters. Heike had grown up with the distinct impression that the atrocities of the Second World War had been committed by West German fascists and that the good socialists of the DDR had looked on in powerless horror, or resisted and been punished themselves. It was more useful to the authorities to conflate the crimes of the Third Reich with the crimes of the Federal Republic.

Both her grandfathers had seen military service, but the family mythology had been carefully constructed to suggest that they were conscripts and not disciples. It was different now, of course. Young people had absorbed their history, visited the memorials, were quick to decry anything that smacked of fascism. The war belonged to their great-grandparents, known mostly through photographs in textbooks and TV documentaries. Even the Wall – that totem of Heike's childhood – had been demolished before their birth. And now, on Potsdamer Platz, only a small section of it remained as monument.

'The city's become so gentrified,' Yusuf said. 'All the old alternative culture places have gone – like the Tacheles compound. Or the Berghain nightclub. Nowadays it's just full of tourists taking selfies.'

'And I thought I was the nostalgist.'

'Oh, I'm happiest in the past. The future's just a place full of the mistakes I haven't made yet.'

She laughed, but then Yusuf suddenly pulled away from her. Perhaps he'd realised she was a mistake.

'I think you should come to my place of work.'

His look was a challenge.

'Now?'

'Not now. But soon.'

'In the near-future?'

'In the near-future.'

And then he stepped forward and kissed her.

Back at Friedrichstraße, she sat with Leonie on the sofa, the traditional Saturday night bowl of popcorn between them, *Schlag den Star* on the TV.

'There's someone I'd like you to meet.'

'Yusuf.'

'How do you know his name?'

'I've seen it on your phone. Yusuf – three thousand two hundred and thirty-eight messages.'

'Well, I think that's a bit of an—'

'Is he your boyfriend?'

'No. Well. Yes. It's early days, but I . . . I think it would be good for you to meet each other. I think you'll like him.'

'Is he going to move in here?'

'Oh no. No.' She tried to imagine Yusuf in the armchair opposite them, laughing at *Schlag den Star*, spilling popcorn on the rug. 'Nothing like that.'

'Is he a terrorist?'

'What do you mean?'

'Isn't Yusuf a Muslim name?'

'It can be, but . . . Leonie? Why did you say that? You know only a tiny, tiny handful of people are terrorists – and they're mostly crazy, brainwashed people – and anyway when I was growing up, most of the terrorists in Germany were white

Germans.' She was getting herself into a tangle here. 'I mean non-Muslims. Muslims can still be German. And white, of course. And most of them aren't terrorists. Muslims, I mean.'

Oh God. Heike tipped a palmful of popcorn into her mouth to dam the stream of inanity. Together they watched the two contestants race each other to hammer ten nails into a piece of wood, monitored, inexplicably, by two extras dressed as cowboys. She suddenly felt overwhelmed with inadequacy. The world was burning up, the oceans were filling with plastic, the far right was once more on the rise, her ex-husband was depressed, she was failing to address her daughter's cultural stereotyping, she was too afraid to suggest to her boyfriend that they have sex and she didn't know which of the two contestants was the celebrity.

'Anyway, Yusuf's Jewish. But not practising.'
She immediately distrusted her addition of the qualifier.
Leonie's eyes never strayed from the TV screen.
'I thought all the Jewish people were dead.'

There was a commotion on the landing outside the apartment. Heike ran to open the door and discovered two women from the floor below remonstrating with a pigeon that had somehow become trapped in the stairwell. It was now throwing itself in panic towards the moonlit glass of the skylight. The hapless creature flew up and down through the stairwell, occasionally perching on the balustrades before making another bid for freedom. Frustrated by the glass, it flew down to perch on the third floor banister, cooing and looking down at its audience. For a moment, it shuffled along the polished wood, before launching itself once more, failing to learn from experience. Heike thought of the photograph of the diver, transient beauty and imminent death trapped in one image. For a while, the three women stood, heads tilted upwards, watching the bird in ineffectual silence then the tide of sound rises once more. The baby adds his voice to it. The twelve members of the collective encircle her. She watches their mouths opening and closing, their teeth, tongues, saliva. Someone – Rainer, is it? – takes her by the arm, shakes her. *Are you out of your tiny mind?* Others call her many synonyms of fuckwit. Tonja hears them as if at the end of a long tunnel. They quiz her, anxious to determine whether her insane behaviour has compromised the group, given them all away. She manages to answer some of their questions, but cannot provide justification for bringing the child back to the squat. He struggles against the straps of his stroller, red-faced and whining, panicked by the noise and the claustrophobic press of dark figures above him.

She listens to them berate Monika for talking them into allowing her to join the group. All the things they weren't able to say before are now said. Tonja's naive, uneducated, bourgeois, suburban, a liability, clearly stupid for getting knocked up at nineteen. Out of the cacophony, the surprise of Monika's voice. Calm, forceful. *She was being human. It was the human thing to do.* Tonja's eyes meet hers. *Thank you*, they say. But Rainer will not be appeased. *Goddammit we're not misty-eyed social workers. This is fucking war.*

Once the retributions have been released, the discussion turns to the best course of action. The members of the collective relax a little. They like debating a plan. Incredibly, it seems no one has followed her. There are no sirens in the street. No one hammers on the door.

In the living room, the flatmates crowd around the radio, listening to the news anchor solemnly reporting the callous murder of two men and one woman by a terrorist group. The assumption is that the woman's baby has also died, although no body has yet been found. The collective is comforted by this – at least no one is actively looking for the child. And there is no reference to a young woman fleeing the scene with a pushchair.

As they talk, Tonja finds food and heats milk for the baby. Rocks it to sleep, using pillows and blankets to construct a nest for it on the bedroom floor. For the first time, she realises this is know-ledge that no one else in the group shares. For the first time, she is able to take some pride in it.

She knows that Jörg has fathered a kid, but has never been a part of its life. Angelika and Monika have both had abortions. An experience they talk about with a breeziness Tonja's never quite believed. And now, looking at this changeling child in his nest of cushions, she realises how little she's thought about Kurt these last few weeks. Her own child, flesh of her flesh, lying in a distant cot across the city. But here is this infant, for whom she has no feelings, other than the gut clench of guilt. And the instinct that she must somehow do right by him.

By the time she returns to the others, her future has been formulated.

It is communicated to her by Rainer, naturally. He speaks slowly, as if to a foreigner or idiot. She notices that his teeth are studded with poppy seeds. After dark, she is to take the baby to a police station. She will leave it outside in the car park and then phone the front desk to tell them it's there. Then she will hole up in the squat for the next month, so that the collective can manage the situation. After that, she can and must leave. Sentence has been passed. Twelve have voted. Twelve apostles, twelve angry men. She feels simultaneously rejected and liberated. She is suddenly completely alone in the world. Something in her has already started to rebel. But for now, the simplest option is to agree to whatever they suggest.

She waits until dark. Her evening is spent in the little back bedroom feeding and entertaining the baby. Kat and Angelika keep their distance. The child's beginning to be aware of the strangeness of its new situation, beginning to sense the absence of its mother. He chunters on, his mouth exploring vowels and a few favoured consonants, and whatever he is saying sounds questioning, distrustful. She fancies he is saying 'Will you jump? Will you jump?'

At midnight, Tonja lifts the sleeping child from its makeshift bed. He wakes, momentarily, and looks at her without a sound, as if complicit in this plan. The look frightens her a little. She avoids meeting his eyes as she pushes stubby arms into a coat, fastens the pushchair straps around his chest. By the time this is achieved, he is once more fast asleep. With Monika's assistance, she carries the chair down the stairs. Tonja has dressed in several layers of clothes, stuffed wads of money in various pockets. Some of this money is stolen from Kat and Angelika, but she's past guilt now. She hopes Monika won't comment on her eccentrically bulging appearance, but can't risk taking the blue holdall. Monika asks if she should come along to the police station, but Tonja says, no, it's easier on her own. She's astonished when Monika gives her a hug.

She walks south down Friedrichstraße, through Mehringplatz and west along the Landwehrkanal until the house feels a long way behind her. A night bus takes her to the suburbs. The linden trees, the wholesome-looking cream apartment blocks, the cars parked on the tidy road, Stefan's green Volkswagen Golf. She gazes up at the first floor, but the windows of her old flat are blank and unlit. Quietly, she pulls the spare key from her jacket pocket, walks up to the car and fumbles at the lock, pulling gently at the handle to open it. Unstraps the child from the push-chair and transfers it to Kurt's baby seat. The baby stirs, but does not wake. She struggles to fold up the unfamiliar pushchair, cursing as she packs it into the boot, which closes with a tell-tale thunk.

The moment she starts the engine, a light goes on in the apartment. As she manoeuvres out of the parking space, she's aware of Stefan in the upstairs window. She can't hear, but she can imagine the shouts. And just as she reaches the end of the street, her former life receding in the rear-view mirror, Stefan appears on the pavement in his pyjamas. He starts to run towards the car, but it's pointless. Tonja indicates right like a good citizen, turns the wheel and drives.

Takes the transit road that connects West Berlin to West Germany, showing her ID card at the checkpoint, giving the border guard just enough of a smile to indicate harmlessness. There are only a few other cars on the road, but she's careful to keep to the speed limit as she drives the 170 km to the border. Outside, in the darkness, is that other country that also goes by the name of Germany. That other country describes itself as a socialist utopia, but she knows, treacherously, that she wouldn't want to live there.

She's only been on this road a dozen or so times before, to visit relatives or to sightsee – Hanover, Cologne, Heidelberg – although it was usually her mother or Stefan who drove. Being the one at the wheel now is like a coming of age. The road surface consists of temporary concrete blocks and the car thumps rhythmically over them, like a war drum.

As the miles expand between her and Friedrichstraße, Tonja's breathing begins to calm. Occasionally, she imagines a movement in the rear-view mirror and fancies someone is in the back of the car. Kat or Angelika or Jörg. And she is momentarily frightened. But when she turns to check, there is only the baby, asleep in its padded seat. She remembers how the flatmates crowded around her in the hallway. Their unconcealed contempt. How quick they were to denounce her. She sees for the first time that, for all their speeches of solidarity with ordinary workers, those university graduates were always ill at ease with her working classness. They had no idea how to talk to her. She suspects their knowledge of ordinary workers is largely theoretical.

The radio is still talking about the 'terrorist incident'. There is now some question over the fate of a thirteen-month-old baby and the anomaly of a missing pushchair. She learns that relatives are desperate for news of the child. There is a statement from the boy's grandfather, in which his voice cracks mid-sentence. She learns that the baby is called Thomas. The name that is harder to learn is the name of his mother, and her age – twenty-seven. A life is described that has nothing to do with the thing Tonja saw on the tarmac.

She has no definite plan. The only thought in her head is a vague idea of mountains, of vivid green pastures and clear air. She drives west, through the border and then south, only stopping when she must. Luckily, Stefan has filled the tank up only recently. The child in the back seat seems indifferent to her presence, or perhaps he's getting used to her. He sleeps through the sunrise and when he wakes talks animatedly to himself in his own language. By the afternoon, she's exhausted and can drive no further. Spends the night in a damp hotel on the fringes of a midland town. The double bed with its floral eiderdown feels like a boat floating in a vast ocean. Sleeps fitfully, woken by the baby's demands for food or attention and each time she wakes registers a strange sense of seasickness.

*

It's only the next day that she notices the car. A black Audi. It's always in her rear-view mirror, always two or three cars behind, although it is occasionally exposed when one of those cars changes lanes. Tells herself it's just paranoia. But the unlit head-lights of the car burn like eyes on her back. She slows down, just a little, to get a better view of the driver in her mirror. But he's too far back and the bright morning light fills his windscreen with rapidly flickering patterns.

Now she tries to put some distance between them, pressing the pedal to a speed that scares her, just above the legal limit, but faster than feels comfortable. In the back of the car, Thomas senses this acceleration and starts to sing to himself, a repeated four note skat. Sometimes she sings back to him – 'There's no business like showbusiness . . .'

She wonders how she will cope with prison. Scenes from a half-remembered TV documentary – lino floors, white painted bars, the hard faces of seasoned offenders. Girls who grew to woman-hood with the pinched, grey look of the malnourished. She won't think herself one of them. There's nothing intrinsically criminal about her. She's a soldier, a freedom fighter, a guerrilla. But they will sense her weakness and bully her, steal her food, twist her arm behind her back, push her face into the toilet bowl. She imagines what it would be like to go on hunger strike, to have a rubber tube forced down her oesophagus. Or to be kept in the grey-painted chill of solitary confinement. How it would be to fashion a rope from a bedsheet and hang herself, like Meinhof or Ensslin. But she's certain she couldn't do this. Wonders whether Monika will visit her in prison and then realises, with a strange pang, that this will not be possible.

The sky blackens with the promise of a deluge. A little further and the windscreen is strafed with rain. The cars around her slow down, put on their lights, but she holds her nerve, keeps the pedal depressed as far as she dares. The control required by road and machine makes her head feel clear and sharp. Somewhere between Fulda and Würzburg, she thinks she may have lost her tail.

Without consciously making a decision, she's following signs for Oberammergau. It's somewhere she's never been, so it seems as logical a destination as any. In the shop of a petrol station, she fills a bag with food and soft drinks, thinking she will stay on the road until the fuel runs out. Pulls out of the forecourt and back onto the road. And then, in her mirror, she sees it. A black Audi glides out of a layby and rejoins the stream of traffic.

The baby, who's been strapped to his seat for hours, begins to complain. She tries to distract him with chatter, with singing, with food, unwrapping a cake and passing it back to him. He takes one mouthful, drops the rest, irretrievably, into the darkness of the footwell and starts to wail. Tonja fishes with one hand in the bag beside her, eyes fixed to the wet tarmac, the windscreen still pelted with rain. The car swerves a little as she fumbles for bread rolls and when the car in front brakes suddenly, she's forced to push the pedal to the floor. Bag, food and bottles avalanche from the passenger seat.

The baby's crying crescendos. He is red with rage. The stink of a full nappy fills the car. His cry is so shrill that her molars ache with it. An alien cry, so unlike Kurt's more plaintive protests. This baby's cry feels performative, overdone. She finds herself blaming the mother for permitting her baby to develop a cry as piercing as that. And then Tonja remembers that whoever she was, she does not exist any more. The child screams on, certain of his place at the centre of the universe. She shouts at him. He screams even louder. And that is when remorse finally hits. She has yelled at him. This child who is not her son.

*

The effort of concentration is exhausting. She is twenty years old. The rest of life unrolls before her like a dark, wet motorway. The thought of it, of each grey mile, is exhausting. She could simply let the car slide into the one in front. Perhaps that would be for the best. Perhaps she's just not very good at responsibility. Because she never knows when she's lucky (her mother). Because she's selfish and egotistical (Stefan). Because she's stupid for getting knocked up at nineteen. Because she doesn't know how to love her baby. Because something in her kicks against her own sense of powerlessness. Because so much is wrong and corrupt and unfair. Because the police state would kick and kick and kick her and those like her into oblivion. Because she needs to do something that matters. Because doing something feels like a stand against apathy, against ego. But now she realises she feels responsible for the whole world. And that this might be the worst kind of egotism.

The baby finally gives up, worn out by crying. His hot red face collapses into sleep. The rain, too, has eased, and the steady growl of tyres on tarmac is soporific. She has to pull herself from the desire to nap. Drinks a Coke. Unwraps a bar of chocolate with one hand and chomps it down, without tasting it.

She wonders which photo Stefan will give the police. Whether he'll be vindictive and choose something unflattering, a snapshot he knows she hates. And then she thinks of the press coverage of the RAF women, the newspapers printing photos in which they gaze down maternally at their babies, all soft hair and soft focus, the babies these women had chosen to abandon. The implication of German womanhood corrupted. Presumably the same thing will happen to her. The right wing press will use her as *the flip-side of feminism*, belittle her with headlines in which she becomes a *wild fury* or *terrorist girl*. An unwoman. *Patriarchal bullshit*, Monika would say.

*

By Schongau the petrol is running low. The landscape around the car has changed to winter-yellow pasture, forested hills and on the horizon, the first crags of the Alps. When she winds down the window, the air is crisp and fresh. She's glad for the cold hit of it, as the roads have become steep and sharp-bended, requiring all concentration. Up, up, up. Perhaps she will drive all the way to a top of a mountain. Perhaps there, she will stand on a rock and feel alive and let the winds take her. She has no plan. Thomas has slept for the last three hours. She keeps checking in the mirror that he's still breathing.

The black Audi is still out there somewhere. Occasionally she catches the black flash of it in her mirror. It has begun to feel like a necessary part of this, a shadow she cannot rip away. It is almost company.

The light is beginning to dim. Other cars have switched on their lights, but she keeps hers off. The petrol is now on the warning mark. She hopes she can make it as far as the town on the horizon.

Driving into the outskirts, she overshoots a shabby Gasthaus with a car park outside. She turns around a little further up the road. As she retraces her route, the black Audi passes her. There are two men sitting in the front. They do not meet her eyes.

The baby wakes with the halt of the car. It opens its eyes and looks at Tonja, the wrong mother, and its face floods with outrage. And above his angry ululation, another wail echoes around the valley. The sound bounces in such peculiar ways off the surrounding mountains and buildings she's not sure whether there is one siren or two. And now, pulling into the car park to block her exit, the black Audi.

A frame from a heist movie. Perhaps she should pull the baby from the car and threaten to harm it. But she's so tired. And she doesn't have a gun or any kind of weapon. And something in her is curious to see what the Audi men look like. A second police car pulls up onto the pavement. The flashing light distracts the baby and he falls temporarily silent.

Four men, not two. Standing in front of them, she's aware of how small and skinny she must look. In the valley in front of her, a sudden murmuration of starlings fills the sky, rising and diving. She does that thing they do on TV. She raises her arms in the air

SIGI, 1948

& there were so many birds wheeling around the ruins of the Schiller Theatre I think they're starting to come back or anyway I decided to take it as a sign & God knows how but Eric had found a piano & wheeled it half a mile along the road & managed to tune it just enough for it to sound okay though it was missing a couple of keys & I hardly dared trust my voice because it's so tight & scratchy these days but I sang Hollaender & Nelson & Spolianksy like I was summoning their shadows I guess *There is something hypnotic in the air, idiotic in the air* & there was a funny moment when a ring-collared dove flew down & perched on the piano & seemed completely unbothered by the noise perhaps he'd been deafened by the constant planes & he occasionally trundled along the piano top & looked down at Eric as if to say Mein Gott is this really the best girl singer you can find & by the time I got to *Eine kleine Sehnsucht* the tears were pouring down my cheeks so I had to cheer myself & everyone else up with *Wenn die beste Freundin* & two big old girls sang along & others clapped & cheered you

have to hope don't you

& you have to hope for the best in people

*

& I am trying to do my best though you probably thought the worst of me

> think

> I'm not consigning you to the past tense

> > think think think

& you'd be right of course such stupidity such blind faith in words but you can live through the end of the world without knowing because it starts with one crack in the milk jug just a hairline & then it deepens & spreads & bifurcates & fractures & then suddenly the whole jug is in a thousand splinters & you see it at your feet on the floor the milk wasted & you think how did that come to be I don't remember dropping it I don't remember losing control of myself

& it's not just the birds but people are starting to come back soldiers refugees people who went off to do God knows what you see them wandering the streets like ghosts desperately looking for landmarks trying to get their bearings people are coming back

& that was how I met Frau de Groot at first I thought she was another deranged old lady who'd lost her way she was hanging around outside our building when I made it home with only two apples for my pains & she took my arm & kept saying nineteen nineteen & because I was so tired it took me a little while to realise she was asking about the street number so I said yes yes nineteen & she shook her head looking up at the wreckage of it all & I asked whether she was looking for someone & she said she used to live there but that everyone was gone now & I think she meant dead because that's generally what people mean

*

& then she said she'd lived here years ago with her first husband who was some kind of magician maybe a conjuror I think she said but he'd died of the Spanish flu in '18 & she'd eventually married a Dutchman & moved to Rotterdam but she was always too homesick for Berlin & they moved back in '32 which was one of the stupidest decisions of her life she said

& I invited her in & took her up the stairs where I've stretched string across all the gaps in the banisters to prevent mother from doing herself an injury or perhaps to prevent me from chucking myself off ha ha & I led her through to the kitchen & as we walked I noticed she was touching the walls in places as though they held memories she might somehow pull out of the plaster

& I boiled some water & reused the little bit of tea we have to make at least the coloured water that passes for tea these days & she sat at the table & told us she'd had an invitation to go to America she has a son out there I think it was her son who's big in movies an editor or something I think she said he worked with Billy Wilder I think it was Wilder or maybe Lubitsch & he could sort things out for her but she laughed & said wouldn't it be a crazy thing for an old lady to do & anyway she didn't speak American & that's when mother piped up to my amazement she'd been almost completely silent till this point & said if she had an invitation she'd be on the first boat west because what was there left to live for here who cares about the ugly language at least you'd get a decent meal out there & Frau de Groot looked thoughtful for a moment but then shook her head & said she couldn't see it happening & thank you so much for the tea but I must be going now & on the way out she noticed the dragon mirror & she put her hand to her heart & I was scared she was about to keel over but it was just the mirror my God she said my God after everything

& yesterday I spent four hours in the IRO office queuing & shuffling & sitting around & being sent from one part of the building to another & now my back is in a very bad way almost too crocked to walk but I had to go because I suddenly remembered the name of your village it bubbled up out of the bog of my brain & I thought it might be a step closer & my hopes were raised at one point by this lovely young woman because I knew she was trying everything I could just tell she would be fastidious & look through every possible record & she found something on a list that sounded promising & went to get the file but then I looked & I realised the dates didn't work out & just as I was about to give up I suddenly thought of something & asked if I should try the displaced persons camps & she said that all of the Berlin ones had closed in the last few months & that most of the Jews had already been flown out on the same planes that bring us sugar & matches & I

you still could be

you could

still

& sometimes I feel so close to giving up

& then I remember I have mother even though her will is fading & I often hear her weeping quietly in the night I don't know whether it's my duty to keep reviving her with cheery promises or whether really it would be better to let her carry on disappearing it's like she's more translucent every day it's like her skin is turning into rice paper she barely speaks though this evening as we were enjoying ha ha yet another bowl of cabbage soup & she said I'd rather be dead I'd rather be with Vatti which is a load of bollocks because they were always at it Sturm & Drang when he was alive she mostly couldn't stand the sight of him but then she looked up at me her soup spoon suspended in the air & said we brought all this on ourselves you know never mind blaming the Jews or the British or the French or the Russkis this is something self-destructive in us something deep in our psyche she said she didn't even blame Hitler because we were the ones who went along with that madman God knows she said how we produced all those scientists God knows because clearly we Germans are just stupid lazy compliant deferential just wanting someone else to be in charge to make the decisions it's not the madman's fault if people decide to take his ravings for gospel & after this lengthy monologue she closed her eyes

& she was pretending to be asleep

& of course she didn't really mean all Germans are stupid she mostly meant me

& not long after that conversation Eric & Gerhard had an almighty row I know Gerhard can't sleep at night for the noise of the planes & sleep deprivation makes him wired & edgy & there is always fault to be found with one of us usually Eric & this evening poor Eric stumbled in the dark & spilled a whole jug of milk it was a very small jug but still it was all we had & Gerhard flew into a rage & stamped around the apartment so violently I thought he might take the ceiling down with him the building creaks & groans in all sorts of odd ways I often have nightmares about the walls crashing down on us while we're in our beds I think it's quite possible

& later I found Eric on the stairs in tears he said he didn't want Gerhard to know he was upset so I put my arm around his shoulders poor old bugger his emotions are always very close to the surface sometimes I feel like I'm mother to them all yes all right ha ha don't mock me & my lack of maternal instincts perhaps I've changed you know

& I have changed you know

*

& if you came back there is so much I'd say to you there are no excuses none but I have been trying to make sense of myself I guess which started with the revelation that I'm not really as rebellious & free-thinking as I thought despite my running away to the circus & wearing men's clothes & singing to strangers & giving sass despite joining the Party thinking I was rebelling against the parsimonious small-minded conservatism of my parents because there was something in me that wanted to belong to something bigger to be consumed by the tide something in me that believed in the socialism of National Socialism & its promises of equality & restored pride & shared purpose everyone working for the common good & it all sounded so possible so plausible just another form of good old German romanticism good old Gemeinschaft & of course the something in me that needed to be a good girl that wanted the teacher to nod approvingly at my essay written in perfect copperplate something in me that admires certainty in others something in me that is furious at myself for not being normal for choosing this other life & though I love & admire all the other outcasts & rebels & queers I'm mostly nowhere near as brave as any of them for all my talk nowhere near as brave as Gustav & Peter who ended up in Dachau because they refused to be anything other than themselves & I think this is one of the reasons Eric weeps at night because of Peter because he feels like a traitor which is rubbish of course & anyway which of us would be judged the bigger traitor

& if you came back we would walk across the whole city like we used to though you wouldn't know the place the Schwarzer Kater gone the Tingel-Tangel gone the Catacombs Kadeko too I'm guessing though I haven't been over there in an age both churches on the Gendarmenmarkt in ruins the concert hall obliterated all the ministry buildings on Wilhelmstraße now wasteland the thousand-year Reich wasteland the lindens of Unter den Linden blackened stumps the Brandenburger Tor covered in scaffolding the Quadriga missing the Tiergarten divided up into allotments & all the trees gone but still the grass is starting to come back now we'd have to get past the crossing points of course but that's usually okay especially for two girls who say they're taking a walk in the park who am I kidding? *girls*

& I'm lying in bed now & every bone in me aches though it's nothing to do with all the walking I feel there's something living inside me something growing taking over it keeps me awake at night & then I feel even worse in the morning as if I am just one ball of ache mother caught my grimace of pain as I stooped to light the stove & nagged me about it you must find a doctor but it's all too much effort & anyway we've murdered half of them

& I stare at the ceiling now in your apartment & contemplate the criss-cross of lines across the ceiling like an eggshell hammered by an overenthusiastic child the gift of the Yankee bombers & I look at the picture rail even though there aren't any pictures hanging up any more & I look at the picture rail & remember days when people bothered to dust & how you would have kept that picture rail so clean & free from spiderwebs & now I'm thinking about you lying here with your husband & now I'm thinking Matz I'm thinking I could try to find out what happened to Matz because even if he shouts at me shuts the door in my face hits me that might be a step closer

SARA, *1929*

stumbling down the steep stairs of Zimze in her rarely worn dress shoes. Summoning the nerve to walk here had required a shot of brandy. She couldn't remember ever walking by herself down a street after nine in the evening and wondered whether Matz would be shocked at her daring, or titillated by it. Some part of her hoped she wouldn't be able to locate the club, that she'd be forced to admit defeat and return home, but she found it all too easily. She thought the doorman would be able to hear her heart, it seemed to be thumping so loudly. A sweet damp miasma of perfume, cigarette smoke and sweat rose towards her on the stairs. A door painted silver and gold. A room pulsing to the vamp of a small brass band, chatter, cognac-loud laughter.

She looked for a table in the shadows and then realised that all the tables were in shadow, that the whole place had been deliberately lit to suggest something clandestine. She opted for a table in the corner, in the deepest shadows. A tall, brilliantined waiter appeared at her side. He looked like he might be wearing eye make-up. Sara swallowed. He was clearly *one of those*. She tried to avoid brushing against him, as he pulled out a chair for her.

'What will it be?' He read her discomfort. A smile tugged at one corner of his mouth.
Sara had never before ordered a drink for herself. What should one order in a place like this? She suddenly remembered the name of a drink she'd read of in a magazine.
'Negroni.'
She had no idea what this was and hoped she had not failed her first test. Brilliantine's lips twisted into a smile that didn't quite reach his eyes.
'Coming up, ducks.'

On the small stage, a pianist was accompanying a squat, moustachioed man, who sang a satirical song about the Communists. The audience greeted the thumping rhymes with appreciative laughter. Sara found the jokes hard to follow – the political references were beyond her – but the tune was jolly enough.

When she realised that no one seemed to be paying her any attention, she relaxed a little, and began to study the other audience members. They were predominantly men, in groups, or pairs and the occasional couple, although few wedding bands were in evidence; there were also a few women whom Sara realised, with a thrilled shudder, were whores. Across the aisle, two large women in satin frocks sat gazing at the stage and smoking long cigarettes. And then Sara saw that they were holding hands beneath the table. One hand started to stroke the other, tenderly, suggestively. The woman being stroked moved, perceptibly, her body responding. And then she looked candidly at her companion in a way that made Sara's lungs contract. She watched those fingers and felt them on her own hand, the electric charge of it, the way being stroked reveals to you your own skin's softness.

The waiter appeared from nowhere. He had caught the direction of Sara's gaze and having glanced back briefly himself at the satin women, he now smiled openly, like a challenge.

'Your Negroni.'

'Thank you.'

'You waiting for someone?'

She looked up at him.

'Sigi. I'm a friend of Sigrid's.'

'I'm sure you are, ducks.'

The moustachioed man on the stage was joined by another, taller man and together they performed a sketch as two husbands commiserating with each other because their wives had fully embraced the concept of 'the new woman' and with it an alarming sexual voraciousness. This was followed by a comic monologue on the Weimar government that took the form of an extended metaphor about rotten fruit. By the time Sigi appeared on the stage, Sara had drunk two Negronis and her head was swimming. Dressed in an old-fashioned frock coat, white shirt, cravat and trousers, Sigi strode to the microphone. In the white glare of the lights, she no longer looked slight and fragile, but the harbinger of another age.

*

Sara's cheeks burned. She could feel damp circles spreading under her arms. And she realised that her predominant feeling, looking up at this assured, androgynous creature, luminous in the white spotlight, was envy. A solo trumpet played an anticipatory phrase and then Sigi started to sing. Her voice was neither pretty nor powerful, but it had a pleasing reedy clarity as it swelled towards the chorus – *Hannelore! Hannelore! Schönstes Kind vom Hall'schen Tore!* Sara hoped there might be a message coded into the song. She hoped she might be the beautiful child from Hallesches Tor.

The Sigi that fell into the chair beside her thirty minutes later was quite unlike the stage Sigi. This Sigi was flushed and garrulous, words tumbling out of her in a rush. It took a while for Sara to adjust to this new entity.

'You came I'm astonished you came I wasn't sure you had it in you no I think maybe I did think you had it in you but when I saw you from the stage I was well I was really shocked no impressed I mean impressed.' She stopped to draw breath and then, with a wry smile. 'I'm guessing your husband's out of town?'

'He's on business in Hanover.'

'Perfect! Then I can really get to work on corrupting you. Don't look like that, I'm only teasing. You'll be looked after here. Just like you looked after me. Though you know – you fixed those bandages so tight, I nearly lost my leg through lack of blood. I'm teasing you, you donkey. Where's the bloody waiter? I've just been working my arse off. Hey! You son of a dog! I'm dying of thirst here!' This shouted in the direction of Brilliantine, who took the cue and sashayed up to the table.

'Mitzi, what's a girl have to do to get a drink around here?'

'Put on a better act than that, at least.'

'At least I don't spend my evenings spilling gin all over sateened lesbians.'

'I don't spill it darling, I was simply trying to throw it in your direction. Anything to stop you spouting that endless drivel. But your admirer here kept tugging at my arm.'

'I'm glad you've met. Mitzi–Sara, Sara–Mitzi. The oldest showgirl in town.'

A cadaverous man now took to the stage. He had accentuated his deep-set eyes with kohl and the rest of his face was subtly powdered white. He took his time with the audience, eyeballing those on the nearest tables, who tittered nervously, before he began.

The song decried the Jews. The Jews were to blame. For the war. For the reparations. For the inflation of '23. For the weather. For your faithless wife. For your dog's diarrhoea.

Sara could feel the blood pulsing at her temple. She leaned over to Sigi.

'This song?'

'It's satire, darling. Don't worry.'

'You mean – he doesn't mean it?'

'He's sending up the anti-Semites. He's as Jewish as they come. Even more Jewish than you. Can't you see the shape of his nose?'

'But isn't there a danger that some people might agree with him?'

'Oh, yes. There are probably a few dyed-in-the-wool bigots here tonight.'

'I thought cabarets were full of Communists.'

'Oh, we take all sorts here. Raoul is very careful. We can mock. But we must mock everyone. No sacred cows.'

'But doesn't that sort of assume everyone is worthy of mockery?'

'Everyone *is* worthy of mockery.'

'But aren't some political ideas are better than others? Surely? I mean I don't know much about politics, but I know I wouldn't vote for the NSDAP.'

'You're a Commie then?'

'No. I just mean that . . .' she faltered. What did she mean? She usually deferred to Matz on political matters and now felt stupid and unworldly. Language was such a slippery thing. Why did the words she used always fall short of themselves? There was a chasm between the world as she felt it and the world she was able to express.

Sigi, on the other hand, seemed charged with assurance. She was astonishingly beautiful, but her confidence didn't appear to derive from physical vanity. She was a woman certain of the swiftness of her mind.

After three glasses of Negroni which, she'd discovered, were completely delicious, Sara felt no more articulate, but rather less self-conscious. She started to enjoy the banter. Several songs and skits talked about the lives of the poor. The part of her brain that remained sober registered the oddness of this, given that many of the audience had rounded bellies and well-cut suits. A number of the songs ran to sexual innuendo, which she understood without full comprehension of the words. Sigi watched her responses with amusement, but then seemed keen to assert her professionalism by deconstructing the songs for her.

'You see, it's usually a three stanza form.'

'Stanza?'

'Verse. Like a verse in a poem? The first stanza, you set out the situation; the second stanza, you make a little bit naughty; the third stanza, you express your political point.'

'Are you trying to change people's minds?'

'Heaven, no! What would be the point of that?'

'Then why talk about politics at all?'

'Lady's got a point,' said an older man, suddenly leaning over from his table to join the conversation. 'Lady certainly has a point. It's a curious thing, my dear, but the Kabaretts of this town are gripped by the strange ambition of wanting to be aggressive, without actually offending anyone.'

'We've got to keep them coming through the doors, Georg. I don't care what colour his armband's painted, as long as he pays his money.'

By three in the morning, after an uncatalogued number of cocktails, Sara could hardly see. She was aware of Sigi helping her into her coat, and up the stairs. The cold night air of Friedrichstraße sobered her up a little.

'Do you think you can walk?' Sigi asked, laughing at Sara's haphazard posture.

'Maybe?'

Sara put one foot forward and immediately started to wobble.

'Give me your arm. I'll see you get home safely.'

The two women stumbled down the street. Sara had never been out this late before. She was astonished to find the city still alive with pedestrians and lights. As they approached 19, they nearly tripped over a homeless man, with wolfish matted hair, sitting on the pavement. He'd apparently been asleep, because their stumble made him roar with indignation. Sigi responded at equal volume – 'What you making a fuss about, you son of a whore?', for which Sara immediately apologised, frightened he might retaliate. Then she realised that the man was blind, a war veteran, which made her apologise again, before Sigi pulled her away. The two steps up to the front door seemed to require great effort. Sara contemplated the door with bemusement.

'What do we do now?'

Sigi laughed. 'You really can't take your alcohol, can you? I'm going to have to toughen you up. We use a key? Luckily, I'm in full possession of my faculties, so I can unlock the door for both of us. I think we'd better take the lift, though. Don't fancy our chances on the stairs.'

*

Inside the lift's rattling cage, in the familiar smell of the house, Sara's haze began to disperse a little. Sigi was facing her with an expression she couldn't read. There wasn't a great deal of space, but even so they seemed pressed against each other more than was necessary, although neither chose to pull away. They juddered to a halt at the second floor.

'Come on, lady, I'll see you to your door.' She took Sara's arm. 'Can you manage the lock?' Sara fumbled for her key, dropped it, retrieved it, dropped it again. Before she could bend once more to pick it up, Sigrid had stepped towards her, and was kissing her, full on the mouth. Her lips were soft and still wet with gin. A river seemed to rush through Sara's core. She found she was kissing Sigi back. A little fish-tongue darted in and out of her mouth. She mirrored its movements. She realised Sigi's hands were on her breasts. Two floors below them, a door creaked shut.

Sigi stepped back. Even in the landing's half-light, her eyes glittered.

'You're sweet,' she said. 'A sweet Commie Jew.'

Sara spent the next day in a fever. She went out early to the market to buy the ingredients for Matz's supper, planning to make his favourite meal, but when she returned to the apartment, realised she'd forgotten the butter and beetroot. It was ten o'clock. She was unwilling to head out again, because every nerve in her body was listening for Sigi. Three times, she heard a movement on the stairs, and she flew to the door. When the steps sounded not towards her but away, she nevertheless found some reason to open the door. Three times she flung open the door to see another resident, three times she had to pretend she was on her way down to the hall to look for the post.

The day passed and Sigi did not appear. Had she gone out early, when Sara was at the market? Was she still upstairs, just two floors above? What did she do with herself all day? Was she still in bed? Was she thinking about her? Against the kitchen door frame, Sara placed her own hand and formed a pair of lips from fingers. She kissed the fingers again and again, remembering the sugary smell of Sigi's hair, the astonishing softness of her skin. She spent the day twittering between window and door, watching and listening, unable to settle to anything. She felt nauseous, could not eat; felt deranged, loved feeling deranged.

Even the radio seemed to conspire – *Baby, wenn du inartig bist . . . Baby, if you're naughty, you're going to be kissed today.*

As dusk fell, she stayed by the window, squinting hopefully at all who passed by. She almost didn't spot Matz until he was right beneath the apartment. He carried his small case and appeared, implausibly, to be whistling to himself. Seeing him from above, oblivious to her gaze, he seemed like some remote creature, diminished and vulnerable. A stranger. He did not know. He was innocent of it. And what was there to know? It was nothing. A drunken, girlish giddiness. *Wenn du inartig bist.* She felt no guilt. She thought perhaps she should. She thought *I want to kiss her again.*

Once Matz disappeared from view, Sara remained in the window for a few moments, still hoping to see Sigi on her way to the club. As his key turned in the lock, she stepped swiftly into the hallway. He was still whistling. Seeing her, he took off his hat and smiled. She took this as her cue to fly to him and plant a kiss on his cheek. Matz pulled back to look at her.

'You're cheerful.'
Sara answered with exaggerated brightness. 'Did it go well?'

'Yes. Couldn't have been better.' He put down his case, and encircled her with his arms. His hands moved to her buttocks. They played out loving-wife-greets-husband. The customary shyness after having been apart for a night. The trip had gone well. He'd returned with a new contract for a significant amount of business and hopes for a pay rise.

'This economy's on the up at last,' Matz said, squeezing her breast. Only lightly, but it hurt a little. 'People are prepared to pay that little bit more for a dazzling smile.'

They ate dinner at the large mahogany table that had once belonged to her grandparents and Matz talked about his trip. Usually she liked to hear the details of his business life, the different personalities, the tactics, the triumphs. She was glad to populate her own sparse world with characters from his and felt glad he wasn't the sort of man to assume his wife wouldn't be interested in his work.

But tonight she wasn't concentrating. She listened enough to be able to ask prompting questions in the right place, to laugh or tut where required, but she marvelled that Matz didn't look up from his plate and see that she was transformed, that her whole body radiated with new light, that her skin tingled and her bones – yes, how ridiculous – her *bones* thrummed with fear and desire. Matz used his napkin to remove food from between his teeth and appeared to notice nothing.

It was not a Friday night, but the work trip away had given him an appetite, and when he came to her and put his hands up her skirt, she was so full of longing that it was easy to give herself to him. She spent the night awake, feeling curiously guilty. It was hard not to feel she'd been unfaithful. To Sigi.

The following day, her body was heavy with tiredness, but she was too fretful to go back to bed. She decided to distract herself with housework, pulled all the living-room furniture into the centre of the room and cleaned all the skirting boards and crevices. By mid-morning, she was flushed and sweating. Heaving the tweed armchair back into its place, she nearly missed the rap at the door. When she registered it, she ran to the door just in time to see Sigi's back already disappearing down the stairs.

'Sigi!'

She was suddenly conscious of her tousled hair, the damp patches under her arms, her begrimed fingers. She wiped them on her apron. She thought she might be about to be violently sick. And then Sigi turned and came back to her.

They spent the rest of the day in bed. In the middle of the afternoon, Sigi fell asleep. Sara lay next to her, gazing at this alien creature, whose hair on the pillow seemed shockingly dark after Matz's straw-blonde. There was a half-smile on her face. Sara half-wondered whether she were really asleep, or just pretending. She had been so gentle, so sweetly serious, considerate at each stage. Sara had not needed to question what she was doing. Everything felt right, like a truth long known. She had given herself up to it. Something astonishing happened to her body. And it had made her weep, and then Sigi had held her and said things of such simple tenderness that Sara had wept all over again.

When Sigi left, Sara tore around the apartment to restore it to order. She would not have time to make the pie she had planned for Matz's supper, so as she tidied she made a mental list of what food she had, and what might be quickly improvised from it. As she stood over the stove she tried to summon some guilt. But she could not find it. There had been such honesty in that bed that afternoon, it was impossible to believe such feeling wrong. Set against it, her marriage felt fraudulent, performed.

She wondered whether Matz felt as trapped by their life as she did. And she realised, for the first time, that he was not entirely happy either. That he was hoping for more than she could give him. That they were both playing at marriage because it was what they had signed up for, it was what was expected. She saw

157

too that they both knew this, but neither had the language with which to talk to one another. In one afternoon, Sigi had asked her more searching, intimate questions than Matz had asked in their entire courtship. And courtship should have been the time for questions. Once you were married, it was assumed that all questions had been answered, all mysteries revealed. The past was no longer important. The future was the thing – saving and planning for all the things married couples were supposed to save and plan for: children, furniture, a nicer house, holidays if you were lucky. Sara realised she had spent her whole life waiting for a time in which she'd never arrive.

But Sigi was the present. It was impossible to imagine the shape of any future with Sigi, so Sara needed to focus on the now. She'd never known it was possible to make love to a woman. Such things had never been acknowledged in the village she'd grown up in, although she supposed it was possible they went on. She'd occasionally noticed masculine-looking women on the streets of Berlin, but had imagined that something to do with Women's Lib, a rebellion against the constraints of femininity. And though she'd inwardly applauded their nonconformity, she'd never allowed space in her imagination for their intimate lives. There'd been a friend at high school, Clara, who'd had blonde pigtails and a beautiful gap-toothed smile, with whom Sara had shared chocolate and confidences. Looking back now, Sara could see that her clinging devotion to Clara, her pathetic neediness, which had finally pushed Clara away from her, contained a seed of the flower Sigi had now watered.

Three weeks passed since the night at Zimze and they began to fall into a routine. Matz would go to work, Sara would go to shopping for the evening meal and be home by eleven. At twelve, or shortly after (Sigi was not a friend of punctuality), there would be a knock at the door and Sara would fly from the chair on which she'd barely been sitting. They would say hello on the doorstep, like two respectable Hausfrauen about to gossip over lunch, even if Sigi's shirt and slacks hinted at aberration. Once safely inside, Sara would pull Sigi into her arms, and they would kiss and kiss until Sigi, laughing, would break away, take Sara by the hand and lead her back onto the landing and up the stairs to her little apartment under the eaves.

Sara had never known such hunger. The visceral wring of it. The sudden famine when they parted. She was astonished by the intensity of her own desire, by the sounds that would rise, unbidden, from somewhere deep within her. Is this what other people experienced within marriage? Is this what it was meant to be? It was impossible to believe that other people felt this way, that those other wives she knew could be so raw and unguarded. Now she found herself looking in mirrors more often, wondering what Sigi saw there. She noticed new details – her small ear lobes, a childhood scar on her right knee, the two faint creases at the top of her nose, the ammonite pattern of moles above her left breast – features that Sigi had admired and stroked and kissed. Sigi told her she was beautiful and Sara believed her.

To be fair, Matz had also told her this. On their honeymoon, he'd taken her face in his hands and said, 'Your eyes are such a perfect blue. No one would guess your parents were Jewish.'

She felt transformed by love. But trapped by it too. There was a new neediness in her, a new desperation. She loved the nauseous, boneless euphoria as she waited for Sigi's arrival each noon, but she also hated her dependency.

She tried to cook her distractedness away, preparing ever more elaborate meals for Matz's pleasure. One Friday evening, she was filleting a carp, humming to herself as she moved around the kitchen. She heard the key turn in the lock and then Matz was in the doorway, leaning against the wood, smiling at the sight of his pretty, flushed, humming wife.

He moved towards her, pulled up her skirt and undid his fly, pushing her against the counter.

'Let's do it here. I've always wanted to take you standing up. Like a whore.'

A blameless wife could deflect, could make an excuse, could pretend to scold. A guilty wife must submit to something she doesn't want, that scours inside and bruises her skin, her spine pressed against a hard wooden counter edge. And so she endured it. Holding him as he grunted out his climax. He finally pulled away from her, grinning, 'You're a bad girl, Sara, to make me want to do that.' A guilty wife can only smile at that, re-assume coy modesty, go on with the cooking and hope that this represents the culmination of Friday relations.

She tried to talk to Sigi about guilt. Sara was treating them both to tea in a Japanese-inspired cafe on the Spree. There were paper screens and bamboo plants in pots and delicate watercolours of koi carp on the walls. Sigi was quiet for a moment and then she said, 'You know, the Japanese don't have a word for guilt.' Since Sigi had befriended a Japanese architect who frequented the club, she'd become fond of lecturing Sara on Japanese practices and traditions. Usually Sara would conceal her irritation at this by gently mocking Sigi's new-found cultural expertise, but this caught her interest.

'How is that possible?'

'Their culture is based around shame. It's the shame of being caught, rather than a moral anxiety about what you're doing.'

'That can't be true. Surely guilt is a natural human emotion? You can't control whether you feel it or not.'

'Perhaps the Japanese don't feel it.'

'In that case, perhaps I'm really Japanese.'

Sigi took her by both hands.

'I love you whoever you are. Life's too short to feel guilty about a moment's pleasure. You're not hurting anyone, if no one knows.'

Sara didn't hear the second part of this speech. 'You love me?'

'Well, I'm not going to say it again, unless you do.'

'I love you.'

'Good.'

When Matz announced he had to go to Munich for three days, she was elated. She and Sigi had not yet spent a night together and this had become an intimacy Sara had started to long for. Not just the hours in bed, but the falling asleep together, the waking up next to each other. And Sigi had also promised to take her dancing.

The Pyramid Ladies' Club met in the Toppkeller in Schöneberg at nine o'clock on a Monday evening. Sara could never have found it by herself. From Schwerinstrasse, Sigi led her through the labyrinth of three gates and three courtyards, through a door and down a few steps, the damp heat hitting her skin like laundry steam. Admission was 35 pfennigs. A four-piece band played tangos and foxtrots. Sara recognised a couple of melodies from dance concerts on the Telefunken. The room was decked out with garlands of leaves and flowers, so that it could have been a village wedding except that everyone – even those wearing trouser suits – was female.

They pushed their way through the crowd. In every direction, assured, elegant women toked on cigarettes or sipped cognac. From their table, Sigi pointed out a few significant figures – Claire Waldoff, the cabaret star, famous painters from the Seine, a writer from America, a well-known dancer from Budapest, Anita Berber, Celly de Reydt, Susu Wannowsky. The names meant nothing to Sara. She felt shy and provincial. Sigi read her silence and leaned over to whisper in her ear.

'Who cares about them? You're the most beautiful woman in the room.'

And for that moment, as she took Sigi's hand, Sara believed it.

As she watched the room, Sara realised that, as well as the confident, bohemian types, the club attracted dowdier, simply dressed office workers and shopgirls, some of whom looked out on the crowd with coy uncertainty. She wondered if they were also here for the first time. She wondered how much it had cost them to acknowledge the truth of themselves.

The band struck up a jolly dance tune. Sigi filled Sara's glass and then pulled her from her chair.

'It's the cognac polonaise,' explained Sigi, joining in enthusiastically with the ribald lyrics. Many of the other women sang along, flushed and uproarious, the game being to travel around the room by walking across the chairs.

'Catch me, if you can!' shouted Sigi, darting off athletically, fearlessly leaping from one precarious wooden chair to another. Sara set off in pursuit, holding up her skirt in one hand, her glass in the other, worried she might slip and twist her ankle. Most of the other women were also moving around the room in a clockwise direction. Some did fall, to shouts of laughter, or sent the chairs flying. Once their partner was caught, the chase would end with a passionate kiss. Surrounded by flushed couples, Sara's need to get to Sigi felt keener than ever, but Sigi was fast. Sara resorted to cheating and took a short cut across a table before colliding with her. Laughing, dizzy with cognac and freedom, they wrapped themselves around each other, their drinks spilling onto their clothes. Sara could feel Sigi's lightness, her small bones, her muscular arms, the delicious lemony scent of her skin. The electric thrill of kissing Sigi in public. Kissing was all you needed, really, to feel alive.

'What do you want from life?' Sigi asked, as they stumbled back up Friedrichstraße at three in the morning, their feet blistered and bleeding from the long walk home. It was the simplest query, and yet the most impossible to answer. Sara no longer knew. Her life till that point had run along tramlines she had accepted, without question. And now questions were everywhere. They hung above the marriage bed, they shone in the windows of the Friedrichstraße apartment, they formed themselves into the wrought-iron curlicues of the stairwell's banisters. *What do you want? What do you want?* To be in your arms. It was a simplistic, schoolgirl answer, but it felt like the only true response. Though she did not say it out loud.

She spent the night in Sigi's apartment. They now always chose Sigi's bed, as it felt like less of a betrayal and had the practical advantage of not requiring a fresh change of sheets immediately afterwards. And snugged away, at the top of the building, the world outside seemed further away. Sara wished they hadn't stayed out so late. She had so looked forward to spending a whole night together, and now they had danced most of those hours away. As she peeled off her stockings, exhaustion hit her and she imagined they would probably both collapse and immediately fall asleep. But Sigi was having none of that. 'You can sleep when you're dead, my darling.' After that, all traces of tiredness left her.

They woke just after ten and ate their breakfast in bed. Sara's senses danced. She'd never tasted bread so delicious, or coffee so fragrant. After they'd eaten, they lay forehead to forehead, so that Sigi's features were just a blur.

'I knew from very early on,' Sigi whispered. 'When I was twelve, I made a friend at my high school and we spent every moment together – sat next to each other in class just so our knees could touch beneath the desks, went on camping trips together, disappeared for days at a time.'

'And did you—?'

163

'Oh yes. We knew nothing of course. Complete babies. Had to work everything out for ourselves. But that was magical in itself. I worshipped her. And then, I don't know, something or someone got to her. People were gossiping, or her parents were beginning to get wise, or – I don't know – but she dropped me, started hanging out with the in-crowd at school. Completely vapid types. Found herself a boyfriend. I was devastated.'

'What happened to her?'

'Oh, she married some jolly farmer, got fat with three babies in about the same number of years. I hope she's thoroughly miserable and that the farmer grunts his wicked way with her every night.'

'You don't mean that?'

'No. Well, maybe a little.'

'Did your parents ever suspect?'

'Not for years. I don't think they believed in the existence of women like us and anyway they were mostly just struggling to survive after the inflation – they had to strip the house bare, sell everything – curtains, furniture, my battered old piano. I used to see the local kids running around in clothes made out of mother's parlour curtains. But then I had an affair with an older woman. A French artist, who lived in a cottage by the river at the edge of the town. She was completely – you know – no cups in the cupboard, but there was something wonderful and fearless and unapologetic about her and I used to pose for her in the nude and my father found out about this, put two and two together, and came to find me in her cottage. And he saw me, naked, through the window – can you imagine? – and pretty much pummelled the door down. He ordered me to put my clothes on and then dragged me back home, making all kinds of threats, saying if I didn't get married within the year – and he already had a husband in mind for me – the local butcher – I'm not joking – he'd have me put away. And I screamed at him, "Get married? I'd rather jump off this bridge." And he screamed back, "Go on then, jump!"

'So the next day, I hopped on a train to Berlin – the French artist lent me some money – and washed up here and I've never been home since. Stayed the first night in the most appalling flea-pit in Mitte, and next day spent 5 pfennings on some sheet music, took myself off to the Schwarzer Kater – can't quite believe my own balls, now I look back – and made them audition me. Two days later I was on stage.'

'Weren't you afraid?'

'Oh, pissing myself. Even now, I'm not quite sure how I managed to work it all out. I knew nothing about Berlin, where anything was, how to get around. It was like landing on the moon. But the French artist had told me about the Schwarzer Kater – or Le Chat Noir, as she called it – she said Germany had stolen cabaret from the French – so that was my starting point, and thankfully that all worked out.'

'Were you lonely?'

'Oh yes. Horribly. There were the people at the club, of course, but it took a while to feel accepted. But then you realise that hardly anyone in Berlin belongs here – everyone's a blow-in from the back of beyond, or from other countries altogether – and once you realise that, it's a great equaliser.'

'I'd no idea you were a country girl. You seem such a Berliner to me.'

Sigi laughed. 'Rude, you mean?'

'I mean you have a ready turn-of-phrase in insults. Whereas I still feel very provincial.'

'And so you are, darling. But that only makes you all the more alluring.'

And Sigi sprang out from the bedclothes and mimed a buxom country girl abandoning her milking stool, pulled inexorably towards the wanton pleasures of the big city, and Sara cried with laughter until Sigi leapt back onto the bed and covered her in kisses.

Sigi asked her about everything. About the people in her life, the choices she had made, her hopes for the future. And each of

Sara's answers was interrogated, explored. It was as though Sigi were bringing her back to herself. And her disarming tactic of asking the most intimate questions meant that confessions bubbled out of Sara in a way she'd not thought possible. Having to formulate her thoughts into words gave her a new sense of solidity in the world. And Sigi's own capacity for honesty was seductively shocking. She spoke graphically about her fantasies and desires, or gossiped in delicious detail about the romantic dramas of other women in her circle.

But she still felt there was a part of Sigi that remained sealed to her. An inner room to which Sara was not granted access. And she couldn't ask to be admitted, because she didn't have the words to describe what it was she felt shut out from. But for all Sigi's sexual candour and lack of inhibition, something was being omitted.

Some afternoons Sigi would leave the apartment earlier than usual and be vague about her reasons. Once or twice, Sara saw her running across the street to the young man she'd noticed that first time. When she questioned Sigi about him, she just laughed and said, 'Were you jealous, darling? He's just a pianist from the Tingel-Tangel who helps me source new material to sing. He's a bit full of himself, but he's a damned good musician and he knows what works for my voice.' Sara did her best to believe this.

And, anyway, summer was on the march. The trees of the city had burst into life and there was a new hopefulness in the air. After the desperate years of recession and inflation, the economy was stabilising, people were buying things again. It was boom time, baby. Foreign investment poured into Berlin. Sigi and Sara would climb up to the small roof terrace to smoke and sunbathe and gaze down at a city being remade. There seemed to be new buildings going up everywhere. Everywhere, cranes and jack-hammers and metal cutters. Matz had been given a pay rise and was now talking of buying a motorbike in time for Christmas. He occasionally gave Sara extra money and suggested she treat herself to something pretty to wear. She went to the KaDeWe and purchased a new felt hat and a white crêpe de Chine frock with tiny sprigs of yellow roses on it.

Matz was also away on business more frequently. In his absence, Sigi took her to all the clubs and Kabaretts. To The Wasps and the Cabaret of the Nameless, to Küka and the Kadeko. Jazz everywhere. Cigarettes and knock-off champagne, fur coats and sharp-toed shoes. Neon lights and advertising hoardings shouting at each other across the lanes of traffic – *Feel Safe with Sicher Insurance! Ulla's Unisex Hair Styling! All the ladies want Steffi Stockings!* When she first arrived, Sara had been frightened by the speed and scale of the city, by the tall canyons of buildings, the ceaseless flow of strangers, but now she gave herself up to the woozy lurch of the streets, to its noise and anonymity.

Perhaps they became less cautious, perhaps they took more risks than they should have. There were a couple of occasions where the landlady, Frau Kimmel, caught them giggling and tipsy, arm in arm on the stairs. Sara no longer thought much about the future. There seemed little point. The present was too bright and all-consuming. And then the crash came.

On the day America called in its loans to the German government, Matz came home unexpectedly at four in the afternoon. Sara was kneading pastry, her cheeks flushed, sticky dough webbed between her fingers. The effort of the task distracting her from the realisation that she was over a week late.

When he appeared in the kitchen doorway, she turned with surprise, began to wipe her fingers on her apron. The slap caught her off guard. She staggered, her hip crashing hard into the side of the stove. He came for her again, and she instinctively put her hands up to protect her face. He grabbed her wrists and shook her.

'I know what you've been up to. Sneaking around behind my back. With that revolting creature.'

'What are you talking—?'

'Don't try that with me. Frau Kimmel's told me everything. She's seen the two of you. Creeping around. Drunk. Apparently. On more than one occasion. Slobbering over one another. You make me sick. Unnatural. No wonder you can't get pregnant. No wonder you're like a piece of dead meat in the sack. Fucking you makes me sick.'

She could smell the drink on him. He hadn't even had the guts to confront her sober. No, he'd needed to drop a couple of pints first, to fuel himself up to hit her.

'Pack your things.'

'What?'

'Pack. Go on. You've got two minutes.'

'Where will I go?'

'I don't care.'

He threw her onto the floor. She scrambled to her feet, her hands still in front of her face, fearing a beating. In their room, she pulled down the suitcase from the top of the wardrobe, her eyes blind with tears. He followed her. Stood in the doorway, pink-faced with curses. She managed to pile a few clothes into the case, before he grabbed her again. He threw her onto the bed, then lay on top of her, holding her wrists above her head. His weight crushed her lungs. She was too frightened to make a sound.

'I could do it,' he said. 'Do what a man should do.'

*

As he spoke, flecks of saliva landed on her cheek. He thrust himself against her. She saw this man who had told her he'd love her till death was capable of anything. Of murder even. She couldn't cry out, could only wait for him to take her by the neck and do whatever he was going to do.

'My mother warned me.' The words spat into her face. 'She told me.'

The pressure on her chest was unbearable. His knee was against her crotch. She thought the weight of him might break her ribs. He brought his mouth to her ear, in the way he usually did during sex, to whisper encouraging compliments. This was a whisper too.
    'Dirty whoring Kike.'

By the time she reached the steps of Zimze, Sara's arms were burning with the strain of carrying her case. Though the air was icy cold, she was sweating beneath her coat. The door was locked. She hammered at it and began to worry no one would ever answer, but eventually a lock slid back and Mitzi appeared. He took in her bedraggled appearance and shiny face with cool amusement.

    'She's not here, Ducks.'
    'Do you know where she might be?'
    'She's not tucked up at home with you?'
    'No.'
He noticed the suitcase. 'You off on holiday?'
She ignored this. 'Have you any idea where I might find her? It's important.'
    'Yes. You certainly give that impression. Try Friedrichstraße.'
    'No, no. I know she's not at home.'
There was a new, inscrutable expression on his face.
    'I meant the station.'

*

At Friedrichstraße Bahnhof, Sara heaved her case around the main concourse. She looked in the tearoom, squinted down every platform. There was no sign of Sigi. Had Mitzi meant she was catching a train? He had been infuriatingly gnomic. She returned to the tearoom, wiped out, and ordered some tea in an attempt to calm down. But in her distractedness, she drank it too quickly, scalding the roof of her mouth.

She realised she had nowhere to go. Even if she found Sigi, she could hardly move in with her, two floors above Matz. And she couldn't face Melita and Irmgard. She would have to tell them something of the truth, and that would be far too scandalous for them to offer her hospitality. Home then? She counted the few coins left in her purse. Enough for a train ticket. Her mother and father would always give her a home, but she would have to weave them a lie, and the very idea of lying to her innocent, anxious parents felt corrosive. She wasn't sure she could do it.

At the same time, she didn't trust Matz not to write to them, relishing the revenge of setting down every shameful detail. If she left now, she could try to intercept any such letter, or at least devise a plausible counter-story – he had been violent and cruel, he had proved himself an anti-Semite. They would believe her. On some level, they might even be glad to believe her, to know that the conversion experiment had failed. And then she remembered her Aunt Lilli at the wedding. *If you ever need a refuge.* Aunt Lilli with her twinkling eyes and fox furs and French doctor husband and house in Montparnasse. But Paris? That seemed like the other side of the world. And a world away from Sigi.

She finished the tea, although her scalded mouth could take no relief from it. As she rose to her feet and once more took the weight of the case, she formed a plan. She would wait in the cafe opposite Zimze until Sigi appeared. They could talk and Sigi would know what to do. Perhaps Sigi had an open-minded friend Sara could stay with.

As she walked out of the station doors, she was aware of papers fluttering towards her. A gust of wind had caught them, flinging them against walls and lamp posts. One blew against her skirt and she instinctively reached out to catch it. The usual grey fibrous paper of political leaflets, the usual compressed italic type. The paper was crammed with dense paragraphs. No matter what their political persuasion, Berliners had never mastered the art of the brief, arresting catchphrase. No wonder those passers-by who took one immediately cast it to the wind. The main subject seemed to be that of the approaching referendum and a call to oppose the Young Plan, which apparently represented 'the enslavement of the German people' and 'reparations for 60 years'. But one sub-heading caught her eye:

Zur Judenfrage. On the Jewish question. She had seen the words countless times before. *Überfremdung.* Flooding. *Schieberrepublick.* Profiteer republic. *Schmährepublik.* Reviled republic. And all of these were ultimately a *Judenrepublik.* As she read the pamphlet's perfectly phrased, smoothly reasonable arguments on the matter of the *Judenschwein* and their role in the traitorous propositions of the Young Plan, she heard the voice of the woman who must be handing out these leaflets. 'Heil! Heil!' It was shriller than usual, but there was enough familiarity about it to make Sara's heart pound. She didn't read any more, but started to walk in the direction of the voice.

Beneath the railway arch, a woman, in an unfamiliar wool skirt, jacket and heels, but with unmistakeable close-cropped hair, calling out to passing pedestrians, 'Heil! Heil!' Like witnessing someone you know well speak in a foreign language for the first time. The dislocation of hearing their voice form the shapes of another tongue. As though they had momentarily slipped into an alien personality, an alien world with a different set of rules.

She watched Sigi from a distance, clutching the leaflet into a tight scroll in her hand. Most people hurried past, ignoring the proffered paper – Berliners were inured to political campaigning. But a few accepted it, and one or two stopped to talk and nod their heads at whatever Sigi was saying. Sara was suddenly aware of her bruised ribs. She felt close to vomiting. And now she realised that there was a second leafleteer, the young man she had first seen with Sigi all those months ago. And now there was no denying the armband bearing the

HANS, 1969

swastika on the cover was discreetly layered beneath the book title, as if trying to conceal itself. In the history section of the small bookshop on Gneisenaustraße, this was the only book he could find on the Final Solution. A quick scan of the index confirmed at least ten references to Eichmann, the man he had recently discovered to be his mother's former employer. There were things he needed to understand before he confronted her. If he confronted her. As he placed the book on the counter, the shopkeeper gave him a look that made Hans uneasy. It was a look of hope.

He walked on for a few yards before stopping to take his purchase out of its paper bag and after consulting the index, made his way by U-Bahn to Nollendorfplatz. The number of junkies hanging around the station seemed to have increased since he was last here. He ignored the emaciated twenty-something who asked him for money and walked the half mile or so west along Kurfürstenstraße. He was looking for number 115–116, but the grand turn-of-the-century edifice from the book's illustration had vanished. A modern concrete hotel stood on the site, above a basement strip joint. There was nothing here to mark that the area once housed Adolf Eichmann's IV B4 – the Judenreferat, the Department for Jewish Affairs. There was a bench across the street from the hotel and he went to sit on it. He opened the book and found a photograph with accompanying text that told him that the department had been housed in a building originally built for the Jewish Brotherhood. This act of smug desecration flooded him with such rage that his brain found it hard to focus on the page's dense paragraphs, so he returned to the photograph. He tried to work out where the building would have stood on the street in front of him, but everything had been erased and replaced with bland modernity.

He flipped through the later pages of the book, which contained the well-known photographs of the camps, the railway line terminating at Auschwitz-Birkenau, the sign above the gate, the piles of corpses, the emptied-out faces of skeletal people in striped uniforms. These images had become so familiar that they too felt emptied-out. He'd always believed in the power of a photograph to eclipse any other form of expression, that its proximity to reality endowed it with immediately accessible truth. But now he wondered whether this proximity were, in fact, part of the problem. The more we see, the less we remember. The more an image is reproduced, the greater our familiarity. The greater our familiarity, the more likely it is that we slip into dull acquiescence. Here is the past, says the photograph. You can turn the page and leave me behind.

But the past was not something to be mastered, or sealed off. It lived alongside them. It banged on the windows and doors of the city, it demanded acknowledgement. And his generation had to live in the tension between shame and the resentment of a shame bequeathed to them. For they'd been raised by those who had actively participated or passively stood by. All those good, polite Germans apologising to the Jewish colleague they were sacking, the shopkeeper they were boycotting. Shaking their heads sadly,

Not my decision, of course, but you know what those idiots in government are like ... Clinging to their quiet, unconfrontational lives. And when they saw their neighbours rounded up and taken away in army trucks at dawn, how quickly had they fallen back into their quiet lives? Had they forgotten that sad, suitcase-carrying family by the time they arrived at the office, by coffee time, by dinner?

And though Hans had grown up ignorant of his mother's rape, he had nonetheless been fed a narrative in which Germans were the victims. The half-million civilians killed by American and British bombs. The millions who had died on the Eastern Front or as POWs in NKVD camps. The thousands of women and children violated. Taking refuge in a balancing out of figures, in the desperate mathematics of suffering. And it was easier to talk about the Russians, as they were just over there, still a palpable threat. Another brand of totalitarianism. *Look!* said their parents – *we Germans weren't unique in that!*

In need of air, Hans walked the couple of miles back to Friedrichstraße. Near Hallesches Tor, a small group of student protestors accosted him with a crudely printed leaflet about Vietnam. Young people everywhere were sticking two fingers up to their parents' generation, to their conservatism and warmongering, their outmoded values. But in West Germany this rebellion took on a different texture. Everyone knew that parliament, the courts, the universities, the banks, all contained former Nazis, sometimes at the highest levels, even if Willy Brandt's recent election meant that they'd just got rid of Chancellor Kiesinger. The Federal Criminal Police Office alone was stuffed with former members of the SS's Totenkopf division. The protests, the resistance – perhaps they were just a distraction to cover the shame of powerlessness and passivity. So much simmering beneath the surface, ready to combust.

*

He had felt it last year in the demonstrations in response to the attempted assassination of political activist Rudi Dutschke. When *Bild-Zeitung* labelled Dutschke 'an enemy of the people', thousands of students took to the streets of Kreuzberg to march on the Springer building, from where the tabloid was printed. Standing in his front window, Hans had watched the protestors stream along Friedrichstraße. And it had soon turned ugly. Batons and water cannon, young people with bloodied heads. The streets of the city filled once more with angry crowds. As in every decade that had gone before.

Someone was already opening the front door of Friedrichstraße 19. The elderly woman who lived on the top floor, slight, white-haired. He rarely encountered her and in that moment, could not recollect her name, so had to steal a glance behind her at the nameplates beside the buzzer. Frau Babel, that was it. He wished her a good day and she turned, smiled, nodded in recognition.

You like to go up onto the roof to smoke.

Yes. Sorry. Does the smoke bother you? I don't have to—

Oh no. No. I'm just envious. I can't get out there any more. Too awkward. And now the vertigo . . . But I used to sit out there all the time with my lover. We'd smoke and sunbathe and look out over the city.

It's a good place to hide away from everything.

Yes. We thought so.

The way she said this suggested that her lover was dead. He couldn't think of a sensitive way to explore this further, so he fell back on platitudes.

Have you lived here a long time?

Yes, yes. On and off. I used to live in your apartment.

Really?

But it was too big for me. I live in her apartment now. Though of course it's not the same. All rebuilt after the bombs.

He didn't know who she was referring to, but they were already on the move, passing into the hallway. Hans checked his mailbox, but the woman didn't. Instead, she stood gazing upwards to the skylight above the stairwell.

Funny building, this.

Hans wasn't sure what she might mean. She saw his hesitation.

The light.

Ah.

The angle of the skylight. It does such strange things to the shadows.

Yes. I've noticed that. Yes.

He thought of his favourite photo of Ilse. He'd taken it in the stairwell – Ilse sitting on a step, the high sun from the window above streaming through the banisters and transforming her into an abstract object, marbled with curling shadows. He had tilted her chin so that a bar of light had found her eyes, which looked straight into the sun with a defiance that Hans felt was uniquely Ilse.

The woman was already moving on, beginning the long climb up the stairs to the fourth floor. He wondered why she didn't take the lift. He held back, waiting for her to climb ahead, before he followed. Should he take the lift? No, that would be ridiculous. She knew he only lived on the second floor.

The woman moved surprisingly swiftly, her left hand on the handrail. It was then Hans noticed her finger. The top two joints of the middle finger were missing.

What happened to your finger?

He immediately regretted the blurted question. The woman stopped on the stair and turned to look at her hand on the polished wood, as though she'd forgotten the fact of its deformity. Her face twisted oddly.

I was trying to shield my daughter. They wanted me to hand her over to them, but I refused. So they shot her in the head. And the same bullet took my finger.

The Russians?

The SS. The Vel' d'Hiv in Paris. July 1942. A velodrome. A beautiful glass-roofed velodrome for cycling and circuses and boxing and Jew-killing.

He couldn't hear more of that story. If he heard more of that story, he'd never be able to leave this stairwell. And anyway, he didn't need to ask what happened next. They both stood in silence for a while. The air around them was suddenly viscous with loss. But then the woman continued to move upwards. Hans followed slowly behind, keeping three stairs' distance. He couldn't leave the conversation there, but neither could he pursue it. They had reached the first landing. The woman started up the next flight of stairs.

And your lover?

This time she didn't stop, but kept climbing upwards.

Dead. A long time ago.

I'm sorry.

Cancer. She fought so hard to live.

She looked over her shoulder at him. A flicker of challenge in her eyes.

Ah. He tried to indicate with his body that he wasn't fazed.

We both fought. To keep on living. And now I don't know why.

He felt inadequate to this conversation. The responses that came to mind seemed banal, obvious. He shrugged. *What else can we do?*

The woman gave him a half-smile. Something in it chilled him, but he could not say why. She started up the stairs again, reached the second landing and began the third flight. With her back still turned, her right hand went up in a gesture of farewell.

Goodbye.

It was clear he was being dismissed. He hovered uncertainly in front of his apartment door.

Goodbye.

A strange silence greeted him as he entered the flat. Like, he thought fancifully, the sound of dust settling. Ilse's coat was missing from the peg and she appeared to have eaten most of the food in the fridge. He hoped she wasn't with Pieter. It seemed she had at least left him the coffee, so he put a pot on the stove.

But Ilse didn't return that evening. He tried to pretend indifference, but he was jittery, unable to settle to anything. At midnight, he went to bed, but too much clattered around his skull – the anti-Vietnam protestors, Frau Babel saying *they shot her in the head*, Eichmann in his glass courtroom box, Pieter and Ilse on the couch. He gave up on sleep, switched on his bedside light and reached for the history book, studying every photograph, every footnote, but they supplied only facts and no answers. He wasn't going to find his mother here.

By 4 a.m., he was still awake, so took a shower and, in need of distraction, riffled through files of old images he'd previously rejected for the magazine, in case there was anything usable. But his heart wasn't in it. Sifting through his own detritus only fed the inner voice that told him he was washed up, talentless.

By late afternoon, Ilse had still not returned. He hoped she was somewhere safe. He hoped she was warm.

When the buzzer went at 5 p.m., he bounded to the door and it took him a moment to adjust to the not-Ilse who stood there.
    One of your neighbours let me in downstairs.
Although her belted mac and headscarf belonged to the year they both stood in, something about Gisela's hairstyle, shade of lipstick and stockinged neatness remained stuck in the 1930s of her youth. His immediate thought was that his mother must have died, but his aunt's expression, though characteristically hard-set, contained something less resolved.

May I come in?
Of course.

As he gestured for her to enter the apartment, Hans remembered his work laid out across the mahogany table in the kitchen. He managed to divert Gisela towards the living room and offered her tea. When she raised an eyebrow at this, he upped his bid to vodka, the only alcohol in the flat. Back in the kitchen, he hastily covered over the nudes on the table with a newspaper. When he returned with the glasses, Gisela was gazing down into the street.

She's not well, Hans. They think it's pre-senile dementia.
Dementia? But she's only – what – forty-eight?
Forty-seven. Yes. That's why they call it 'pre-senile'. It's rare, but . . . Gisela shrugged in a way that indicated bad luck.
Jesus.
It's come on pretty quickly. You ought to see her. But she's not herself. Her memory is all over the place. Sometimes she doesn't seem to know who I am. She finds it hard to pin down words. Other days, she seems much clearer. It's impossible to predict.
Is she in hospital?
No. She was, but it was little better than a prison. Anyway, there's nothing a hospital can do for her. But I've found somewhere to take her. A home. It's not perfect, but perfect wasn't on offer. Gisela produced a postcard showing 'Beautiful lighthouses of Schleswig-Holstein'. *I've written down the address.*

Hans had always assumed there would be a reckoning, a future conversation with his mother in which they finally spoke frankly to each other. And after seeing the newsreel the urgency for that conversation had become more acute. But now, perhaps, it was too late.

She asks about you.

Yeah. Well. I don't have anything to say to her.

There's always something to say.

He looked into Gisela's still startlingly blue eyes and hated that she was right.

Okay. Well, let me ask you something.

All right.

I saw her, the other day, on an old newsreel about Adolf Eichmann.

Gisela's eyes narrowed defensively.

It was clearly her. I thought you two worked together in the war. I thought you were both secretaries. Something boring and bureaucratic, just to keep your heads down. I mean, I always knew you were a paid-up Party member, but Mum – she was so young, I imagined she just had to go along with it all. But Eichmann?

Gisela put her glass down on the windowsill and folded her hands neatly in her lap.

Yes. We both worked there. It was a big place. Hilde and I were very junior – your mother was only seventeen when she started. We needed the money. It wasn't a question of political affiliation.

Oh come on. You were in your twenties. You knew exactly what you were doing.

I am not going to talk about this. The tendons in her hands were raised and white.

I just want to know what's true and not true. All along, I've been fed lies and evasions. I used to think it was done to protect me, but now—

She was trying to protect you.

Well, you weren't. You were the one who told me what had happened. And what pleasure it must have given you – to tell me. What a two-faced bitch.

Gisela looked frightened. *I won't be spoken to like that.*

No? How should one speak to a Nazi?

Her hands clutched at each other in her lap. *I only told you because . . . I thought you should know. So that you could understand your mother.*

Hans stood up. *I want you to go.*

Gisela drained her glass deliberately, before rising to her feet and coolly picking up her bag. Hans's irritation intensified. Her appearance had nothing to do with altruism or empathy – only her need to believe she had done her duty. At the door, she turned with a final thought.

Don't give your mother grief. You know all she has suffered.
She set off down the stairs, retying her headscarf as she went. He was about to shut the apartment door, when another female voice rose from the landing below.

Herr Schneider, is that you? One of your trollops is outside, high on God knows what.

Outside the front door, Ilse was crouched over a pool of her own vomit. As he put a hand on her shoulder, he was dimly aware of Gisela's heels clacking hurriedly across the street. She must have had to step around Ilse's curled body to get away. The girl's eyes were unfocused, her expression beatific, all personality erased. He wasn't entirely sure she recognised him, but he pulled her to her feet.

Come on then, let's get you inside.

She staggered against him, allowing him to take most of her weight. Once inside, he briefly considered picking her up and carrying her up the two flights, but he couldn't be certain that he'd be strong enough. Instead, they did a comical shuffle towards the lift, a ventriloquist dragging his dummy. Ilse's legs started to buckle and it required some effort to keep her upright. She smelled bad. Vomit and sweat and stale cigarettes. But he clung to her with relief and, he realised, something like happiness.

※

He lay her down on his bed, and carefully peeled off her jacket and shoes, before pulling the blankets over her. She had her eyes closed through most of this, smiling in apparently blissful oblivion. His efforts over, Hans sat beside her on the bed. Her skin was pale, unwashed and breaking into acne, her fine hair dark with grease. He did not understand his own tenderness for this unknowable creature, but it was tenderness that made him reach out a hand and stroke her cheek. As he did this, Ilse's eyes suddenly flicked open and looked directly at him. He jerked his hand away, as if he'd been caught molesting her, but he did not move from the bed. His eyes held her gaze until she gave in to sleep.

While Ilse slept it off, Hans sat at the kitchen table and tried to work. But his attention kept returning to the 'Beautiful lighthouses of Schleswig-Holstein' propped up against the lamp.

When Ilse came to, complaining of an aching head, he made her coffee and warmed up a pastry left over from breakfast. She had the grace to look a little sheepish, even if no apology was offered. Hans had thought about lecturing her, about laying down conditions for her continued stay in the apartment, but when it came to it, it all seemed entirely unimportant. Instead of asking where she'd been the last two days, he found himself confiding in her about the shock of seeing the newsreel, Gisela's visit and his mother's illness. Ilse shrugged.

You should go see her. It's not so unusual to be the child of a Nazi.

The care home was in Steglitz. They walked along a wide residential street, deserted apart from the occasional passing car. The bare trees that lined each side of the road were fuzzed with frost and a low mist veiled the houses. He was grateful for Ilse's presence, touched by her offer to accompany him. As they approached the house, Ilse took his arm, an uncharacteristic intimacy that only heightened his nerves.

The home was set a little way back from the road. It looked closed in – the ivy hung too thickly about the walls, the peeling paintwork an unenticing shade of brown. Ilse sensed his hesitation as he approached the door, and he felt her tug him forward. And when the door was opened, it was Ilse who spoke and told the nurse who they'd come to see. A spindly Christmas tree sat in a corner of the reception area, draped with angel hair tinsel. Hans wondered vaguely whether he should have thought to bring a gift.

They were led down a long corridor towards the day room, which overlooked the garden at the back of the house. The whole place reeked of urine and unwashed ageing bodies. The nurse gestured at a blue faux-leather armchair in the window, and then retreated.

The woman in the chair might have been anyone. She bore no relation to the athletic blonde in scarf and slacks he had once known as his mother. A shrivelled thing, in a grey cardigan and oyster-pink blouse, tan stockings, velour slippers – a costume too old for her forty-seven years. There were several other women in the day room, all two or three decades ahead of her. Some were slumped forwards, asleep and drooling; one woman in a brown smock gurned and chewed on nothing, another waved animatedly at Hans and Ilse. *Hello, hello. Hello, hello.* Hilde did not look up.

Ilse released Hans's arm and let him approach first.
   Mutti? It's me. Hans.
   She shook her head. *No.*
   It's me, Mutti.
   I don't know where I put it.

What? Have you lost something?
Don't be angry with me.
I'm not—
Don't be angry with me, Papa.

He hadn't been prepared for this. He'd imagined forgetfulness and frustration, but not erasure. He was about to correct her, but then he stopped himself. There seemed little point in breaking the news of her father's death to her. He'd spent the journey here formulating questions, but his mother was no longer in the room. Neither the mother he'd known, nor the reimagined version of her.

He drew up a chair at her side and leaned towards her.
I'm not angry.
She laughed then. A surprisingly girlish laugh. It was not a sound he recognised, not the laugh he associated with her. She began to hum. Something wandering and tuneless, but she smiled as she did so, and turned her gaze away from him to look out of the window. They sat for some time this way. Occasionally, she would make some cryptic remark to which Hans did not know how to respond. Should he nod encouragingly at her non sequiturs, or should he just talk at her and attempt to communicate something about the person he'd become? He felt as though he were treading water above a whirlpool that threatened to suck him under. Everything was falling away from him. He had left it all too late.

It was Ilse who began to speak. Talking to Hilde in a low, measured voice, she started to tell her a story about a young woman who had decided to run away from her own life. And Hilde turned towards her with genuine interest in her eyes. She listened politely to the girl's tale and, though Hans doubted she understood a word of what was being said, somehow managed to nod and laugh in the appropriate places. He was in such a stupor, it took him a little while to realise that Ilse was telling her own story, one that she had never before shared with him.

She'd crossed the border in a petrol tank.

After her mother died, she'd started working in a hotel bar in East Berlin. An older Western businessman had taken a shine to her and she'd realised she could capitalise on this. Ilse grinned when she realised she'd used the verb 'capitalise' – *You see, I was never meant to be a socialist.* And so she'd seduced him, *the old paedo.* He'd presented her with a plan that at first sounded ludicrous, but as he talked it through, began to sound entirely rational. *And of course I was high on grief at that point so I wasn't really thinking anything through.*

The petrol tank of an Isetta was cleaned out and its underside fitted with a hidden door. Above this, the mechanics mounted a second, much smaller tank, which held 5 litres of fuel. Just enough for the journey from East to West. Despite her height, Ilse was slim and pliable enough to be able to lie inside the adulterated tank, her knees tucked under her chin.

I thought I was going to die. I thought I would suffocate in there, or choke on my own vomit, or that the petrol tank would somehow explode. The smell made me retch, every muscle screamed with the pain of the position I had to hold, and the movement . . . The shaking and the bumping and the noise and the terrible heat. We only drove about ten miles, but it felt like an eternity. I realised how stupid I'd been. That nothing could be worth dying for in that way, in that metal tomb.

Once in West Berlin, she'd quickly cast off the older lover. Run away via the fire escape of the Charlottenburg hotel he'd taken her to. Hans found himself pitying the man for a moment. All that ingenuity and risk suggested more than lust. But when Hans pressed her, Ilse shrugged. *He got his kicks. He should never have imagined it would last.*

He didn't buy her performance of world-weary hardness. But he knew better than to challenge her. Any such probing only resulted in the shutters being pulled firmly down. And what did it matter if it wasn't genuine? Her toughness wasn't entirely feigned. He imagined those spindly legs folded into the foetal position inside a stinking tank. How she must have held her breath at the border checkpoint, listening to the muffled voices of the guards, the dogs straining at their leashes—

Brave girl.

For a second, he wondered where the voice had come from. And then he realised that Hilde was smiling at Ilse with an expression of complete lucidity. *She's a brave girl, isn't she, Hans?* A quivering finger was raised and pointed accusingly at Hans's chest

RUDI, 1906

He will murder me.

Nothing was ever said again about this ridiculous allegation. At least not to my face. But Erholtz's response to me changed in some profound way that day, for all he tried to conceal it with civility. I saw the way he kept one step further away from me than he might have done, the way he could never hold my gaze for more than a second. And though I did not believe him to be a gossip, I was sure word of Fräulein Gottschalk's slur had spread around the Academy. Rooms fell quiet when I walked into them; there was no longer any of the easy banter I had enjoyed with Otto or Hetty. And Wolf, although never a man of many words, was now a man of decidedly fewer. I felt him battling against the notion of my innate murderousness, but he had bought in to her prophetic photographs along with the rest of them.

There were more visions. Wolf and I were kept busy in the dark-room, but I was now excluded from the 'transference' sessions in the studio. Errands were found for me that took me away from the building for two or three hours and I was happy to be out and about in the city, beyond the aura of the interloper's malice.

The infatuated Erholtz remained in ecstasies over her product-ivity. According to him, the girl's arrival at the Academy had ignited something in her brain, just as he had hoped. 'There is something electric in these walls! I knew it the first time I entered the building. These walls contain all ages, all times – past and future. And this little Mädchen is the conduit!'

Some of the visions were abstracted images, subjects of fierce conjecture among the Academy members – did the Star of David represent the establishment of a Jewish State in Palestine, or a Jewish Chancellor at the Reichstag? And what of the hammer encircled by a laurel wreath? Others were more obviously local – a building that appeared to represent our own house on Friedrichstraße, but brutally truncated, the upper two storeys vanished into thin air. Then there was a series of skeleton-like images – the scorched remains of trees holding their branches to the sky in attitudes of surrender; a wall of coiled barbed wire; the frame of a motor vehicle, its metal twisted and blackened by some great heat; the mechanical parts of an upended perambulator, stripped of any fabric. I did not understand Erholtz's excitement. If Fräulein Gottschalk truly had prophetic powers, the pictures she presented of the future were not comforting ones. But the one image that haunted me most, although I could not for certain say why, other than its perfect composition, was that of the silhouetted diver curving through light and space.

*

The case for my innocence wasn't helped when one of the Fräulein's visions was apparently proved true. One of the glass plates had revealed the image of an elderly man in the uniform of a Prussian captain. It was an unremarkable picture, other than the mysteriously bulging cloth bag in the figure's right hand. There had been the usual debate as to its meaning, but the identity of the portrait could not be determined.

But then a shoemaker called Wilhelm Voigt was arrested in Berlin for impersonating a Prussian captain and commandeering a number of soldiers – the soldiers so indoctrinated by the Kaiser to worship the fetish of uniform that they followed this stranger without question. They marched the twenty miles to Köpenick, and there helped Voigt to occupy the city hall and arrest the mayor and treasurer on charges of embezzlement. Though not before Voigt had pocketed 4,002 marks and 36 pfennigs. As soon as the case was reported in the Berlin newspapers, Wolf and Erholtz recognised the Fräulein's vision as proof of her augury.

The Academy was immediately beset with reporters. The *Berliner Morgenpost*, *B.Z. am Mittag*, *Berliner Tageblatt*, *Frankfurter Zeitung*, *Hamburger Abendblatt*, the English *Telegraph* and *Times*, the *Washington Post*. All wanting a piece of our diminutive psychic. *A Cassandra of Our Times! The Girl Who Knows! The Pretty Prophetess! The Divine Diviner!*

I didn't think Fräulein Gottschalk in any sense pretty, but I suppose journalists see what they want to see. I noticed that they lit her very carefully for their shots, attempting to make their moneymaking soothsayer as toothsome as possible. One photographer insisted on positioning a china doll on a small chair beside her, to emphasise her youth. Another employed a hairdresser to arrange her hair in perfect ringlets, finished with a large pink bow. And she simpered along with all of this. Not that she simpered in any of the photographs. She had clearly spent some time practising her sibylline expression in the mirror – making her eyes as saucer-like and inscrutable as possible.

But the one person who could truly capture her was Wolf. It was not an easy face to photograph. She was all eye and shadow, with angular features and a prominent lower lip. But when Wolf lit her, the photographs he produced were extraordinary. Her eyes seemed illuminated from within by a wisdom far beyond her years. Even I had to admit she looked like the oracle she claimed to be.

Alongside Fräulein Gottschalk's portrait, reproductions of her visions appeared in papers all over the world. But these only enhanced the murkiness of the images, so the reporters had to translate the shadows for their readers. And the range of the newspapers' interpretations was ludicrous, swayed by the political leanings of their proprietors, so that I might have derived entertainment from them, had the whole charade not augmented her standing within the household.

She now seemed unassailable, whereas I had become a ghost in my own life. Loneliness bit into my heart like Fräulein Gottschalk's teeth into my forearm. I avoided her as far as I could, but when circumstances forced us into each other's company, I seethed and burned. This incomer had more than displaced me, she had stolen my reputation. No one could act on her allegation, because it was all conjecture. But a story is the most powerful thing of all, especially a salacious one, because, at heart, everyone wants a story of someone else's misdeeds to be true. That way, we can hoodwink ourselves that our own sins are less worthy of attention.

Only Margo remained unaffected. 'I take people as they come. I don't need anyone else telling me what to think about a person.'

And I clung to her and to her clear-sighted version of the truth. But Margo's duties – and mine – meant we were rarely alone together, although she still stole into my room most mornings. And at the evening meal, which was largely her responsibility, she would briefly press a comforting hand on my head as she placed my plate before me.

Time ticked on, oblivious and unjudging. The Academy went about its business. I helped Wolf design programmes and posters, helped Margo to paste them up all over Kreuzberg, carried props and costumes up and down Friedrichstraße. There were performances in the Wintergarten, where Caspar and Hannus de Groot shared the bill with the famed juggler Rastelli, a revue at the Metropol compered by Erholtz, and demonstrations of Madame Czigany's spiritualist visions in grand private houses in Charlottenburg.

And then I began to have visions of my own. Visions that had the solidity of celluloid and, as it turned out, the power to change the course of my life.

One of the many errands on which I was sent was to purchase glass plates. Wolf had been fortunate to find a first-class supplier just a few doors down the street – the glass factory of Oskar Messter. I'd never met Herr Messter himself, although I'd heard a great deal about him. Not only did his factory manufacture optical equipment for scientists and medical men, it also made devices for showmen and magicians. But most exciting of all were Messter's moving pictures. He had personally engineered film projectors and cameras that captured moving images, and now his factory housed a film studio, the first in Germany – right here on Friedrichstraße. The southern side of the building was largely constructed from glass, to allow him to film with natural light, and he had installed a motor-driven suspension bridge beneath the glass roof, so that he could move subject or camera as necessary. There seemed no end to his ingenuity.

Margo had once taken me to the Apollo to see one of his sound films. Two women, one dressed as a man, had danced on the screen in front of me with as much animation and vitality as if they were in the room with us. The one in male clothes put her arm around the smaller woman, and gazed at her with such intensity, my whole body had flooded with heat and confusion. I hoped Margo, sitting next to me, couldn't feel the shameful warmth rising from me. But then the two women opened their mouths and sang the most beautiful thing I'd ever heard – *Ist ein Traum kann nicht wirklich sein, This is a dream that cannot be true*. My own mouth fell open – I'd seen moving pictures before, but never singing ones, and it seemed as though the music emanated from the screen itself, as though the singers stood immediately behind it. Margo explained to me that Messter had devised a machine that enabled the perfect synchronisation of the film with a gramophone. It was more wondrous than any of the conjuring tricks I had witnessed at the Academy.

My visits to his glassworks fizzed with the awareness of this proximity to genius, although I had never once clapped eyes on the great impresario himself. I was even more keen to catch a glimpse of the famous 'Messter girl', the new star of his films, whose image graced posters the length of Friedrichstraße. No one knew her name, as it was rumoured that Messter was worried she'd ask for more money if she became famous in her own right. But when Wolf caught me lingering over her portrait in a magazine, he told me her name was Frieda Porten, a disappointingly lumpen name for such a beautiful woman.

Messter's studio always thrummed with activity – secretaries and carpenters, lighting technicians and costume ladies. I always tried to find an excuse to loiter a little, in order to inhale some of that glamour. And then one Thursday, as I was reluctantly heading out the door with my parcel, I was aware of a man in his fifties, with prominent elfin ears, hurrying down the corridor towards me.

'Are you the magician's boy?'

'Yes, sir.'

'I wish to film the little Fräulein who has the visions.'

'Fräulein Gottschalk?' I said, as if the question needed to be asked.

'Yes. Would you give her my card? Or perhaps she has a guardian?'

'That would be Herr Erholtz, sir.'

'Yes, yes. Of course. Please ask Herr Erholtz to call on me, at his convenience.'

'Yes, sir.'

'You're a photographer's assistant?'

'Yes, sir.'

'Know all about printing?'

'Of course, sir.'

'Well, if you're learning from Wolf, you'll know what you're about. Ever seen a moving picture printer?'

'No, sir.'

His eyes gleamed. 'Come with me.'

He set off at a sprightly pace along the corridor towards the back of the building. I followed him through a door on the left, which he closed behind us. The room was completely dark. It seemed the windows had been boarded up with wooden panels, painted black. Messter flicked on a dim table lamp, before moving to a machine that resembled one of Wolf's cameras. He opened it up to show me its innards.

'This is my latest model. It contains my secret weapon! What does that remind you of?' He pointed to a brass structure at the centre of the box.

'A Maltese Cross?'

'Clever boy! Good! Good!' He pointed to a strip of celluloid. 'You see, there's a positive film – and a negative film – and I only bring them together in the printer gate. They are held together in the gate with compressed air. Can you see? Underneath? Two sprockets to separate them out again. I call this my Maltese Cross Gear. It changes everything!'

The mechanism looked familiar to me. And then I remembered.

'I've seen something like this before, sir. In a Geneva watch.'

'Yes! Exactly. Those clever Swiss watchmakers were my inspiration.' He stood back to look at me. 'You've studied the mechanics of watches?'

'My father was a clockmaker and repairer of watches. I was his apprentice.'

Messter squinted at me for a moment, his lips pulled into a moue. 'How interesting. Come over here.'

He walked over to another wooden box, made a few adjustments and then beckoned me towards him. I put my eye to the slot and Messter began to turn the hand crank, so that with a few clicks and whirrs, a film was pulled across my field of vision. Ladies on bicycles cycled through a park, smiling at the camera, looking every bit as real and present as I knew the man beside me to be. I even smiled back at them. One daring lady took a hand from the bars and waved at me. This made me laugh with pleasure.

'Like what you see?'

'Yes, sir.'

'Pretty ladies, huh?'

'Yes, sir.'

'Let me show you something even better.'

Messter replaced the reel with another. The can he took it from was labelled 'The Artist's Muse'. Once more I placed my eye against the slot.

*

A naked lady stood like a statue. A real-life naked lady, standing completely still, in a pose that might have been from one of the paintings in the Nationalgalerie, where Margo had once taken me for a Saturday treat. I swallowed hard, aware that I was being watched. And then the picture jumped, and the naked lady was sitting on a plinth and the camera seemed to move around her. Or was it that the platform she sat on rotated? The woman didn't appear to be aware of the camera, maintaining an expression of serene disinterest. The picture jumped again. Now she was standing, holding a ball, bent forward as if about to bowl. I could see the hair on her thingummy. I could see her small nipples. I could imagine the smoothness of her pale skin. I was aware of the heat of Messter's body just beside me. And now she stretched and held a pose like a Greek sculpture.

'She's a beauty, isn't she?'

I couldn't answer, without betraying my acute embarrassment, so made only a grunt of assent.

'A whore, of course. But totally at ease in front of the camera. That's a rare gift.'

This, at least, I knew to be true. I grunted again, more persuasively.

'And this, I call "Adam and Eve".'

Now the naked woman was joined by a naked man. He put an arm around her, and together they held an apple. I hoped Messter couldn't see the bulge in my trousers from his place behind me. I wished the naked woman didn't look so like Margo.

'And this is the famous Rape of the Sabine Women.'

Now the two actors held a position that I took to be another sculpture, the man suspending the woman across his thighs. It was too much for me. I stepped away from the camera. I said the only thing I could think of to say.

'Thank you, sir.'

Messter looked at me and laughed.

'Bet you'd like to make films like that?'

'Well, I—'

'You know the world's first moving picture was screened here?' I gestured uncomprehendingly at the room.

'Here?'

Messter laughed.

'Not here. Further up Friedrichstraße. In the Wintergarten. Two months before those Lumière brothers got in on the act. Moving pictures are Berlin's gift to the world – never forget that.'

'No, sir.'

'What's your name?'

'Rudi, sir.'

'Do you think Wolf could spare you, occasionally? With your knowledge of printing and clock mechanics, you could be extremely useful to us here.'

'Really? That would be . . .'

An adjective equal to my desire eluded me.

'Leave it with me.'

And so I came to spend half of my week working in Messter's studio. At first, I was assigned to the printing room, work for which I had a natural affinity, since it drew on both the mechanical skills I had learned from my father, and the chemical processing of Wolf's darkroom. Margo was full of enthusiasm.

This is the future, Rudi. And you'll be making it.

As the youngest employee, I was also called upon as general errand boy and dogsbody, but I didn't mind. Every encounter was an opportunity to learn and most of the technicians were happy to lecture a young boy on their area of expertise. They were alchemists, inventors, pioneers. The latest films from France and Denmark and Britain were pored over and discussed animatedly – each new technique or style deconstructed and replicated.

So absorbed was I in my new endeavour that I was only dimly aware of the negotiations between the houses of Messter and Erholtz over the Pretty Prophetess. Erholtz finally agreed to the filmmaker attempting to replicate the Fräulein's visions, but this time her mind would be exposed to moving celluloid, rather than static glass. In exchange, Messter promised Erholtz a film projector for use in his stage conjuring act.

The Fräulein was duly brought into Messter's studio and seated before the camera. But no lights were wheeled into position, no set or props decorated the scene. Instead, once the take was slated, the room was dimmed. I stood in the dark alongside the rest of the crew in sceptical anticipation. For a good while nothing happened. I could sense a restlessness in my unseen neighbours, one or two shuffled their feet, changed position, quietly cleared their throat. But then, suddenly, the air in the room altered. I could feel everyone become still, hold their breath. Later, a couple of witnesses said they had heard a strange humming or musical note, as though from a stringed instrument. Then, just as suddenly, the girl gasped in anguish and could be heard to collapse into her chair. Erholtz touched Messter's arm to indicate that the trance was over, light was restored and Fräulein Gottschalk led away to recover in her dressing room. The film was promptly dispatched to the processing room.

Once printed, a small group of us assembled in the projection room to view the results. To our mutual incredulity, the screen flickered into life. A human figure, crouched, poised to run. An athlete. A lean, muscular black man, in a white vest and shorts. And then he runs. And then with complete control, he lifts into the air. He flies. And lands. And immediately springs forward once more. But then the image suddenly sputtered into darkness, bubbles of white popping and fizzing on the frames. And then black.

An electric charge passed through the small audience. Even I, chief sceptic, could not deny the evidence of my own eyes.

*

The next day, after allowing 'the little Fräulein' time to rest, Messter repeated the experiment. Once again, the studio lamps were lowered, the camera rolled. Afterwards, an even larger number of those present now claimed to hear the strange humming noise that accompanied the transference of the vision onto celluloid. But when, with great anticipation, the newly printed film was spooled through the projector, the images flickering on the screen were, frame by frame, identical to those the day before. At first Messter thought there must have been some mistake, that the reels of film had become confused, but when it was proved that there was no error, irritation gave way to bewilderment and a suppressed disappointment.

The experiment was repeated three more times. But with each printing, the vision remained the same. It appeared there were to be no more celluloid visions. The jumper was a miracle, a moment of cinematic history, but a few frames of cinematic history did not make a film.

Messter now began to plot a sensation that would share the Fräulein's visions with the world, while simultaneously offering jaw-dropping special effects to surpass even Méliès's greatest achievements. He planned to stage dramatic scenes representing 'the future', inspired by the images Wolf and I had developed in the darkroom. The only problem was that actors required some kind of narrative, and very few of the pictures offered enough detail to suggest plot. But Messter refused to be discouraged. He hired a writer to talk to Fräulein Gottschalk, in an attempt to draw out more story from the images in her mind. The fellow he booked for this job seemed at first entirely unprepossessing – a playwright by the name of Johann Klütz, who specialised in tawdry melodramas for the stage. Nevertheless, Klütz's interviews with the girl proved fruitful and he and Messter spent days talking through the various scenarios teased from the girl's 'revelations'.

*

But the film's *pièce de résistance* was to be the framing device and Messter had already determined that I would be the one to help him realise it. One morning, he summoned me into his office and unrolled a vast scroll of paper, on which he had sketched the entire sequence of the film. As soon as I saw the title, I had a premonition of what was about to be asked of me.

The film would be called *The Clockmaker's Dream*. It was to tell the tale of an eccentric white-haired clockmaker called Zeittraumer, who builds himself a vast and incredible clock that controls time itself. At the beginning of the film, we see Zeittraumer experimenting with speeded-up time. As the hands of his wondrous clock accelerate around the dial, we cut to accelerated frames of horse-drawn buses, motor vehicles and pedestrians propelled along Friedrichstraße as though by some unseen force. Zeittraumer then experiments with slowing time down – the minute hand of the clock now seems to judder uncertainly, stalled – and then we cut to a ballerina pirouetting across a stage, but with an improbable slow grace that defies gravity.

And then the obsessive clockmaker, his white hair now sticking up from his head to indicate burgeoning madness, pushes the power of his clock further. We cut to the interior of a house. A despairing mother holds a baby who won't stop crying, despite all her attempts at consolation. She passes the swaddled infant to her husband, who rocks it back and forth in his arms, but as he rocks, the baby grows and grows, first to a toddler, then to a child, and within a few seconds the husband is rocking an adult-sized baby, still clothed in a white blanket and bonnet.

We cut back to the clockmaker's workshop. He's dizzy with pleasure at his wonderful machine, rubs his hands gleefully. Then he notices a copy of the *Berliner Morgenpost* lying on a nearby table and picks it up, revealing to the camera Fräulein Gottschalk's pale face gazing out inscrutably from the front page. We can see

Zeittraumer reading about the *Pretty Prophetess!* with her *Astonishing Visions of the Future!* He studies the article with great intensity, before looking directly into the camera with wild-eyed enthusiasm – he has a brilliant idea!

In the next scene, Zeittraumer lures Fräulein Gottschalk, in bonnet and ringlets, into his shop. At first he seems kindly, paternal, demonstrating the great variety of his wares, his prettiest cuckoo clock, but then he leads her before a towering grandfather with a large and glittering pendulum swinging to and fro. He makes sure the girl watches the pendulum, to and fro, to and fro, which causes her to fall into a trance. The film fades to black and when the camera iris opens up once more on the clockmaker's workshop, Fräulein Gottschalk is nowhere to be seen.

Now in the centre of the room sits a mysterious large object concealed beneath a sheet. Zeittraumer whips this away to reveal the most incredible machine – an even larger version of the clock device we saw before. There are mysterious symbols carved into its case, intricately wrought iron hands, and the clock face itself appears to glow. Above the dial is a pair of doors. A wooden cuckoo's entrance, perhaps?

The clockmaker winds his clock, steps back and watches as the hands move towards the hour. The hour strikes, the doors fly open, but no cuckoo. Instead the face of a mysterious, ethereal girl-child appears. She seems familiar. Could this be the ringleted Fräulein Gottschalk we saw moments earlier? But now she is clothed entirely in white; her face and hair luminescent with white paint. Her eyes are closed. Her head is positioned so that her face and the face of the clock are two glowing white circles, one above the other. The device is now half-girl, half-machine.

The clockmaker sets the clock to run at an insanely fast pace and we see hours, days, months, years flash past. Then all of a sudden, the girl opens her large saucer eyes, rimmed in dark kohl, and the clock hands freeze. The picture dissolves to show a barren landscape of jagged trees, blackened and deformed. A solitary man with wild salt-and-pepper hair stumbles across this pitted terrain, his eyes bandaged, his clothes caked with mud.

We cut back to the clock. The girl's eyes are closed. Zeittraumer sets the hands in motion once more. They fly round and round until, as before, the girl's eyes open and time stops. This happens several times and we see, severally:

A man with patched, baggy clothes and shoes with flapping soles pushes a wheelbarrow along Friedrichstraße. As he approaches the camera, we can see that the wheelbarrow is full of paper money bundled up with bits of string.

A woman stands on top of a high wall which splits the frame precisely in half, left and right. There are crowds of people on both sides who appear to be calling up to her. They seem excited, agitated. She swithers. Which side should she listen to? Then she turns to the crowd on the left-hand side and we notice a man, holding his arms up, gesturing to her to jump. They lock eyes. And then she jumps.

A group of anarchists hides in some bushes at the side of a road. We know they are anarchists because of their flat workers' caps, round-frame spectacles and the short pointed cuts of their beards. A motor car chugs towards them, but as it approaches the chief anarchist pushes down a detonator and the car vanishes in a puff of smoke.

A tall silver contraption that looks like a hypodermic needle. Scientists in white coats move around it, scratching their heads and debating with each other, confounded by this machine that has apparently landed in their midst. And then a door opens in its side. A man in a metallic suit with a black face appears in the doorway. The intertitle declares 'I come to you from 2019, from Deutsch-Südwestafrika, southernmost territory of the great German Reich!'

Messter stepped back from the storyboard, breathless from his impassioned narration.

What do you think?

It's wonderful. Is that where it ends?

No. No. I'm still working on the finale, but I think the magical clock has to explode and then in the final scene we see the clock-maker as a patient in the madhouse. I think that's what has to happen.

So we don't know whether his visions are real or hallucinations?

Precisely. But the most important question is – can you build it?

Build?

The clock. If my carpenters construct the case, could you build the clock mechanism?

I was possessed by hubris and a sudden image of Margo's admiring face.

Of course.

Messter spoke to Erholtz to secure some dedicated time away from the Academy. While Johann the carpenter and I worked on the construction of the clock, Messter set about filming the dramatised visions. I had brought two of my father's old handbooks with me from Oranienburg and these were my constant study. Because of the size of device required, I based my design not on a grandfather clock, but on that of a turret-tower mechanism, as you might find in a church, or in a public square, but scaled down to match the proportions of our studio model.

*

Of course, I was merely a fledgling in clock construction, but I disguised my ineptitude with a show of confidence, while learning my craft through many curse-filled hours of painful experiment and error. And as I worked, my determination to succeed was fortified by the realisation that I was building this marvellous machine for Margo. To create something that would make her proud, that would make her see me as more than a boy.

Zeittraumer's magical clock stood at an imposing ten-feet five. Its wood was carved with mystical symbols and Egyptian hiero-glyphs. The clock face itself was five feet in diameter, the square ornamental drum made of gunmetal, the winding weight a mighty sixty pounds. Inside the body of the clock was a steep ladder, leading to a narrow wooden platform on which Fräulein Gottschalk would stand, her chin resting on a support concealed just inside the doors. On cue, these would fly open to reveal her face above the dial – the cuckoo in the clock.

And when it was complete, I wound the weight until it was fully up, controlling the winding handle gently, gently, allowing it to travel backwards slightly when the winding was done, so that I didn't wind the weight too high and strain the line anchorage. And then, when I finally released it and heard the clock spring into life, I felt as though I'd created something that breathed and lived.

The day of filming arrived.

We rehearsed the scene all morning. The timing proved problem-atic, with so many moving parts, but by lunchtime Messter was confident that we were sufficiently slick to attempt a shoot. Cast and crew broke for a short repast and then we reassembled at one o'clock for the first take.

*

The lights blazed and Fräulein Gottschalk, swaddled in white robes, a muslin cap covering her hair, face glowing with thick white paint, eyes kohl-rimmed, climbed onto her platform inside the clock. The actor playing Zeittraumer bouffed up his hair, adjusted his cravat and found his mark. The camera rattled into life. Slate. Shout. Action.

The first take went relatively smoothly. Messter shouted cut with evident satisfaction and told us he wanted to re-block some of the movement. This done, he went for a second take. I once more assumed my position behind the clock, operating the various parts of the mechanism on cue. The camera rolled again. Messter talked through the action as Zeittraumer gesticulated to express his excitement at his marvellous machine. But as this was happening, I was suddenly aware of a movement within the clock tower – I could hear the girl moving backwards down the wooden ladder. This was not part of the plan. Any moment now the wooden doors were due to fly open and reveal her face.

Who knows why she decided to move at that particular moment? Perhaps something startled her. Perhaps she suddenly felt faint under all the lights, swathed in heavy fabric. But whatever the reason, as she stepped back and descended into the body of the clock, her small hands gripping the ladder sides, a loose drape of fabric from her costume must have caught somehow in the clock mechanism. The wheels tugged and pulled her away from the ladder, her feet slipping from the rungs, the material winding tighter and tighter, dragging her into the heart of the machine. There was an appalling grinding sound, as the cogs struggled to move. Everything within the mechanism strained and sucked her in, before casting her down to the concrete floor. And then, high above her head, the cord that held the clock weight frayed and broke. Sixty pounds of metal hurtled downwards. She didn't even have time to cry out.

*

After the appalling crash, there was a moment of stunned silence on the studio floor. Then everyone sprang into action. I was the first to reach her. Even in the shadow of the clock tower, I could tell she wouldn't survive this. The blood from her head wound already pooled around her, soaking my trousers as I knelt beside her. But she was still conscious. Her eyes flicked open for a moment and found mine.

Later, it was impossible not to think there was something triumphant in that gaze. Later still, I wondered whether she'd not cried out because she'd known all along that this is how it would end.

I had to accept her visions as truth. I had murdered her. In the heat of my panic, I could not begin to think why the mechanism had failed so badly. As those around me yelled and wailed and cleared a space, I stood paralysed at the edge of the set, my skin clammy, my thoughts misted. And then something emerged from the fog, something I had possibly known all along, but had pushed to one side.

I had miscalculated. Following the examples in my handbooks, I'd designed the weight for an exterior clock in winter, not taking into account the additional heat of the studio under all the lights. As a result, the weight put too much pressure on the system, the cord broke and with it the girl's dreadful prophecy had come true.

Most people blamed me. I accepted this as due punishment. I knew Erholtz would never forgive me and that my time in the Academy was over. For days I hid myself away in my room. No one visited. I did not expect them to. I was aware of Wolf at work across the hall in the studio, but he never once called in. Only Margo – steadfast, loving, forgiving Margo – came to see me. She would appear with trays of food and attempt to draw me into conversation, but words had abandoned me. I picked at the meals she left, but she never once complained about my ingratitude. The accumulation of losses was overwhelming. I was about to lose her, to lose Wolf, my home, my employment. I thought about ending it all, running into the path of a trolley bus on Friedrichstraße, or jumping into the Spree, or from the roof of the Academy. The image of Fräulein Gottschalk's diver kept playing before my eyes. I imagined it might be me, curving through the air. But I didn't have the courage. Instead, I shut myself down, numbed every nerve ending.

But one evening, Margo brought an accomplice. Messter, looking a little older, his cheeks more sunken than before. He pulled a chair up to the side of the bed and I rearranged myself into a sitting position, like an invalid receiving a visitor.

'First things first,' he said, with his typical briskness. 'You cannot stay in Berlin. That much seems clear. I have been in correspondence with a friend of mine in New York who works for the Biograph company. He has kindly arranged for an apprenticeship for you.' I began to protest, but he waved a hand at me dismissively. 'There is no need to concern yourself with the cost of the passage. I am happy to pay all expenses.' He patted my arm. 'America is the future, Rudi.'

What did I know of America? Beyond reproductions of the Flatiron Building and the Statue of Liberty, I had no other images for that vast country. And then I remembered the Red Indians on display at the Panopticon. Margo had taken me to see them – real Red Indians brought over to America and installed beside imitation wigwams and campfires, a painted background of russet rocks, cacti. I remembered Margo taking my arm to point out a tiny Indian baby in a papoose on its mother's back. I remembered the tears in Margo's eyes as she gazed on the sleeping child. I remembered catching the mother's eye and realising I was the exhibit.

'I don't think I can,' I said. 'I'm too afraid of going wrong. I don't trust my own hands any more.'

Messter leaned forward.

'Fräulein Gottschalk's death is a terrible terrible thing, but we all must share the burden of culpability – I most of all. You are very young and because you are very talented I entrusted too much to you. That is my miscalculation, not yours.'

And he emphasised this point by patting my arm on each word.

'If there is one thing my long life has taught me, Rudi, it is about the importance of acknowledging one's errors of judgement. Erholtz and I must take the responsibility for treating Fräulein Gottschalk as a pretty puppet. And you – you will also have to square up to your own role in that young woman's death. It is something we shall carry with us for the rest of our lives. It will haunt us and hound us and bring us to the edge of despair, but we shall endure. What else can we do?'

—————⟶◦⟵—————

Three weeks have passed since that conversation. Now I'm on board a ship, gazing on the bleak grey churn of the ocean. I cling to the rail, waiting for my seasickness to subside, hoping the cold Atlantic air will calm my stomach and sharpen my thoughts. An emigrant. A lonely word in any language. Margo's last gift to me was an English primer, which I study each day, although some of the pronunciations baffle me. I try to practise on the British and Irish people I encounter, but no one person says a word in the same way, and the Scots are completely incomprehensible. No matter. Images are the future. Pictures that can speak to people across lands and languages, across time. Fräulein Gottschalk had taught me that at least – of people's need for visions, for conjurations of our dreams in all their comedy and chaos, fear and desire. Perhaps a man who can master the art of images can do a little good in the world. Perhaps it will be a way to atone for her small lifeless body, pale as a clock face. But I still haven't decided

HEIKE, 2019

how close to death she wanted to get. She saw Yusuf before she saw the shop. His face, smiling broadly, on a plasticated panel, MM & Son, Funeral Managers of the Year, 2016. She wasn't sure it wasn't a little obscene – to parade one's professional success in the window of such a terminal kind of establishment. The interior also surprised her, as she'd imagined something kitsch, or reassuringly old-fashioned, designed to appeal to the old. Instead it was corporate, carpeted, sensitively lit. When she pointed this out, Yusuf said, 'The old come in by another door.'

They'd been dating for three months now, but seeing him in his charcoal suit, his polished shoes on the tastefully patterned carpet, was to see him in context for the first time. Heike could imagine his sensitivity with grieving relatives, the way he'd be able to guide them, in their most irrational moments, through a rational process of decision-making. But something about his calm was unnerving. She wondered whether maintaining such serenity required great efforts of suppression. Perhaps one day the dam would finally burst and Yusuf's mugshot would appear on the evening news. *'We're in shock,' said a neighbour, 'he seemed like such a lovely man.'*

She'd not been there when her dad died, but away working in Florence on a radio job. He'd been ill, on and off, for several years, following complications from a perforated bowel, his decline eked out to the extent that Heike registered every goodbye as a potential final farewell. Every time she left her parents' house she would kiss him, walk away and then turn back for one exaggeratedly cheerful wave. And then, of course, when he did die, she couldn't remember the exact details of their final goodbye – it had merged into all the others – and in her inability to remember, felt she was letting him down in some terrible, cataclysmic way.

Yusuf broke into her thoughts, placed a hand on her arm.

'Do you want to come through?'

'Through?'

He indicated the door to the Trauerhalle.

'Oh.' She felt small and childish. 'I've never seen a dead body.'

'Don't be frightened. Death is just another stage of life.'

'But do I really want to look it in the face?'

'I don't know. I suppose I think that seeing it makes it easier to understand.'

An odd formality overtook her.

'All right then. Yes, I will. Thank you.'

He led her through heavy pine doors whose sprung hinges sighed mournfully behind them.

'His family are coming in later.'

And now she and Yusuf stood beside an old man in a coffin. White satin around his head.

'Was he Jewish?'

'Lutheran.'

So this is a death's head, Heike thought. *Ein Totenkopf.* It was not as they said. He did not look asleep, he looked absent from himself. Without knowing why she whispered, she leant towards Yusuf and said, 'Do you think his real self has gone somewhere else?'

'His soul, you mean?'

A medieval word. She had a vague notion of what it was meant to mean, but nothing concrete. She repeated it anyway.

'Yes. His soul.'

'The dust returns to the earth as it was, and the spirit returns to God who gave it.'

In the end, Heike wondered, what was truly ours? If our atoms belonged to the earth and our soul belonged to God. Perhaps, in the end, all we really owned were our names – on the certificate, the flyleaf, the register, the grave. She thought of saying this out loud to Yusuf, but an odd introversion consumed her. He made tea for her in his office and she steered the conversation back to more workaday subjects. As he handed her a mug, he touched her shoulder.

'Are you all right?'

'Yes. Sorry. I think it was just God. You talking about souls and God and . . .' She felt simultaneously hostile and defensive. 'You see, I don't do divine beings. I don't have any instinct that there's anything out there beyond the material.'

'And yet you think you hear disembodied voices in buildings?'

She laughed then. 'No one said that atheists can't be fanciful.'

She said goodbye to Yusuf, whose working day was not yet over. He kissed her briefly on the lips and she held on to him a little longer than he seemed to feel comfortable with. She felt overtaken by the urge to push herself against the living heat of him, but he stepped back, with an apologetic smile. Heike had the fleeting sensation that she had just failed some kind of test.

The streets outside the funeral home seemed larger, brighter than before. A little way off, the solid clock tower and red-tiled roof of Rathaus Neukölln, and in the far distance the hypodermic needle of the Fernsehturm gleaming bright in the late afternoon sun. The man in the coffin would have oriented himself by these towers. Perhaps his father and his grandfather too. The stage set of our lives remains, Heike thought. It's just us who disappear into the wings.

Her car was parked a couple of streets away. She sat in the driver's seat, her skin stinging with desire. They'd still not slept together. There was an odd reserve in both of them, and though they'd referenced sex a few times, it was always obliquely. Heike worried that there was an optimum number of dates before jumping into bed, and they'd missed it, condemned to be platonic friends for ever. As the engine shuddered to life, she tuned the radio to an old-timers' station she never listened to. They were playing a song by Friedrich Hollaender, a song from the Weimar Kabaretts. She turned it up to full volume and sang along. *Eine kleine Sehnsucht*. At the traffic lights, a car pulled up beside hers and the young man in the driver's seat looked across at her, and mimed 'crazy'. She didn't care. *Everyone needs a little longing.* And then her phone buzzed.

She swapped to hands free and suddenly Martin was in her ear in full self-righteous quality.

'Leonie told me about Yusuf.'

'Did she?'

'You didn't think to ask me?'

'About whether I could date someone else?'

'About whether our daughter should meet him. About whether that might be distressing for her?'

'It wasn't distressing. We had burgers. They got on well. It was very brief. I'm not about to ask him to move in with me.'

She could hear Martin's breath at the other end of the line, debating whether to pursue the argument, or let it go. He let it go.

'Anyway. I didn't phone up to argue. I phoned to say that I can pick Leonie up from school on Friday.'

'You bunking off?'

'I've quit.'

Heike laughed and then realised this wasn't a joke.

'You've quit? Why?'

'I need a break. A few weeks off. Then I'm going to start my own business. Yes. I reckon I'll do that.'

'Your own business? Doing what?'

'I don't know. I'll figure something out.'

Heike didn't recognise this breezy proto-entrepreneur. His apparent recklessness scared her a little. She wasn't sure how to interrogate that, so she spooled the conversation back to an earlier point.

'How about you, then? Are you seeing anyone?'

'No. I don't think about that sort of thing any more.'

A sudden flash of memory. Leaving their marital home for the last time. The finality of the latch's click, the relief of release. She couldn't resist a dig.

'Did you *ever* think about it?'

'There's more to life than sex, Heike.'

'Of course. But most people require some basic human affection.'

'I loved you, Heike.' Ah. There it was. The past tense.

'It's a shame you were never able to show it.'

'You just weren't looking at it right.'

She had to end the call before she said something volcanic.

The next morning she phoned Yusuf at work. She'd rehearsed her opening gambit, not wanting to lose her nerve.

'I think it's time we slept together.'

There was a slight pause at the other end. She heard him clear his throat.

'Right. Very good. I'm with a client at the moment. Can we talk later?'

She spent the rest of the day fretting about her clumsy timing and Yusuf's obvious lack of enthusiasm. She was training up a new engineer at work and was aware that everything she said to him was badly phrased, lacking in clarity. The younger man was trying hard not to appear as though he were questioning her authority, but was clearly confused by her instructions. She hated herself for her own distractibility. She was a bad feminist, a bad mother, a bad line manager. She found herself in a bar at 4 p.m., drinking a large glass of Pinot Noir on her own. Now, on top of everything else, she was turning into an alcoholic.

Yusuf called her back that evening. She'd only just put Leonie to bed, so she whispered into the phone, aware of her wakeful daughter in the next room.

'Sorry about earlier.' Dammit. Why was she apologising?

'I don't often get propositioned at 9.30 in the morning.'

'I just think it's time we moved things along.'

'Well, if that's what the instruction manual says.'

She laughed, embarrassed, but would not be deterred. 'How are you fixed for Friday?'

'Well, I'm not sure I can perform on Shabbat.'

'Oh. I'm sorry. I didn't—'

'I'm teasing you. You Germans. You're so bloody guilty all the time.'

'It's not that.' Though, she reflected, it probably was.

He cleared his throat. 'I feel a bit strange about scheduling it in. I guess I was hoping that it might just happen naturally. When the moment felt right.'

'I have to fit things around Leonie.'

'I know. So. Your place or mine?'

'Yours.'

On Thursday, she met Alice for lunch, in a cafe overlooking the Landwehrkanal. Alice's interpretation of Martin's decision to quit his job was that he was finally *finding himself*. Heike thought 'finding yourself' was a New Age excuse for fucking everyone else over.

'The arrogance of it. The arrogance of believing there might be something more to be found, when perhaps you're really just as boring and meaningless as everyone else.'

Alice's expression suggested she felt personally affronted by such nihilism, but Heike ploughed on regardless.

'As if finding yourself would suddenly determine that you should take up snowboarding, or make a pilgrimage to Santiago de Compostela, or realise you're the wrong gender.'

Although this, admittedly, had happened to her friend Ove, and the subsequent life transformation had proved a great relief to everyone. 'Funny how no one ever "finds themself" and realises that what they really ought to be is an accountant for a small pharmaceuticals company in Spiegelau.'

'You've become very hard, Heike,' Alice said. 'Don't you get it? It's all about slippage.'

'Slippage?'

'Turning fifty. An awareness that we're closer to death than to birth. When I meet up with friends, I can almost see the disappointments circling our heads. Doesn't matter about the outward success – the hard-won careers, the nice house, the violin-playing children – there's a sense of dissatisfaction, of things undone. A sense that we've lost something of ourselves along the way.'

Heike had suddenly lost her appetite for the croque-monsieur she'd ordered. She put the half she was holding back on her plate. The cheese leaked oil onto the white porcelain.

'You think Martin's disappointed by life?'

'He's a fifty-one-year-old man. I think that's entirely possible.'

Alice's shrug said *That's just the way it is*. It also said *It's all your fault*.

After school, she took Leonie to her weekly swimming club. Heike sat in the pool's spectator gallery, scrolling through Twitter, occasionally looking up to see her daughter attacking the water in a confident butterfly stroke, or diving from the springboard. Leonie's affinity with water was a source of genetic delight to her, a talent she believed inherited from her. In her teens, she'd been a dedicated swimmer, to the extent that she'd hoped to be selected for sports college by the DDR scouts. She'd felt crushed when this hadn't materialised, but with hindsight knew she'd been spared a punishing training regime and Stasi-sanctioned steroids. And competition wasn't really the point. She loved the solitude of swimming, the sense of being at one with a different element, the liquid in her body responding to the liquid outside. Swimming pools were less pleasurable, with their chlorine and regulated lanes, but she and Leonie both looked forward to the summer months, when they could go swimming in the Weißer See.

She unrolled a lengthy thread of tweets, which started with an accusation of transphobia and developed into an unedifying chain of name-calling. But she nevertheless scrolled through the whole thing with a weary fascination. Heike rarely posted on social media. She was too afraid of getting it wrong, a cowardice no doubt due to her lack of character. Perhaps half the fascination of Twitter spats was to observe those who had no such cowardice. The mob was beguiling, even in virtual form. You could stand at the side and watch others beat themselves to a bloody pulp and still convince yourself that you were only looking in the interests of intellectual curiosity. But it was voyeurism just the same.

Heike looked up from her phone to see Leonie climb onto the diving board. Even from this distance, she could see her daughter wanted assurance of her attention, so she waved to indicate that she was watching. Leonie turned her back, bouncing a little on the board, bounce, bounce, before springing confidently into a backflip. Her body arched briefly through the air, a sudden flare of low sun through the fugged windows casting all the specifics of Leonie – the purple swimming costume studded with yellow flowers, the tightly twisted bun of hair, the blonde down on her legs, the mole on her right cheek – into a curved silhouette. As her body arrowed down towards the water, Leonie's head struck the edge of the board with an impact that made everyone gasp. Her body jerked back and she landed awkwardly in the water, disappearing down into the depths of the pool. Heike's breath stuck in her throat as she rose from the bench, willing her daughter to resurface.

Everything that followed seemed to happen through dense fog.

Air bubbles rose from the darkness of the deep end, before Leonie herself bobbed back up. She seemed to swim for a few seconds before suddenly lolling to one side, her head dipping once more under the water. Heike felt a scream trapped in her chest. The swimming instructor pulled off his trainers and dived in, reaching Leonie in a couple of strokes, scooping her up and gently guiding her back to the side of the pool. The child's eyes were closed, her head flopped against her shoulder. A stripe of blood appeared on the bridge of her nose. Heike was dimly aware of other members of staff gathering at the pool's edge, as she stumbled from her seat and ran down the stairs.

Here it was – the worst thing. And she hadn't seen it coming. All those rehearsals of grief – imagined road accidents, playground falls, kidnappings, faulty fairground rides – and she'd not thought of the obvious possibility right in front of her. As she ran, she made bargains with the god she didn't believe in – she could cope with anything, so long as Leonie didn't die. She could cope with disability, she could cope with a wheelchair – no, no bargains.

Martin met her at the hospital. He didn't say it, but she felt blamed, as though the accident had been caused by her inattention. And she was ready to believe this. If she hadn't been looking at her phone, if Leonie hadn't been trying to catch her eye just moments before, if she hadn't forced swimming lessons on her daughter, if she hadn't needed the validation of inherited talent. Events had been set in train and they were all down to her. But then she glanced at Martin. He looked like a man under arrest. They sat side by side in the disinfectant tang of the waiting room, grey-faced and guilty.

The surgeon appeared, with an expression that was terrifyingly unreadable. He nodded at them.

'Her nose is broken in six places, her cheekbone is fractured and she has a nasty neck sprain, but that will mend.'

'And her head?'

'She'll have a bad headache for a few days, but no sign of any damage.'

There was no wave of relief, no sudden rush of joy. Heike felt like a criminal who'd got away with it. The corridor behind the surgeon suddenly seemed to hold all the darkness of a future that wouldn't arrive. A future of forms and phone calls and white coffins and drugged night-times and void. For a moment, they had felt the hem of disaster's skirt brush against them.

They sat on either side of their daughter's bed. Leonie's pale skin and wispy dark hair just visible beyond all the bandages. Gradually, she came to consciousness and after initial confusion began to cry. It was not a sound Heike had ever heard her make. Such a lonely, despairing cry that she would have done anything – jumped out of the window – just to take the pain of that sound away from her daughter. They stroked Leonie's hair, her hands, told her everything would be all right, everything would mend, she'd be back to normal in no time. They told her they loved her. After a few minutes, she drifted back to sleep.

*

They sat for an hour, watching her without talking, and then a new fear floated up in Heike.

'Do you think she'll be disfigured?'

'Well, she might have an odd bump in her nose and a little scar on her forehead. But she could always cover that up with her hair.'

'Right.'

'Anyway,' Martin smiled, 'we wouldn't want her to be too beautiful. Imagine the stress.'

She managed to access a laugh. 'That's true.'

In whispers, they started to talk. She avoided the subject of his new business venture. He avoided the subject of Yusuf. They talked mostly about Leonie – her little mannerisms, her implacability, their pride in her intelligence and stubbornness. They laughed about the projected teenage battles ahead.

'I'm glad we can talk like this.'

Heike blushed, like a first date. 'Me too.'

'I don't want things left unresolved.'

She didn't quite understand what he meant by this, but decided to take it in the spirit of reconciliation. The leatherette chair suddenly seemed to pull her into its depths, and she closed her eyes, giving way to exhaustion. Her head fell to one side and she had to jerk herself back to consciousness.

Martin said softly, 'You get home.'

'No. I should stay.'

'I'll stay. She'll be all right. I'll call you if there's any change.'

'You sure?'

It felt wrong to be the parent who left.

'I'll be back first thing.'

'Of course you will. She won't even notice you've gone.'

When they said goodbye, he kissed her on both cheeks. It was the most physical he had been with her in years. The familiar smell of him, the particular texture of his stubble, floored her for a moment. She felt a profound need to see Yusuf.

In the back of a cab, she called him. Her fingers fumbled at the touchscreen. When he answered, her jaws felt dislocated, so loose in their moorings that she could barely speak, but as each appalling detail came back to her, the retelling sped up, finally playing out the panic she'd so far suppressed. When she finished, there was a small pause. And then his voice. Calm, all knowing. She lay on it like a raft.

'I'll be right over. If you'd like me to—'

'Yes. Please.'

'This is not your fault. Okay? It's very important you should know that.'

'Okay.'

He was about to ring off and then he remembered, 'I'll need the address.'

By the time Yusuf appeared at her door, it was after 9.30. Standing in her hallway, she could sense he was about to give her a hug and she dodged this, not quite ready for intimacy.

'Have you eaten?'

She shook her head.

'Let me make you something.'

'Okay.'

She sat in the kitchen and watched him cook ratatouille, navigating her kitchen without questions, wordlessly finding everything he needed. But when he finally served it up, she felt too nauseous to eat. Instead, she moved to the sofa and patted the cushion beside her.

'Could you come over here?'

He sat down and took the cue to put his arms around her. The dam in her finally burst and the tears came, uninhibited, soaking the shoulder of his shirt. He said nothing, but as she cried, she realised he was rocking her, ever so gently, just as she had once rocked a baby Leonie. She felt as though she were grieving. The accident was not a reprieve, but a reminder of the fragility of things, the nearness of loss.

Afterwards, when she'd reached the raw, emptied-out stage of post-weeping, they sat together for a long time, saying nothing. And then she turned to Yusuf and kissed him with an intensity that surprised them both. She pulled him down onto the cushions and they made love without speaking. And as Heike watched Yusuf's face above her, she thought of her daughter in a hospital bed in another part of the city, Martin dozing next to her. The wrong parent fulfilling the duty that was hers. And she acknowledged the monster in her and wondered if this were the truth of a world without

HANS, 1970

angels, garlanding the editor's head. His desk was positioned in front of a framed blow-up of a recent cover, in which the model had been dressed entirely in white, golden wings sprouting from her shoulders, waved hair cascading down her back like a Botticelli.

It was important not to betray neediness, so he suppressed the urge to speak when Müller skipped over his best print with barely a pause. It was the one of Ilse, taken in the stairwell of Friedrichstraße, dappled with shadows. Trying not to stare at his assessor, Hans focused on the second hand of the clock that hung high on the wall behind him. This allowed him to time things. Müller spent exactly 95 seconds riffling through the portfolio.

Not bad. Though nothing truly original, I'd say. But something like this . . . He flicked back to a more conventional fashion pose,

Ilse feeding the ducks by the lake. *An image like that we could use*. Hans tried to look grateful and ready for immediate deployment. A few contracts with a magazine like this would allow him to leave the porn behind.

But we have our regular photographers, as you know, so it's unlikely I'll be able to offer you much beyond occasional free-lance work.

I'm happy to be called at short notice.

You have a phone?

My landlady, Frau Käsemann. She takes messages for me.

Hans tried to picture Herr Müller leaving a message with the monosyllabic Frau Käsemann, but found he could not conjure it. The meeting was clearly over. Müller closed the folder and pushed it back towards Hans, who rose to his feet.

Well, thank you for your time.

It's a competitive business you're trying to break into.

I know, but still I—

If I were you, I'd stick to what you know. Müller pulled his trousers away from his crotch. *Nice work if you can get it*. The man then actually licked his lower lip. Hans knew he should play along with the banter, but as ever, something in him resisted it, refused the pretence.

It's a business. Like any other.

Well, of course. But with unique advantages, yes? Mind you, I don't do too badly here. So many of the staff here are pansies, the girls are desperate for a bit of attention, you know?

Hans knew the direction this conversation was taking. He had been here countless times before, once a man got wind of what he did for a living. If he couldn't slide them a free copy of the magazine, they wanted him to give them an anecdote they could jerk off to later.

Who's the girl?

The girl?

In the photos.

Her name's Ilse.

Does she pose for you? I bet she'd—

No.

She got an agent?

No.

Next time you see her, will you give her my card? There might be some modelling work for her here.

Hans gathered up his portfolio, thanked Müller for his time and left through the ranks of secretaries, whose eyes burned through the back of his jacket.

Ilse laughed when he recounted the meeting to her. He was glad to hear that schoolgirl giggle, which hadn't been much in evidence lately. She'd now been living in the apartment for five months. At his suggestion, she'd enrolled at a nearby art college, where she was studying photography. Initially, she'd returned from the classes jabbering breathlessly about all the ideas she might pursue, but several weeks on and she mostly complained about the tutor, about the amount of homework, about the stuck-up Wessis in her class.

Hans, who regretted surrendering his own dream of studying photography so easily, buttoned in his irritation at her apparent lack of gratitude. At first, she'd shared her course notes and books with him, and he'd fed upon all she could remember from her classes about composition, or the latest lighting styles, or the early photographers, Atget, Cameron, Lartigue, Zille, Stieglitz. She would laugh at his forensic questioning, when she wasn't irritated by it. But now she rarely came home immediately after class. He couldn't imagine her hanging out with her classmates, given the way she spoke so disparagingly about them, and he worried about the company she kept. He wondered whether he was too generous with the allowance he gave her, but then he worried she would earn the cash by selling herself.

*

There'd been no more revelations since that first visit to his mother's nursing home. Hans had attempted questions about Ilse's family, her schooldays in the DDR, her early perceptions of the West, but she would not be drawn. She had crossed the border from that old life and there was to be no return.

But her presence in the flat released something in him. It was a novel experience, to have a companion, a confidante, even if he couldn't tell whether his anecdotes bored or amused her. She tended to listen in silence, her expression impassive. But just when he'd thought she was no longer paying attention, she'd suddenly interrupt with an observation or question that caught him off guard. And he found himself confessing things he'd never before articulated to another person.

He couldn't explain why he'd come to feel so close to her, especially when she often infuriated him. He couldn't say exactly what he wanted from her. But must all human relationships depend upon something as transactional as want? He didn't make any demands on her, but neither could he claim that his attachment to her was selfless.

I'm going to shadow a film director.
This was news. *Really? Who?*
Just some guy I met at college. From the way she said this, Hans knew she was sleeping with him. *He's making a movie. I'm going to go away for a couple of weeks. We're shooting some of it in the woods.* She hooked a stray curl of hair behind her ear. He could tell she wanted him to be impressed and something in him felt disinclined to give her what she wanted.
What about your course?
She shrugged. *I'm not really learning much from it any more.*
But you're not far off getting your certificate.
No one cares. She bit on her bottom lip with a deliberate nonchalance that made him furious.

You're going to throw all of that away? All the money I've spent on books and equipment? He hadn't meant to say this second part, to cast himself as aggrieved Dad. Ilse sprang up in a fury, knocking over a cup of coffee as she did so.

Oh yes, that's what this is about, isn't it? Your fucking patronage. Why do you do it? Do you get some weird self-righteous kick from funding impoverished East Berliners through college? Or do you just want me to do the things you never had the guts to do?

A buzz at the front door. Pieter, with the week's takings. Hans hoped he could dispense with him quickly, but Pieter invited himself into the apartment with the entitlement of a close family member. Hans saw him take in Ilse's flushed face, the spilled mug. He smirked at Hans.

Lovers' tiff?

Before he could answer, Pieter continued. *But you're not really up to that, are you, Hans? Lovers aren't really your thing.* He sucked one cheek in, creating a dimple which, on Pieter's fleshy face, looked somehow obscene.

So she'd told him. Ilse at least had the good grace to look down at her feet. Hans realised that he didn't care, that none of it mattered. He didn't care if Pieter knew that his entire life was a contradiction. It was a stinking business to be in, especially when you had to deal with arseholes like Pieter, but it was a business he knew how to play. To his surprise, Pieter seemed unwilling to poke the wasps' nest further and quickly changed the subject, claiming he wanted to sit down and discuss business. Eager to move him out of the flat, Hans suggested they both go to a local bar. Pieter blew Ilse a kiss on the way out and she flashed a wide smile back at him. The smile wasn't hers – it had the performed brightness of a cover model.

There was an Eckkneipe on the corner a couple of blocks west. The walls and ceiling were a dark nicotine, the linoleum floor looked like it hadn't been scrubbed in a decade and the air was so thick with smoke that Hans's eyes immediately started to water. Three elderly drinkers in one corner were playing skat. They looked like they might have been sitting there since the war.

They took stools at the bar and Hans ordered two Schultheiss – cold, bitter and cheap. Pieter's urgent business conversation proved to be nothing more than laying claim to the small victory of expanding their market to a couple of shops in Hamburg. But he was in ebullient mood, and it was easier to let him chunter on.

In his peripheral vision, Hans was aware of a woman coming into the bar. This wasn't territory many women entered. She wore a belted mac and high heels, which clacked towards him.

Your girlfriend told me I'd find you here.
The tone of 'girlfriend' indicated her disapproval. He shrugged, an adolescent emulation of Ilse.

It's about your mum. This was not a conversation he wanted to have in front of Pieter.

Let's go outside. And he steered Gisela out of the door.

It was raining, so they walked a few doors down the street to stand beneath a shop awning. Several other people had already gathered there for shelter, so Hans was forced to stand under the awning's dripping edge. His shoulders were quickly soaked through.

She's not been well. His aunt lit a cigarette with a tortoiseshell lighter. *She's had pneumonia.*

Oh God.

She's pulled through. But it's left her pretty fragile. You should go see her.

She doesn't know who I am.

Yes she does. She talks about you. Some days she's clearer than others. Some days . . . Gisela flicked the ash off her cigarette . . . *some days she doesn't seem to recognise anyone, or have any idea of who she was.*

Hans registered the past tense.

I don't know what I can do for her.

Gisela fixed him with a look. *Do? What you have to do is be there. That's your duty as her son.*

Duty. An old word. A Bismarckian word. A Third Reich word. But it still cut deep, could not be ignored.

His mother appeared to have lost several pounds. Her cheeks were sunken, her white blonde hair straggly and in need of a wash. She didn't look at him, but stared out of the window. This time, the nurse took him up to her bedroom, a narrow rectangle on the second floor, overlooking the street. There was a single picture – a print of Monet's water lilies that had faded in the sun. Beauty receding into the mist.

Mutti? He briefly placed his hand on hers. *It's me. Hans. I haven't been to see you because I couldn't think what I'd say. I'm sorry you've been ill. I hope you're feeling better?*

He stopped. What was the point? Why was he trying to explain himself to a creature whose brain cells were rapidly burning out? She moved her head slightly, apparently following the movement of something outside window.

How many people died? Her voice was reedy with disuse.

What?

In this city. Thousands? Millions?

You mean – in the war?

Her eyes were suddenly bright. She leaned forward slightly in her chair to make sure he was listening.

When it was over, there were bodies everywhere. Rotting. Buried beneath rubble, or just left on the street. Sometimes I still smell it. Between the buildings, under the pavements. But nobody talks about this now. Everyone in here . . . She gestured vaguely at the door. *We're afraid to say the words.*

He was shocked to find himself once more in the company of a living person. He worried that any moment the clockwork would grind to a halt and she'd disappear again. She shook her head.

No one wants to talk about the past.

He moved his chair closer to hers. *Because of guilt?*

She shook her head again. A half-smile.

Because of pride.

Is that how you feel, Mutti? Proud?

I just wanted to be good at my job. For people to say, ah yes, Hilde, she's a good worker.

And did they? Say that?

Oh yes.

Do you remember where you worked?

I was just a secretary. Yes, a secretary. A good secretary.

And where did you work?

At the . . . At the . . . She shook her head. *I'm losing . . . I start a sentence and I think I know where it's . . . and then I can't find the . . . Can't find the . . .*

Word?

There was a long pause while she searched for it.

Meaning. I can't find the meaning.

Let me help you. I need to know something. I think I saw a photo of you with Eichmann. Adolf Eichmann.

He could see this set the clockwork whirring.

Do you remember who that was?

No, no.

I was watching a newsreel, at the cinema, and there were some shots of Eichmann taking a tour of his office, and there was a young woman who was the spit of you.

No.

The spit, Mutti.

Her hands fluttered momentarily above her lap, as though she were trying to contain a small creature there.

Did you work for the RSHA?

She looked at him, imploringly, but he was not to be bought this way.

You did, didn't you? You were very young, you were just a secretary, but you must have known what your job involved. What it meant. Ultimately.

There was a brief knock at the door, but without waiting for an answer a nurse came in with a trolley.

Tea?

Thank you.

How are you doing, Frau Gumpel?

All right. All right.

That's good. You've perked right up. Is this your boy?

Hilde made a noise that might have been assent. The nurse chirruped on.

I thought he must be. Do you good to have a visitor.

Hans responded to this unsubtle guilt-trip by focusing on the woman's puckered and meaty calves. Having provided them both with tea and a plate of unappetisingly beige biscuits, she finally left the room. He took a sip of the tepid tea before starting again.

You were young, but you knew what your job meant.

You can know and not know. At the same time. Don't you think?

He held this for a moment, and then shook his head.

No. I don't. I think that's just lying to yourself.

Hilde stared out of the window, drew in a long, laboured breath. Something inside her appeared to solidify, to transform once more into the woman he remembered from his teenage years. Although she was saying things he had never heard her say before.

I knew Jews were being deported before I started there. Resettled, they called it. I had a Jewish friend who had

disappeared. Rosalie. Her name was Rosalie. She was very pretty.
She played the violin. I went round to her flat and her neighbour
wouldn't speak to me. I could tell she was looking me up and
down to work out whether I was a Jew too.

It was an effort to keep his voice low and calm.

And where did you think she had gone? To the seaside?

If her cannibalised brain understood the sarcasm, she didn't let
it register on her face.

No. I knew about the camps. But I didn't know what was
going on there. All I knew was that words began to change their
meaning. Sonderbehandlung. *I used to see* Sonderbehandlung *a*
lot on documents. Special treatment. *I knew what that meant. A*
death sentence. I think I also knew that it meant death by hang-
ing, but I can't tell you how I knew this. It was a kind of code, I
guess.

A euphemism.

Yes.

Like selekzionieren.

Yes.

Like lösen

Yes.

Words that used to be innocent. To select. To solve.

Yes.

Who were the euphemisms protecting?

Again the hands fluttered above her lap. *I don't know.* Her lips
twisted beneath her teeth. *Me, I guess. People like me.*

His whole body felt leaden. He leaned forward in his chair, held
the weight of his head in his hands. Was that what had happened
to her mind? All that language of camouflage and concealment
crushing down on the tender fibres of the brain. If you started to
misuse words, did that destroy true connections, meanings?

But for now she was still speaking. With complete clarity.

*

We had Jewish people working for us. They didn't have to wear stars. They helped to track down Jews in hiding.

They weren't deported?

No. Because they were useful to the department.

Collaborators.

They didn't have a choice. You think you'd have chosen differently? I can guarantee you wouldn't have.

No. Perhaps not. He sat back in his chair.

I was young. I wanted to please. I just wanted to get on with my life and go to the cinema and find a boyfriend and not attract attention. That's what you did.

What was he expecting? This was not a courtroom. If a confession were owed, it was not owed to him. But still he couldn't resist the bayonet.

Who was my father? Cleanly in, cleanly out.

I don't know. I don't remember.

You don't remember who it was? Or you don't remember the lie you told me growing up?

I don't know. Don't remember.

She began to cry, silently. Viscous tears pooled at the corners of her eyes, but did not overflow.

There's no point in lying any more. Gisela told me everything. Years ago.

From somewhere, a surge of energy in his mother's diminished body. She threw herself forward and lunged at him in something between an embrace and an assault. Her hands pulled at his clothes. *Please, Hans. Please.* He was repelled by her stained pink cardigan, her yellowed teeth, her watery self-pitying eyes. Repelled by her victimhood. And for an insane moment he wrestled with her, trying to push her away, but simultaneously gripping her arms tightly, wanting to hurt her. *Please, please.*

She was so light against him. It would not take much to snap her in two. He shook her with an inarticulate cry of frustration and fury. And then shame overpowered him and he let her go, and she slid back into her chair. She was a small sack of nothing. Her hair was wild, her cheeks a delta of tears. She returned her gaze to the window and started to rock slightly in the chair. Very quietly, she started to mutter something. *Ist ein Traum kann nicht wirklich sein.* She repeated this phrase, but this time it took on a melody. Hans stood there, helpless.

What's a dream? What do you mean?

But she had shut down again. It was clear there was to be no more conversation. For a moment he wondered whether the dementia itself was a lie. An excuse to close in, to keep the world out, to pretend to forget. As he walked out the care home door, ignoring the nurse who called after him, he decided he would never see her again.

Riding the U-Bahn home, he noticed a young woman seated a little way down the carriage from him, hunched into herself, weeping. He could see she was attempting to hold it together, but the tears would not be stayed, and they dripped from her chin onto her jacket. There were only two other passengers in their section of the carriage, but they had noticed her too. They exchanged uncertain looks with each other – should they intervene? This wordless transaction appeared to prompt the middle-aged woman sitting opposite the girl to lean forward and touch her knee. *Are you all right?* The girl nodded and drew her chin even further back into her chest. The woman hesitated for a moment, unsure whether to press things, but then pulled back into her seat. When she stood up to leave at the next stop, she glanced behind her at the weeping girl as she stepped from the carriage.

Now the only witnesses were Hans and an elderly man with a stick, who was sitting next to the young woman. The two men looked at each other in a conspiracy of indecision. The train rattled on to the next station. Then the elderly man suddenly leaned towards the girl and patted her hand. *You will endure*, he said. His tone was neither patronising nor paternalistic. It was a simple statement of fact. The girl looked up at him, surprised. Her mouth twisted into something almost like a smile and she nodded slightly. *You will endure. What else can we do?*

How was one to understand it all? The compassion of an elderly man, a man who thirty years before might have been an SA thug, kicking another man to death, or a concentration camp guard, sending a girl exactly the same age to the gas chamber. How did one reconcile this in humans? The capacity for empathy and tenderness with the impulse to power, control, torture?

You think you'd have chosen differently? He thought of his seventeen-year-old self, smoking on the garden steps of a hotel at one in the morning, listening to his aunt, in her cups, as she delivered the bombshell. Wanting in that moment to kill her for the undisguised pleasure with which she revealed the true nature of his origins. He thought of Ilse, probably only slightly younger than his mother had been when she'd taken on that job at the RSHA. Seventeen. Terrible things could happen because ordinary seventeen-year-olds and ordinary thirty-year-olds and ordinary fifty-year-olds discovered they were capable of anything.

Hans stepped off the train, feeling the whole weight of the absent building at Kurfürstenstraße bear down on his neck and shoulders. Surely Eichmann's world could never re-emerge. It could never happen again. No. At least not in the same way.

He was filled with the urgent need to talk to Ilse. But he opened the door on a flat abandoned. She'd cleared out – he sensed it immediately. And this was confirmed by the empty clothes rails, the missing bottles in the bathroom. This was more final than a jaunt to the Grunewald with her new friends. The sudden loss of her surged through him. She had not needed him. He had wanted to prove himself more than a pornographer, more than a motherless son adrift in the city, but he'd been fooling himself that a teenager might understand anything of this. And why should she? Why should she want anything more than the freedom she had taken such risks to acquire?

There was a note too, weighted down with a dirty mug on a table in the hallway. A scrawl on a scrap of torn-out notebook paper. *Thanks for being a sport.* And her full name – oddly formal – *Ilse Singer.*

He heard a movement in the stairwell beyond the door and his heart instinctively pounded. She'd changed her mind! He left the note on the table and hurried to the door of his apartment, but there was no one on the landing. Hans stood for a moment, paralysed by his own absurdity. Then he heard a rustle above, so he went to the banisters and looked up. On the fourth floor landing, directly beneath the skylight, her white hair glowing, as if illuminated from within, stood Frau Babel.

Even from two floors below, Hans could see she was swaying slightly. He wondered whether she was having a stroke.

Are you all right?

Yes. Yes.

But her voice was thin and unconvincing. Hans climbed up the two flights of stairs towards her. The landing on the fourth floor was too narrow for them both, so he hovered a couple of stairs below her. From this distance, he noticed for the first time that her eyes were a deep cornflower blue.

Can I help at all? I'm Hans. I live on the second floor.

I know.

The woman gave him a half-smile, acknowledging that she was being patronised. She waved a hand at him. The one with half a finger missing.

You've been kind. But I'm fine. Really.

He took one step backwards down a stair.

Well, if you're sure?

She nodded and turned, as if to go into her apartment. Hans wished her good day and started back down the stairs. He was hurrying for some reason, eager to escape into his own space, away from the shadows of the stairwell and into the light of his apartment. But as he put his hand against the apartment door, he heard a sudden noise above him. He turned just in time to see a shape falling through the stairwell. For a moment, he thought it must be a large black binbag. But then the impact. A dull thud on the tiles of the hallway. He stood frozen by his front door. Understanding coursed through him like toxin.

He forced himself to take the few steps towards the balustrade. He heard his own cry – an alien noise that did not seem to belong to him – echo down through the stairwell. The woman herself had made no noise, had fallen as silently as a kite. And on the tiles below, the blood already pooling around her head, her limbs arranged in impossible angles. In his daze, he noted that her body was arranged like a swastika.

People began to come out of their apartment doors. A man appeared in the hallway and knelt beside her, cursing. A woman from the floor below Hans shouted that she'd call for an ambulance and disappeared back into her apartment. Another woman started tearfully muttering prayers. Hans remained frozen on the second floor landing, his mind already replaying what had just happened, adding detail – the perfect parabola of her fall, the silhouette of her body against the bright white of the sun in the stairwell, an Olympic diver swooping down through curlicued patterns of light and dark. He wasn't sure whether this image was remembered or imagined, but he kept seeing it like one of those nineteenth-century zoetropes with the horse galloping endlessly through the bars, but now it was the woman's shadow falling over and over.

Had she had a heart attack and lost her footing? How was that possible? But the alternative, a self-willed act of destruction, seemed equally implausible. To survive so much and then to choose . . . But he didn't want to believe this. No escape from history, replaying and replaying eternally, like a cinema newsreel. A shadow falling over and over. No. Perhaps this death was in defiance of history. Perhaps that was the point – the autonomy of choice. To own one's end. The ultimate self-possession. To live, to die. To endure, to stop. Or perhaps it had nothing to do with the war and everything to do with love. Her lover had died and the desire for life had guttered

SIGI, 1949

& I've been thinking about something you said to me all those years ago about how we all need something to believe in

& on my way to the records office I stopped in the little church off Askanischer Platz & lit a candle something I haven't done in years not since school though I hadn't planned to do it even when I pushed open the church door I didn't really know why I was there

& I must have known somehow because that day there was a new file & there was his name Matthias Babel died Ukraine January 1944 which must have been a cold terrible death & I didn't think there were any tears left in me but as I went down the steps of the building I cried not for him so much but all those men all that waste & what we were thinking of what was all of it for

& my tears were also for you because I feared this might be my last hope the end of the trail but then when I was halfway home I realised the records office might be able to give me a more recent address or the address of his parents so I limped back cursing my aching hips all the way & joined another queue but it was easy really a filing cabinet a slip of paper & I was out the door with the name of a street in my hand & a town your town or the town near your village those letters in that order so familiar but so strange

& so last week I caught a train everything is slowly starting to work again now that the blockade is over & though the train was packed it was curiously thrilling the normality of tickets & officious conductors & the sag of the seat springs under my arse & the fog of cigarettes & I enjoyed the journey like some kind of Sunday excursion like I should have packed a picnic but then a sign came into view & those letters & suddenly the place was a real place & I stepped onto it onto the platform & felt oh all sorts of things but also a strange nip of excitement & I kept asking people to point the way but it didn't take me too long to find it though of course there was no one home so I thought about waiting outside but there wasn't really anywhere to loiter without looking suspicious so I'd just made up my mind to find a cafe where I could buy a coffee when a woman walking past spotted me & came over asked if I was looking for Fräulein Babel & I said yes yes & the woman said oh she'll be at work over at Grüner's so she waved a hand in the right direction & I hobbled off as fast as my spine would let me

& I found the shop a haberdasher's so incredible to see a building that still looks like a building every roof slate still intact every window to see a life that looks like life used to be

235

& I opened the door & a little bell rang oh just like a life-before bell & the smell of the rolls of fabric was so clean & warm & there was a woman behind the counter & another woman folding up swatches of floral cottons for a display & I said I'm looking for Fräulein Babel & the folding woman straightened up & put a hand to her hair & said yes that's me & then I realised that I hadn't prepared what I was going to say & so I just fumbled for a bit & said that I had known her brother a little in Berlin & that I had only just learned of his death & how sorry etc. & would it be possible to talk to her & the older woman behind the counter said Hanna you go you go we're not busy take as long as you like why don't you take her for tea & Hanna looked a little uncertain but she fetched her coat & we went to a little cafe

& she said she hadn't seen Matz for three years but then the telegram arrived & their father almost lost his mind with grief but fortunately their mother had already lost her mind so wasn't able to take it in which was just as well & there was a wife in Berlin with two kids but they'd not seen her since the telegram she'd taken the children west to escape the bombs & my heart jumped for a moment & I said your name but she frowned & said oh no they were divorced years ago I'm talking about Lotte don't you know Lotte?

& I had to say no & make some excuse about having moved away from the area & then of course I wondered how much Matz had told her so I took a while to get to the point but then I had to ask whether she knew what had happened to you the electric jolt of saying your name out loud but she shrugged & said the last she'd heard you were staying with your aunt in Paris though I knew that already of course after I wrote to your parents back in '33 & I wondered for a moment whether she might have guessed everything about the sort of person I am but she didn't seem to see that in me there was a kind of small-town innocence about her I guess our sort probably don't even exist in her consciousness & now I'm pretty certain Matz never told anyone the truth about us out of some sense of insult to his masculinity or some such

& then I asked about your family did any of them still live in the town & she gave me a look & said they had all been taken away to the east & so far no one had come back but they had been very old so it was hardly to be expected & I was trying to work out how she felt about that though she was impossible to read but then of course I had to ask whether she knew what had happened to you had you been taken away too & she just looked out of the window & said well perhaps she got out of France in time & of course I've been clinging to that too & I had so many questions after that but I could see I was beginning to alarm her & I could also see that she had nothing more to tell me so I paid for our tea & thanked her & said again I was sorry for her loss & took the next train back to Berlin

& of course hope is dangerous

& of course I am wired with it now

> but you could still

& I should know better than to trust in miracles & optimism is a burden because perhaps it is better to be resigned to the smallness of our lives to the grind of it to the potato & cabbageness of now

& seeing Hanna has made me wonder whether you ever received my letter & if you had whether it would have made any difference or whether my apology sounded hollow & self-deluding & far too late God knows what I wrote or if I expressed myself badly in fact I'm sure I expressed myself badly & why had I waited so long to write it when I had already got together with Herta by then & if you'd come to find me would I have turned you away out of loyalty to her even if not to be unfair to Herta who was only ever good & loving & saw me through a lot but she was a friend & companion & you were the thing itself

& if you came back now how could you possibly love me

& I have tried to dive into myself to understand all that happened to discover all the secrets I've kept from myself

& you should know Herta was the one who first made me see sense she came back one night & pulled me out of bed & made me go out with her into the street walking up past the Gütschow-Keller past the soldiers on the gate & she pulled me in & whispered what do you hear what do you hear & there was no way to pretend I couldn't hear the screaming or that I didn't realise the screams were a man being tortured somewhere inside the building not too far from the gate perhaps the basement it was the building owned by the Gütschow brothers remember them they lived just along from us & they'd leased their outbuildings on the opposite side of the street to the SA who used it as a prison for trade unionists & Communists & social democrats & Jews & people locally called it the Castle of Blood when we got home Herta shook me & said don't you get it that's your lot that's the order & reason you think you believe in that's the ambition & purpose & optimism you're always banging on about & okay it wasn't that the scales suddenly fell from my eyes road to Damascus bad comparison it wasn't immediate but it was the beginning of doubt & some nights Herta left the windows open I think she did it deliberately & in the middle of the night when the traffic of the city was quiet I could hear the cries from that building & once it was a woman & I thought my God they'd don't discriminate at all

*

& of course by then most of the people who had once hired me had already left though Trude Hesterberg stayed on & Werner Finck kept going for a while until one of Goebbels's cronies paid a visit which meant the end of the Catacombs the end of the Tingel-Tangel I heard that Paul Nikolaus of the Kadeko committed suicide Gottschalk too Paul Schneider-Duncker offered me work but I couldn't bear the way he pretended that his old partner Rudolf Nelson had never existed & I'd lost all heart by then anyway I'm not quite the whore you might imagine me to be & under the Nazis the cabarets just became all dancing girls tits & arse no one wanted a dyke singing satirical songs the party was over & the Party was over I left the Party yes I finally did something brave & I was lucky that leaving didn't get me into too much hot water though I'm sure I was on some kind of watch list for years

& though sometimes I wanted to end it all I just kept going because

what else can we do

& we all need something to believe in

& Mother has taken herself off to bed desperate to leave this day behind & Eric & Gerhard are out somewhere & I'm feeling as weary as all sin but then there's a small miracle & the lights flicker on electricity at 11 p.m. & I'm going to make the most of being on my own in this luxury so I turn the radio on & there's an orchestra playing but all they seem to play is bloody Mahler which is too big & maudlin for me so I switch it off & collapse in the chair by the window & idly twitch at the curtain to watch the world going by & the moon is very bright tonight making even the ruins look beautiful like a classical painting & a pair of lovers stumble down the street their torsos welded together their legs unsteady I don't think they're drunk I think they just want to climb into each other but then they disappear from view & for a few minutes it's just the moon & me gazing down at the street but now someone is coming along the pavement looking up at the window a tall thin woman in a green coat & now she sees me & she's still looking up & she's still coming & she lifts her hand & waves solemnly & she's still coming & I jump up & run to the door & down the stairs & my whole chest feels like it will burst & I run as the doorbell rings like a siren & I nearly lose my footing on the last few steps & I thunder to the door & fumble at the catch but then I open it & the street & the sky & the whole world surges in

& there is you

Author's Note

Oskar Messter was a German film pioneer who had a workshop and studio on Friedrichstrasse in the early 1900s. But *The Clockmaker's Dream* is my own invention.

Erholtz's Academy of Magical Arts was loosely inspired by Conradi-Horster's 'Magic Headquarters' housed at Friedrichstrasse 17.

Acknowledgements

Thank you to the brilliant team at John Murray, especially my astute and sensitive editor Jocasta Hamilton. And to Lucy Luck at C & W for sage counsel and endless enthusiasm.

Grateful thanks to my early readers Alice Dvořáková, Ralph Ruge and Di Speirs for their insight and encouragement. And to Marc Beeby, whose tireless reading, wisdom and occasional raised eyebrow helped to shape each draft of this novel.

And to John Brewer for advice on early photography.

And to Elena Dalrymple, Miranda Emmerson, Kate Horsley, Victoria Howard, Wei Yee Shiu, Claudine Toutoungi, Simon and Sue Harding – the best and truest cheerleaders.

And to Geoff and Edward, with my love.